BALTIC BELLES:
THE DEDALUS BOOK OF
LATVIAN WOMEN WRITERS

EDITED BY

EVA EGLĀJA-KRISTSONE

Dedalus

This book has been published with the assistance of Latvian Literature.

Published in the UK by Dedalus Limited
24-26, St Judith's Lane, Sawtry, Cambs, PE28 5XE
info@dedalusbooks.com
www.dedalusbooks.com

ISBN printed book 978 1 912868 37 7
ISBN ebook 978 1 915568 11 3

Dedalus is distributed in the USA & Canada by SCB Distributors
15608 South New Century Drive, Gardena, CA 90248
info@scbdistributors.com   www.scbdistributors.com

Dedalus is distributed in Australia by Peribo Pty Ltd
58, Beaumont Road, Mount Kuring-gai, N.S.W. 2080
info@peribo.com.au   www.peribo.com.au

First published by Dedalus in 2022
Translations are copyright the translator and their name appears at the beginning of each text.
Texts which are in copyright are copyright their individual authors or their estates.

The right of Eva Eglāja-Kristsone to be identified as the editor of this work has been asserted by her in accordance with the Copyright, Designs and Patents Act, 1988.

Printed and bound in the UK by Clays Elcograf S.p.A.
Typeset by Marie Lane

THE EDITOR

Eva Eglāja-Kristsone, Dr Philology, is a leading researcher and director of the Institute of Literature, Folklore and Art at the University of Latvia (2021). She is the head of two digital resources: *literatura.lv* the first digital academic literary resource in Latvia (2015) and the resource of women history *womage.lv* (2021).

Her research is mainly in literary studies, literary anthropology, autobiographical studies and women's writing.

She is the author of several books, and with Becca Parkinson edited *The Book of Riga* in 2018.

THE AUTHORS

Inga Ābele (née Ingrīda Ābele, born 1972) is a prose writer, poet and playwright. Her plays have seen numerous productions both in Latvia and abroad. Her novels and short story collections have won the Annual Latvian Literature Award in the category for Best Prose Work, as well as the Dzintars Sodums Award for innovation and creativity in Latvian literature. Recent English translations of her work include *The Year the River Froze Twice* (Norvik, 2020).

Alija Baumane (1891–1941) was a Latvian writer and poet. Her poetry depicted the inner and outer contact of a person with the surrounding world and its nuances of experience, while her short story collections *The Howling City* (Auļojošā pilsēta, 1924) and *Honey of the Earth* (Zemes medus, 1926) showed newcomers to the big city and their disappointment at its soullessness, along with their scepticism of the cult of material things and hurried nature of the times.

Mirdza Bendrupe (1910–1995) was a Latvian writer, poet, and translator. Her poetry is defined by original storylines and a rich language that prized innovation, while her short stories often depicted modern city inhabitants with their agitated and fragmented psyches, which rank among the best of her generation.

Anna Brigadere (1861–1933) was a Latvian writer, playwright, and poet. Her plays, such as *The Tale of Sprīdītis* (Sprīdītis) about a young boy from a Latvian peasant family, and later autobiographical trilogy *God, Nature, Work* (Dievs, daba, darbs, 1926), *In Harsh Winds* (Skarbos vējos, 1930), and *In a Stone Trap* (Akmeņu sprostā, 1930) are considered classics of Latvian literature.

Regīna Ezera (1930–2002) was one of Latvia's most important novelists and short story writers of the latter half of the 20th century. She published her first literary work in 1955. Considered a master of what could be called "silent drama" as well as nuanced psychological portraits, her work pays great attention to detail in human relationships. Among her most important works is her novel *The Well* (Aka, 1972) and short story collection *The Trap* (Slazds, 1979).

Angelika Gailīte (1884–1975) was a Latvian fiction writer. In her prose, she depicted the internal conflicts and experiences of the modern woman, the freeing of a woman from a feeling of dependency on a man, and attempts for spiritual independence, and conscious awareness of harmony and wholeness.

Nora Ikstena (born 1969) is one of Latvia's most celebrated writers. In her novels and short stories, she often reflects on life, love, death and faith. Her novel *Soviet Milk* quickly became a bestseller when it first came out in Latvia, and was subsequently translated into several languages. It was also shortlisted for the 2019 EBRD Translation Prize.

Andra Neiburga (1957–2019) was a prose writer and short story writer. A graduate of the Latvian Academy of Art, she worked as a designer for literary magazines in Latvia. Though she only published three books in her lifetime, two of which being the short story collections *Stuffed Birds and Caged Birds* (Izbāzti putni un putni būros, Liesma Publishing, 1988) and *Push push* (Stum stum, Valters un Rapa Publishing, 2004), her work has been enormously influential on subsequent generations of Latvian authors.

Gundega Repše (born 1960) is a novelist, short story writer, and essayist. She has worked as an editor and contributor in various magazines and other media discussing culture and literature. Her novels and short stories have won several national literary awards, as well as the Baltic Assembly Prize in 2018. She was instrumental in initiating a series of historical novels written by Latvian authors called *We. Latvia. 20th Century* which deals with Latvia's recent past.

Anna Rūmane-Ķeniņa (1877–1950) was a Latvian writer and cultural activist, who was an early proponent of an independent Latvia in the foreign press, and who garnered state awards for her service to both Latvia and France, improving cultural ties between the two countries. Her work in establishing schools for young girls and her involvement in women's organisations helped to promote women's rights in the country.

Ilze Šķipsna (1928–1981) was a Latvian novelist, short story writer and poet. Her family emigrated to Germany in 1944, and in 1949 she received a scholarship to study in the US, where she spent the rest of her life. Writing primarily in Latvian, but also in English, she strove to find answers to the great and eternal questions of being, the meaning of life, national identity, and the ties between people.

Inga Žolude (born 1984) is a Latvian novelist and short story writer. She studied English literature at the University of Latvia, where she also received a PhD in literature, and attended Southern Illinois University as a Fulbright scholar. She received the 2011 EU Prize for Literature for her short story collection *A Solace for Adam's Tree* (Mierinājums Ādama kokam, Dienas Grāmata, 2010), and has continued to receive accolades for her work, which has been translated into several languages

THE TRANSLATORS

Laura Adlers is a Latvian-Canadian cultural administrator and translator. She has a BA in French and German language, literature and translation from the University of Toronto (1991) and a Master in International Arts Management from HEC Montréal (2015). She has been a professional culture administrator since 1995, working primarily with performing arts and arts funding organizations. Laura is also a published translator, introducing Latvian literature to the world one story at a time. Born in 1952 in Sydney, Australia, she studied Drama and Fine Arts at Flinders University, South Australia and Baltic Languages at Stockholm University after moving to Sweden in 1981. She worked at Radio Sweden, writing and directing plays for the Latvian theatre in Sydney and Sweden, as well as teaching English at bilingual primary and secondary schools in Stockholm. She has translated the poetry of a number of Latvian poets including Belševica, Kronbergs and Godiņš. She lives in Rīga.

Ieva Lešinska (born 1958) is a journalist and translator who returned to Latvia in 1994, after sixteen years spent in the United States, Sweden and Germany. As a journalist, she has conducted many interviews, including with a number of world-renowned literary figures. As a translator, she has been the English voice of many Latvian poets, both classical and contemporary. She has also translated the major works of T. S. Eliot, Ezra Pound, Allen Ginsberg, Toni Morrison, and others into Latvian. Ieva's current projects include a new translation of James Joyce's *Ulysses*.

Zan McQuade is a writer, editor and translator living in Cincinnati, Ohio

Žanete Vēvere Pasqualini was born in Riga. She graduated from the Faculty of Foreign Languages, University of Latvia at the same time completing a course in Italian language at the University of Perugia. She was the first Latvian Consul in Rome after Latvia regained independence which has led to her now dividing her time between Latvia and Italy. Presently she works as a Literary Agent for Latvia dedicating some of her time to literary translation.

Māra Rozītis (born 1952) is an actress, director, playwright, and translator. She studied drama theory at Flinders University, Adelaide, graduating with a BA. At Stockholm University, she furthered her knowledge of Baltic languages and literature. She has translated the poetry of Juris Kronbergs, Guntars Godiņš and Vizma Belševica, and the prose of Gundega Repše into English.

CONTENTS

Contents

Introduction

Eva Eglāja-Kristsone

In the spring of 2022, I went to Paris to see the exhibition *Pioneers: Artists in the Paris of the Roaring Twenties* at the Luxembourg Museum, which aimed to reinstate the role of women in the changing history of art and also in the world of architecture, dance, design, literature, fashion and scientific discovery. The exhibition also included one piece of art from Latvia — the legendary painting *Tennis Player* by Aleksandra Beļcova (1892–1981). The biography of the artist Aleksandra Beļcova spans almost the entire 20th century, and her work echoes many of its artistic movements. Though I have seen this painting in various exhibitions, it was vital for me to see it in the context of other women artists from the time. The collection revealed a complex and informed point of view of educated and ambitious women determined to represent the world as they see it, starting with their bodies. The female gaze, through their art, described the female experience and body differently. The painting *Tennis Player* is considered an icon — a woman athlete portrayed by a woman artist.

This painting was chosen as the leitmotif for this collection of Latvian women's prose. Just as this painting is part of a broader narrative about the era, emancipation and art made by women, this prose collection is part of a series that highlights women's writing through the 20th century and extends to the 21st century. It presents the local nuances while framing a broader narrative about women's role in culture and society.

The beginning of Latvian women's writing can be dated back to 1809 when the Christian song book included three spiritual songs by Bormaņu Anna (1785–?). During later decades, some widows of Baltic German pastors wrote enlightening texts, didactic short prose works, and practical and medical advice published in Latvian newspapers. The beginning of an active presence of women in the field of Latvian literature dates back to the 1870s when women writers contributed to drama, prose, poetry, travel writings and other genres. The literary activity of Marija Pēkšēna (1845–1903), Marija Medinska (1830–1888) and Minna Freimane (1847–?) are the main milestones. Pēkšēnas' play *Gertrude* won the Riga Latvian Society's original drama competition in 1870, while Medinska's first story, *Oak, His Life and End*, was printed in 1872. Moreover, Karoline Kronvalde (1836–1913) began the first discussion on the situation of Latvian women and their need for a proper education in her article in 1870. It was not widely read at the time but can be seen to have started the process of women's issues being more widely discussed by the press. Katrīna Reinovska's collection of poems *Latvijas jūrmalas puķites* (1875) was published, and Minna Freimane's travelogues about the Caucasus (1878) appeared in the newspaper *Baltijas Vēstnesis*.

In the formation of the Latvian national literary canon, two women authors, poet and dramatist Aspazija, and fiction author and dramatist Anna Brigadere represented Latvian women's writing from the *fin-de-siècle* till the First World War. By the end of the century, works by several other women writers (Birznieku Latiņa, Tirzmaliete, Emīlija Prūsa and others) were published in periodicals, and the number of women writers grew at the beginning of the 20th century. This collection opens with the story of Anna Brigadere, one of the most distinguished Latvian writers of the twentieth century.

Anna Brigadere started her writing career in 1896 when the literary supplement of the newspaper *Baltic Herald* printed her story *In the Hospital*. Her second short story *Old Karlīne* appeared in the same newspaper in 1897. Brigadere portrays a Latvian mother and her tragedy in her story. Old Karlīne brought up a son who strayed from the right path. He commits theft, is convicted, and the mother goes mad with grief. While earlier writers focused on the prodigal son's life, Anna Brigadere captured the mother's tragedy and her great suffering.

Anna Rūmane-Ķeniņa continues the theme of motherhood. But unlike Anna Brigadere, who never became a mother herself and used empathy and observations from life around her to create maternal characters, Rūmane's story is intensely autobiographical. Anna Rūmane-Keniņa (1877–1950) was one of Latvia's most outstanding and politically active women. She was also a great promoter of French culture in Latvia. She graduated from the Jelgava girls' gymnasium in 1895, where only a few Latvian girls studied among the daughters of German noblemen and the highest Russian officials. At school, she became passionate about French literature and modern poetry, and in 1898 she published her article about the history of 19th-century French literature, *Fragments from French literature.* She married the teacher, poet and politician Atis Ķeniņš and had six children. In 1905 Anna Rūmane-Ķeniņa's daughter Maija, who was only two years old, died of scarlet fever. This loss inspired *Mother's Sorrow* which was published in 1912. *Mother's Sorrow* is an emotionally profound depiction of a mother's experience of losing a child. However, *Mother's Sorrow* was Anna Rūmane-Ķeniņa's last published literary work because it met with harsh criticism from male critics.

The aim of both stories is to focus on the different expressions and emotions of motherhood without giving any counter-arguments to the traditional role and association of women with home and family. However, in the first decades of the 20th century, women characters emerged from the confined spaces of the home to the broader open spaces of nature, with women becoming freer to travel abroad. The following story, *Honeymoon* by Angelika Gailīte, is about the transformation of a young woman, Elza, during a honeymoon trip to Germany. In the early stages of her honeymoon, she is overwhelmed by a new carnal passion. But everything changes when Elza and her new husband go to the opera in Dresden to see Richard Wagner's romantic opera *Lohengrin.*

When Lohengrin arrives on the opera stage in a boat led by a swan, Elza realises that he is her idol, the friend of her youthful dreams and imagination. That fateful evening in Dresden, Lohengrin extinguishes her passion for her husband. And now she is again burning with spiritual love for the light warrior Lohengrin, with whom she identifies King Ludwig II.

Elza visits Ludwig II's last, unfinished castle on an island in Lake Chiemsee in Bavaria. There she drives herself to an unconscious catharsis and goes into the lake to confront Lohengrin. Elza's death is described as tragic but quickly forgotten. On the one hand, the author in her story shows a fascination with romanticised legends, Elza invites everyone to renounce normal life, indulges in the cult of King Ludwig II and enters into a marriage of souls with an imaginary being; on the other hand, the liberation of a sexual body proposed by Oscar Wilde also enters into Gailīte's story.

With the establishment of the Republic of Latvia in 1918, legislation, including in the area of family and law, changed significantly, affecting the life of every woman. However, from the point of view of the changes in the legal situation of Latvian women, it was not until 1920 that they were able to exercise their right to vote for the first time. It is in the period between 1870 and the end of the First World War that Latvian writing actively reflects on the various aspects and constraints on women's lives. The novelist, publicist and political activist Ivande Kaija (1876–1942), who studied philosophy in Berne and Leipzig, lectured at the Sorbonne University, and from 1910 published articles on women's issues and socio-political questions in periodicals. She wrote several novels, the best known being *Original Sin* (1913), which defends women's rights by considering marriage without love to be immoral and making demands for the equal rights of men and women.

Alija Baumane's story *Process* (1927) depicts the exaggerated and misunderstood use of moral criteria against a vulnerable young woman. It also emphasises the role of education in a woman's life. From the story's beginning, the author confirms that schools have been transformed after the war, using Latvian instead of Russian and German. Also, the learning process is livelier for students of both sexes when they study together. The flashback recalls events before the First World War when a significant uproar erupts at the girls' school. Some students discovered that their classmate, Marga Sala, was expecting a baby. Although the final exam is only a few weeks away, Marga is expelled from the school because the headmistress has to respect the objections of many students to what they see as immorality. Baumane shows this absurd thinking through several students who believe that if they finish school with Marga, they will be considered immoral women. On the other hand, there is Marga's humble plea to be allowed to finish school, in which she explains the importance of education: "In our times, without a diploma, I am nothing. If I don't finish school, you know that my earnings will be insignificant. Then I have nowhere to go…" Baumane uses emotionally turbulent psychological depictions of human emotions to speak about misunderstood justice and a woman's right to education in all situations.

The mystery of the search for the ideal but imaginary lover, begun by Alija Baumane, is also solved by Mirdza Bendrupe in her novella *Helēna*. A young architecture student falls in love with a woman he meets in a cemetery, who turns out to be a ghost. This novella is from the collection *God's Whirlwinds*. The unusual incident at the centre of the novella, stirring up deeply hidden feelings and inclinations in people and tearing apart their accepted superficial shell, comes upon them like a whirlwind, bringing a reassessment of values. *Helēna* shows the sensuality and obsession of love in a somewhat mystical light.

On the one hand, Bendrupe looks at people with the gaze of a sympathiser, lovingly suffering for their mistakes and misfortunes or turning their imaginary beauty into a caricature with an ironic smile. On the other hand, the writer's gaze looks beyond, to a search for the meaning of our lives and our contact with the eternal and the divine. She approaches people from a peculiar, aesthetically mystical point of view, and the content of her psychological novellas and short stories is extraordinary.

In the 1920s and 1930s, several other women writers made their mark, for example, Lūcija Zamaiča (1893–1965), Zenta Maurina (1897–1978), Vilma Delle (1892–1980), Austra Krauze-Ozolina (1890–1941), Elīna Zalite (1898–1955), Aīda Niedra (1899–1972). Their works show a variety of genres and themes, with a particular focus on the life of the modern woman, women's education, mobility; alongside their efforts in the field of modernist prose, the genre of the intellectual essay and popular literature have also entered the scene.

The end of the Second World War generated a massive wave of migration from East-Central Europe, including the Baltics. Refugees accompanied the retreating German troops in 1944–45 and landed as displaced persons in German and Austrian camps, waiting for permission to move on. Most of the Baltic refugees eventually went to the US or Canada. In the post-war years, the most formally visible authors in Soviet Latvia were those who followed the dictates of Socialist Realism, such as Anna Sakse and Anna Brodele. At the same time, those pre-war writers who remained in Latvia and did not want to conform to the regime's demands continued their creative activity by translating or writing books for children (Bendrupe, Austra Dāle, Marta Grimma, Elza Stērste, etc). In the 1960s, a strong and visible generation of women writers entered Latvian literature on both sides of the Iron Curtain; in Soviet Latvia, there were fiction writers like Regīna Ezera, Ilze Indrāne (born 1926), and Dagnija Zigmonte (1931–1997), and poets like Vizma Belševica (1931–2005), Cecīlija Dinere (1919–1996) and Daina Avotiņa (born 1926). Ilze Šķipsna, Benita Veisberga (1928–2019) and Erna Ķikurei (1906–2003) published their first books in exile. It should be noted that the works of authors like Regīna Ezera and Ilze Indrāne were known to a wide readership while the books of exiled writers were published in limited editions.

Foreigners, by Ilze Šķipsna continues the line of auto-biographical narrative, but this is the only story in this anthology originally written in English by the author herself. She embodies her own life story and the life stories of many women in exile in the form of a young girl, Biruta. Biruta was a Latvian girl who came to Texas at eighteen as a displaced person sponsored by a church group that had collected enough money in donations to give a female foreign student a year at a college. Similarly, after the Displaced Person Camps, Šķipsna ended up in the USA and lived most of her life in Texas, married to an American.

Biruta is trying hard to explore and adapt to the local society, and learn English in order to be treated equally. As the story continues, Biruta appears as Bee, with an American fiancé, Hayden, who is not particularly interested in Biruta's origin and nationality. But this factor turns out to be important for his family: "Bee's a foreigner, and foreigners may be fascinating, but there's no point in marrying them. If you do, you'll come to grief." They marry and have children who speak both English and Latvian. The complication began when letters arrived from Soviet Latvia from aunts very close to Biruta. And the double meaning of the stranger enters the story: the Latvian Biruta, called Bee, is a stranger in the eyes of the family of the man she loves, while Biruta's family can never admit to their relatives in Latvia that Biruta married a foreigner.

There is a clear awareness that returning to one's homeland is impossible because the places that are remembered no longer exist. The past is not only another country but also another time outside the present. Through bodily sensations connected to the senses, the narrators can not only access the past and their homeland, but also create new connections and find their place wherever they are.

Regīna Ezera is one of Latvian literature's most outstanding fiction authors, and essentially an innovator. The interaction between man and nature, the beauty and diversity of life, the mission of a human, especially a woman, and the multifaceted complexity of her inner life are the main themes in Ezera's fiction.

For Ezera, nature is a measure of humanity, which she reveals in a series of zoological novelettes. These are stories about human and animal attitudes, animal in human and human in animal. In *The Hoopoes' Dance*, a family discovers that hoopoes have built a nest on the verandah of their summer home. An attempt to evict the hoopoes reveals both people's urban, narrow-minded views of bird life and their admiration for the persistent desire of hoopoes to live alongside humans, for their daily habits, familiarity and beautiful appearance. There is a kind of catharsis when, during a party, wine is spilt in the garden, and the hoopoes get drunk. They start a grotesque dance in which the house party hosts find parallels with their own lives and relationships with their fellow human beings.

A central purpose of these zoological novelettes is to reveal a significant peculiarity in human society and in individual character. She juxtaposes the "heroes" of the novelette, the representatives of the zoo-state, with the human being, through parallels, indirect comparisons, and transitions from one state to another.

The 1980s in Latvian (as in Baltic and Central European) literature were characterised by an unprecedented involvement of women in writing. In the mid-1980s, with the changes in the political situation, a new generation of women authors entered Latvian literature, including Gundega Repše, Andra Neiburga, Eva Rubene and Rudīte Kalpiņa. The entry of these new authors into literature marks a turning point in the direction of female dominance in Latvian prose, which gained even more ground in the 1990s and later.

When Gundega Repše's first stories appeared in the 1980s, they immediately attracted attention. In 1987, Repše's first book, *A Concert for My Friends in an Ashtray*, was published to great acclaim. It depicts a domestic environment, a profane time in which the story's protagonists feel out of place with their romanticism, longing for something they cannot articulate. Real-psychological imagery predominates and reveals the direct influence of the artworks on the lives of the characters and society. In the story *Čiks and Maija*, the two main teenage characters have troubled families: Maija is raised by a single mother, and Čiks's parents share the same living space but are emotionally separated. Čiks has studied a lot of art books at a friend's house, and his idea of the ideal world is shaped by them. Art has shaped the boy's understanding of how life should be. Čiks has built himself a shelter, a hut, the walls of which are adorned with reproductions of artworks by Latvian artists cut out of magazines. A landscape by Vilhelms Purvītis (1872–1945) is named and contrasted, significantly, with grotesque paintings of folk art by Maija Tabaka (born 1939) and Miervalds Polis (born 1948) — a metaphor for broken families. The children's characters approach absolute symbolism, their conversations are at times too clever and abstract. The author's typical attention to detail, her ability to use a score of colours, sounds and scents, create the individual tonality of each story. A precisely targeted detail can bring an unexpected additional emotion, a new depth of thought.

Nora Ikstena and Inga Ābele also represent this trend, and were joined later by Andra Manfelde, Inga Žolude, Inga Gaile and others.

Fiction written by women at the turn of the century focuses on the inner dimension of life. Dace Rukšāne's *Romance* (2002) became an important event, taking a frank look at the relationship between a man and a woman and female sexuality. For example, Laima Muktupāvela's first book, *The Champignon Covenant* (2002), is gaining wider recognition because it is based on the still relevant realities of her search for work and her experiences in Ireland. Life stories are becoming particularly topical, where the projection of one's own identity and sense of family is used. This period can be called the renaissance of the short story, with the publication of collections of short stories by Nora Ikstena and Inga Ābele and *Push Push* by Andra Neiburga. Everyday events, sensations, smells and textures are essential to the stories.

Inga Ābele has her own unique style, which encompasses the richness of language and human psychology, as well as different contexts, historical periods and current issues. Her prose is characterised by strong imagery and atmosphere. Abel's characters are created by psychologically exploring their souls. Thus, the characters resonate precisely in any space and time in which they are portrayed, whether it is a typical Latvian household, a Latvian rural landscape or an actual historical era of the past. The story *Nettles* shows two generations of women, a mother-in-law and a daughter-in-law, in the everyday situation of rural life. But in the story, Ābele records the inability of a young woman who has entered her husband's farm to identify herself with the place symbolised by the broken and withered but uncut ash tree. She hides her longing and pain behind a callousness, like the nettles she picks with her bare hands, feeling no pain. Fear of monotony and routine, when there is no time to look up at the sky, and all illusions must be abandoned.

Nora Ikstena is known for her sophisticated writing style and her careful attention to language. Ikstena's prose is often analysed in the context of women's writing and feminism, as it is full of vivid and psychologically rich female characters and relationships between women of different generations, especially mothers and daughters. *A Day in Her Life* is the story of a young girl having to choose between the physical and spiritual love embodied by her friends, the young boys

Kirje and Timotejs. Her boyfriend is Timotejs, a seminarian who is devoted to theology and the church, and the heroine of the story finds it challenging to accept this and fight her feelings for this young man. Ikstena's story has the theological motif found elsewhere, a child born in a dream, amaryllis in bloom. Ikstena's thesis is that the human body is not a prison of the soul or the worst enemy, but a valuable creation of nature that can also be beautiful, so there is no need to be too ashamed of nudity and sensual experiences.

Andra Neiburga (1957–2019) made her debut in Latvian literature in the mid-1980s, was actively published in periodicals in the early 1990s, and then took a literary hiatus until 2004, when her second collection of short stories, *Push Push*, was published. At that time, the book was widely acclaimed by critics and readers and recognised as one of the most brilliant examples of storytelling in 21st-century Latvian literature. The style of expression is unrefined, and the characters are without make-up and in their everyday lives seem just like us.

Inga Žolude's fiction is marked by defiant and fierce femininity, in which she relates to the best Latvian women's writing — Ezera, Repše, Ikstena, Ābele, Manfelde, etc. At the same time, this prose also inscribes itself in a kind of national-ecological lineage of Latvian literature, with its romanticised settings of country houses, forests, gardens and the sea. The plot of Inga Žolude's short story *Lichens* (2015) is based on a married woman named Brita and her search for herself, which is closely connected to bodily experience, where a woman in the existing patriarchal order takes the position of a victim and is subordinated to a man's lust and desires, which are embodied in the story by her husband. Brita remains passive in the relationship, which is closely linked to the construction of traditional femininity. Žolude uses a range of natural images, starting with lichens, which Brita explores out of professional interest, but also water, waterfalls, rocks, forests, the natural world as a space in which it is possible to reclaim oneself, but at the same time shows the impossibility of doing so. Žolude has one of the most precise and honest anatomies of the relationship between a woman and a man in recent Latvian literature. The story's stylistically and emotionally diverse characters are real people who, by their actions, along with the sublime and the fragile, also create an aftertaste of bitterness and meanness.

In the last decade, several new writers have entered Latvian prose, which makes us talk about a new renaissance of the short story genre, including Jana Egle, Dace Vīgante, Sabīne Košeļeva, and Laura Vinogradova. But that's another story, continuing the line of women's writing in Latvia in the 21st century.

Old Karlīne (1897)
Anna Brigadere (1861–1933)
Translated by Laura Adlers

It's autumn. A middle-aged woman, poorly but neatly dressed, walked along a wide path through the woods. She was about forty to forty-five years old, but she looked much older: hard work, worry and heartbreak had left their marks. Who could have imagined this face had once been beautiful and lovely? And yet Dārte Kārklin had once been the prettiest girl in the district. Whether at dances in the tavern or at festivities, Dārte was the brightest shining star to the boys, even when they were deep in the drink and not thinking straight. The pretty girl knew her power and in the arrogance of youth she often poked and teased her poor admirers. There was a rumour that Dārte hated all the servants and only liked the landowners' sons, and fat Juris in particular, Dārte's most ardent suitor to date, was the greatest slanderer of all. Other boys, whom the proud maiden had also teased, listened to Juris' words as if they were from the Wisdom of Sirach. The girls scoffed and rejoiced that they had broken "the stubborn one's" upturned nose. Dārte herself seemed not to notice. It didn't seem to matter to her if they were praising her or slandering her. She had become very, very quiet. She no longer went to the tavern, nor to festivities, and so through her indifference she silenced the idle gossip. And yet people continued talking about her. In the middle of winter, still three months from St. George's Day, Dārte suddenly went missing. She left one night with all her things, no one knew where. The landowner's wife grumbled and worried about how she would manage, especially with her second son setting up a new home and planning a wedding. But when her neighbour urged her to drive off and find the runaway, she exclaimed angrily: "Ha! Why? I don't need aimless wanderers, there is no shortage of hard-working girls!"

So the landowner's wife did know what had happened to Dārte and where she had gone.

On Sunday after church the parishioners were talking about Dārte. "Well, sister," the old shepherd girl Grieta nudged her friend, "I had already noticed long ago there was something wrong there, you know? That landowner's son Andžus pursued her, never letting up; and now — now she has disappeared, Andžus has married into the Gailis family and you see, things have not worked out for Dārte."

"Oh, dear God, then that's what happened. Yes, yes, she aimed high! She destroyed all of the servant boys, and then there was the landowner's son!"

The rumours continued to grow and pretty soon had spread throughout the district as if they were the truth, that proud Dārte had been cheated, and in order to hide her shame, she had escaped to another district.

It's possible that similar memories replayed behind the wrinkled forehead of the lonely wanderer. Big blue eyes, which bore further testimony to her past beauty, looked on, serious and hard, her pinched lips often twitched slowly. The wind had completely stopped, and the woods had fallen silent. The sun wound her threads around the trees and shrubs. Here under a spruce a hare, frightened by the footsteps, ran off into the woods; here again a slender deer ran across the path in long jumps. Dārte, emerging from the woods, noticed in front of her a potato field that stretched along the side of the road. A short distance away a group of workers were harvesting the crop. That was the Lielmanis' field, and there on the other side, at the edge of the woods, the Lielmanis' stately buildings could be seen. Dārte remained standing. She watched the workers for a long time, her hand shielding her eyes. Finally, disgruntled, she shook her head and started towards the Lielmanis' road, when she heard a happy whistling behind her. She turned around to see a boy, about twelve years old. He was carrying two large baskets hanging on a yoke, and to pass the time, whistling joyfully, he threw tiny stones at the sparrows which had gathered on the ground in front of him, picking at the crumbs that had fallen from his baskets. The yoke often slid off his shoulders and the baskets pulled him down towards the ground, but the boy wasn't bothered. Now he suddenly stopped his loud whistling as his hand holding the stone froze in midair. From out of nowhere there stood an old woman, whom he had never seen before.

"A witch!" the frightened boy thought. "What else could there be out here on the edge of the woods but a witch!" Juris knew about spirits, dead people, witches and ghosts. He knew old Mārcis' stories better than the Lord's Prayer and the Ten Commandments. He was the bravest and most carefree boy when there were no woods, cemeteries or old barns nearby and when the sun was still high up in the sky. But at dusk and around the middle of the day Juris tiptoed around, his eyes darting around in all directions. Every strange creature he met when he was alone, whether it was a person or an animal, he regarded as "evil". "It appears in so many different forms," he thought. There were very few who escaped the devil's claws like Juris. He once left a wallet on the main road untouched, afraid that it was cursed. And now right near the woods in the middle of the day an old woman appeared, as if from out of the ground!

"Hello, little boy! Where are you going?"

"Yes, hello, little boy, that's how they all start."

"Are you from the Lielmanis' farm, bringing lunch to the workers? Is everyone in the field, is Karlīne there too?"

"The servant girl Karlīne? Yes, of course, where else would she be? Everyone set out this morning together."

What did this strange woman not know, even about Karlīne, and she is from a completely different region. "Listen, when you go down there, could you tell Karlīne to come to the edge of the woods for a short while during her lunch break? Tell her that — that a little old lady is waiting for her, will you tell her? And here," the strange woman searched in her sack and pulled out a red apple, "here is something for you."

"No, no," the boy waved it off, "I don't eat apples! I will tell her all the same!"

The boy left, the baskets swinging as he went. Dārte watched him go with compassion. "Such a nervous boy. Perhaps he's an orphan," she sighed. "Yes indeed, it's a tough life to be treated like a footrest by others." She sat on a tree stump by the road and watched the boy impatiently. He had reached the workers, and a couple of minutes later a figure left the group and quickly rushed towards the woods. It was a young girl, with a medium build and a pretty face. Her kerchief had slid off her braided hair, her large eyes sparkled with joy. Dārte reached both arms out to her.

"Mother, dear Mother! Where did you come from?"

"My girl, my darling! I wanted to see how you are faring."

"So you came all this way just to see me?"

"Well yes, that is how it ended up. My landowner's wife sent me to Gailenis, you see — you know, where her daughter was married and moved to last autumn — to go there and ask if I could find out about a new fashionable drink. The people at Gailenis live like lords, and so I stayed the night and today I decided to take a slight detour. I really wanted to see you. I haven't heard from you in half a year."

"That's quite a detour! That's half of your normal journey, Mother, how will you make it home today?"

"Not to worry, perhaps a traveller will take me with him; if nothing else, I will stay at Zirnis overnight, where I know a servant's wife. But tell me, how are you? Are your landowners happy?"

"Me? I'm very well — very well, my landowners are happy, and I have no complaints."

This she said quickly, almost harshly, and even though her words indicated all was well, her mother's ear heard something else. She was quiet for a moment and then said in a sombre voice: "Yes, child, it was your choice. You know I would have preferred for you to have stayed with the Puselnieks — close by!"

"I'm not complaining, not at all!" Karlīne replied, her lip trembling and then, with bursting into tears, hid her head in her mother's lap. "My girl! Who cries like that!" her mother exclaimed, frightened, and started to calm her down, at first almost yelling, until her voice became more slow and soft until she finally collapsed in tears. They sat this way for a while, until each had unburdened their hearts through tears. Karlīne was the first to pull herself together and leapt to her feet.

"Oh, Mother, I must go, otherwise lunch will be finished, and you still have a long way to go on foot."

Her mother also got up and wiped her tears. "Yes, girl, yes, go now, go to work, don't be late. God be with you and guide your path!"

Karlīne kissed both of her mother's hands, picked up her kerchief from the ground, tied it onto her head, pulled it over her swollen eyes and half ran back to the field to work, turning a couple more times to wave goodbye to her mother.

Dārte went on her way with a heavy heart. Not one word, not one complaint from her daughter's mouth, and yet she knew what was bothering her, she knew better than could have been explained in a hundred words. The sun had almost set when she emerged from the woods. She turned around and looked for a long time at the road she had just travelled, and then folded her hands and said in a loud, almost impatient voice: "Lord, forgive us our trespasses, as we forgive those who trespass against us!"

Countless stars already filled the clear night sky as people finished their work for the day and left for home. They met big Ansis on the road driving home from the mill. The girls wanted to go for a ride, but Ansis rejected their pleas bluntly, lashed his horse and led it along the trail into the woods. Everyone else went straight across the field to their home. When their voices could no longer be heard, Ansis slowly turned the horse around and returned to the edge of the woods. Here he stopped, got out of the wagon and stared like a hawk into the darkness of the night. Soon he noticed something black moving and began to work around his horse, listening with a beating heart to the gentle steps that came ever closer.

"Oh, it's you, Ansis," he heard a pleasant voice, "how you scared me! What is it? Has something happened?"

"The trail ended," Ansis lied, "but everything is fine again."

"Well! Get on. We'll drive home together like real noblemen. Why are you so late?"

"I couldn't dig up my section so quickly, I was late back from lunch. This is just fine, that I can drive home with you, the landowner's wife will scold me for being last anyway."

"Well, then, we'll just have to drive faster!" And lashing the horse, Ansis went at a fast pace along the dark road. The horse arrived exhausted in the middle of the homestead.

Karlīne took her milking pail and went to the barn. She found her cow, crouched down and started milking her. On the other side she heard the "little" boy Mikus cursing and swearing. He was grooming the horses, which was impossible to do without swearing. Then she heard a joyful whistle. Ansis had unharnessed his horse and had brought it to the stall to be groomed.

"Aha," Mikus scoffed, "the miller is also home. He must have been delayed, picking up girls along the side of the road; the mayor's girl is always lagging behind."

"I guess she wasn't interested in going with you?"

"What would I have to do with her? Do I not have enough respectable girls to go with, rather than with that tramp?"

"Shut your mouth!" Ansis yelled.

"Who are you to tell me to shut my mouth, the whole world already knows what this proud Karlīne is all about. Where's her father, huh? What good mother's child would get involved with her. She knows this very well herself, that's why…"

And then there was a sudden roar, and Mikus calling out: "Oh Lord! Murderer! Save me! Save me!"

Karlīne had dashed to the other side with lightning speed. Mikus was lying on the floor. Ansis had pushed one foot down on his chest and grabbed him by the collar. Mikus was held as if in a vice, and unable to express his anger any other way, was yelling with all his might.

"I'll teach you to slander girls," Ansis whispered, hissing with anger.

Karlīne grabbed his hand. "Let him be!" she said quickly.

Ansis came to his senses. "The scoundrel," he cursed.

Several people from the house ran into the stalls. Mikus wanted to say something, but took one look at Ansis' threatening face and dragged himself off to his room, swearing under his breath. No one learned the reason for the fight, each was left to interpret the incident as they wished.

After that day, Karlīne became even quieter than before, she almost never spoke to Ansis any more and avoided crossing his path. "That Karlīne's like a mute," the girls said, "you couldn't chop a word out of her with an axe." Only the landowner's wife praised her: "You should all be more like her, first to work, and last to talk!"

Soon spring arrived, an early spring with her warm sun and her cold winds. It was the first few days of March. At Lielmanis, the servants and landowners were going to the tavern to celebrate contract day. The landowner's wife had called Karlīne into her room first thing that morning to discuss her new contract for the next year. She offered her cake and cooked ham, embraced her and praised her and promised to raise her pay. But Karlīne didn't want to stay. "Well, I'm sure we'll chat at the tavern," the wife said, unconcerned. She knew from experience that agreements were best made at the tavern.

This week was Karlīne's group's week, and for this reason she was also last to the contract day celebrations. A cold dry wind blew with all its might, fluttering her skirt, pulling at her kerchief, blowing through her curly hair, as if inviting her: "Come on, let's fight!" Karlīne was overcome with reckless joy. Like an electric spark she felt the vigour and joy of youth. She pushed ahead into the reckless wind and started running. She stopped in the shade at the edge of the woods, gasping for air. "This is where I met Ansis that night," she thought slowly, looking all around her. "My God! He's standing right there again like before, and I thought he was already at the tavern ages ago."

"Shall we go together, Karlīne? It will be a shorter trip; that's why I waited for you at the edge of the forest, I saw you run out of the house in a hurry."

"For all I care, we can go together, the road is wide enough." Her words were rather curt, but her voice sounded happy. Ansis was hopeful.

"But you are arriving so late, all of the good landowners

will be taken, now only the husks will be left."

"You should worry more about yourself," Karlīne snapped back. "You are also arriving late."

Both of them fell silent. Karlīne's sharp response had scared Ansis, he was struggling to think of something that would bring him closer to his desired outcome, but he could think of nothing. His brow was sweaty, they had almost arrived at their destination, and still nothing accomplished; but how should he start, what should he say? He was tongue-tied. Karlīne also felt she should say something. "Would you not like to stay right here at Lielmanis?" she finally started. "Me? No! I want to become a manor servant. It's different there: a good contract and a place to call my own, that's worth having!"

"I see! A manor servant! But how could you — I have only ever heard that they accept married men at the manor."

"This is true, so if I want to be a servant in a manor, then there is only one thing to do..."

He looked sideways at his walking companion. She blushed a deep red and looked straight ahead at the road, biting her lip; two big tears fell from her wide eyes and rolled down her cheeks, without her even noticing. Suddenly he was beside her, embracing her: "Karlīne, darling Karlīne! What do you think, the two of us together? Do you not like me even a little?"

Karlīne pulled herself away from his arms. "Let me go! Do you not remember back in autumn? What Mikus said? It's true!"

"Karlīne!" Ansis exclaimed happily. "Is that why you were so quiet and harsh? Do you think I don't know? Do you think it matters to me? I like you, and even if you were the child of a gypsy, I would still want nobody but you." He held her tight once more. "And that is also why I want to work in a manor, because our lives would be nobody else's business, we would live there like noblemen in our room. And then I thought, we could also bring your mother to live with us, manor wives also have to go out on days, and who would stay home. Your mother has lived a long life and will be tired of living off someone else." Now Karlīne had no idea what to say, but Ansis read on her lips the most understandable reply. And so there in the woods they had their own "contract day", at which they came to an agreement about their big life contract.

The sun was already setting when they started back towards home, in order to avoid meeting up with the revellers from the tavern.

On the last Sunday before St. George's Day our couple stood as newlyweds in the grove at Lielmanis by the old leafy linden tree. Although sorry he was unable to retain a hardworking young man and woman for the next year, the Lielmanis owner spared nothing for the wedding reception — he and his wife ordered a pig to be slaughtered and cakes to be baked. Only the members of the household were invited to the wedding, amongst them Mikus, who, having drowned his anger in home-brewed beer, was the most animated dancer. The only relative of the newlyweds in attendance was the bride's mother, as this was her only family, and the groom's family lived too far away and springtime was usually not the best time for a wedding, since everyone's granaries and silos would be empty and what could they offer for the wedding? Although the wedding guests were few, it was a very jovial affair. The newlyweds danced at the beginning, but towards evening they somehow ended up walking together out to the birches to see if there was any birch sap to offer their wedding guests. And luckily, the jovial guests forgot to wait for them, because they stood there for a long time, as if in a trance, and forgot to go home — the world just seemed that different and wonderful to them that day.

Listen! What were those noises, flowing and vibrating through the still night air? Had the sunken castle risen up from the moss-covered hill in the middle of the forest, was the tower guard ringing the giant bells? One could almost imagine there was a supernatural cause for these sounds, they floated through the air so beautifully, bouncing and echoing throughout the forest nearby. Ah! They could be heard again on the other side and there again! And now right there in the nearby birch grove! Those were our little songbirds, greeting the spring. These songs of springtime were not songs of rejoicing, the long-drawn sounds were more like crying, and resounding from grove to grove and blending in the air, they rippled in the distance like the continuous sound of a clock.

If it's true that the happiest person is one who would not trade places with anyone in the world, then Ansis certainly belonged to this group of enviable mortals. His wife's eyes were worth more to him than all the treasures of the world, and not one knight returned home from a hard battle searching with such longing for the glow from the windows of his high castle the way Ansis, upon returning home from work, longed to see the little flames glowing from his home. And if there was anything that could make Karlīne even happier, it was the little curly-haired blue-eyed child whom she cradled about a year later.

Little Krišītis grew big, but remained the only child. "The

only child, a troublesome child," his grandmother was known to say, but Karlīne laughed and replied that Krišītis had caused no trouble so far and she didn't believe this saying to be true.

The time came when the sun set on Dārte's life. One beautiful autumn day she set out on a great journey from which no one returns. "Don't cry, my daughter," she calmed Karlīne in an almost happy voice, "I'm going home, and what a beautiful departure God has given me! I know you are with a good man — Ansis is pure gold — and Krišītis! My little boy, my darling! Bring him to me once more, so I may see his sweet face." And she held the little boy's soft hand tightly in her own cold hand, as her breaths started to fade. The child watched her with wide eyes full of wonder and recoiled, screaming loudly. The dying woman's eyes widened again as she looked around her with a strange expression on her face. The child cried even louder, and Karlīne carried him away to comfort him; when she returned, her mother's heart had stopped beating.

Karlīne cried bitter tears for her mother, but these wounds were bandaged and treated with loving hands and soon she grew accustomed to the empty corner, and after a while Krišītis only occasionally remembered his grandmother as if in a dream.

It's Saturday at Christmas. Everywhere you looked, since early in the morning, there was smoke coming from the chimneys; in the morning, the smoke was thick and black, in the evening it was thinner; in the morning, the landowners baked pies and flat cakes, towards evening — the servants' wives continued. In the kitchen, savoury meat and sausages were boiling in big pots on hooks; everything smelled like Christmas, and everyone, big or small, was working hard to prepare a worthy feast.

Karlīne's small home was also nice and tidy, lovely to see. Even the little windowsills had shed the old thick layer of ice and now, as evening approached, it was adorned with a new, ornate tapestry.

Krišītis got in the way of the mysterious, charming weavers, destroying their fine work with his warm breath. He looked impatiently at the snow-covered clearing and the lonely road: "Father is still not coming!"

"I'm sure he will be home soon. The dark forest is far away, and the roads are all snowed in." His mother calmed him down, thinking to herself: "He should have been home by now, he promised to leave earlier on Christmas Eve."

"Mother, will Christmas be here soon, has it already arrived in Riga?" the boy asked again a bit later.

"It will certainly already be there," his mother answered, taking the good clothes out of the chest. "Oh, Mother! Which fancy shirt will you give me to wear tomorrow?" Krišītis rejoiced. "It must already be Christmas in Jelgava, dusk is falling."

His mother was also looking out of the little window more often, her face looking more and more worried. Krišītis could not keep the cold out, now even the windowsill was being snowed in like a wall. Outside it was already so dark it was difficult to see anything.

"But it must be Christmas now, Mother!"

"Now it is!" His mother replied quietly.

"Hooray!" Krišītis shouted and galloping around the small room he sang:

Christmas has arrived
In a decorated sleigh;

Hurry, children, to greet it
In your bare feet.

Christmas had not yet "arrived" in Karlīne's little home. Until she heard Ansis' voice, she would not feel the festive spirit of the holiday.

"Mother! I'm hungry," Krišītis begged her.

Karlīne put a couple of pieces of bread on the table, then took a pot with broth from the stove and poured it into the boy's cup. "Eat, you must be hungry, I will wait for your Father."

"I want to wait too," Krišītis exclaimed suddenly, reaching for the bread, "I don't want to go to bed yet." When he had satisfied his hunger, he started again: "Mother! I'll recite a song for Father, alright? *I will bring from heaven* or *Say unto the Lord*? No! *I will bring from heaven* is better for me."

And he quickly looked it up in the songbook and started to recite in a monotone voice. But his mother was only half listening. The boy started yawning, his eyes became sleepy, and his head soon fell to his chest. His mother picked him up, carried him to bed and covered him up. She blew out the candle, so as not to waste it, and wrapping a shawl around her, she went outside.

The winter night was dark, the sky was completely overcast, a light snow blew into her eyes. She listened, holding her breath. Nothing! She looked into the dark night for a long time. Nothing there! She walked a few steps further and listened again. She thought she heard a noise. No, those were her feet, sinking and squeaking in the soft snow. She started to shiver. She slowly turned back, retracing her footsteps. She saw candles burning in other workers' rooms, she could hear loud talking and laughter.

Everyone was home, yes, everyone was home! Why was he so late? She knew the black forest was a fair distance — but still — she should run up the hill. There were a couple of other men from the lodgings who went with Ansis to clear the forest; perhaps they were already home and could tell her why Ansis was so late. Karlīne ran up the hill and looked. No! They had not returned home yet either. Old Grieta's mother stood in the door of the building and was looking into the darkness waiting just like her.

"Just like men, girl! Just like men," she tried to calm Karlīne down, "who will give working people a holiday? Yes, and it's even different now, when I was young…"

Karlīne wasn't listening to how things were when Grieta was young; she had heard it a hundred times before. Satisfied, she went inside. Even nature demanded her part. She sat down and started to eat, but was suddenly so consumed with fear that the food caught in her throat and her brow broke out in a cold sweat. "Something bad, yes, something bad! The only thing it could be is that something bad has happened!" she whispered and pushed the bowl away.

And time dragged on slowly between despair and hope, between anxiety and calm.

The thin grease candle had all but burned out. Karlīne focused her gaze on the flickering, crackling little flame. The little room was quiet, except for Krišītis' calm breathing. A dog barked. Karlīne leapt to her feet and ran into the yard. The sky was clear again, there were countless stars against the dark heavens. Pleiades was high up in the sky, so it must have been almost midnight. "God, dear God, have mercy!" Karlīne whispered, wringing her hands.

The dog barked again — this time louder and longer. In the distance she could hear the squeak of a wagon.

"Praise God!" Karlīne called out with heartfelt joy. "He must be starving, poor thing! I have to check if the food is still warm." She ran inside and started to busy herself. She started up the fire in the stove, put a new candle in the lantern and looked through the chest for dry socks and a shirt. "He will be chilled to the bone, my little pigeon." Outside the door she heard a hollow sound, Karlīne's heart beat with joy. "Aha! He's climbing the stairs with heavy steps; he must have ridden through all of the forests!" Karlīne rushed to open the door: "My husband…"

"Don't be alarmed!" answered a slow and unsteady voice.

Karlīne stood as if frozen, and shouted: "Ansis! Where's Ansis!"

"Ansis — don't be alarmed! — a tree in the forest — just don't be alarmed." Karlīne stumbled into the middle of the yard. There! Several figures were moving around the wagon on which lay a dark, still bundle. "Ansis! Ansis!" She'd collapsed onto the wagon, fearfully feeling the stiff limbs, moaning slowly.

"Karlīne! Karlīne!" Someone was shaking her. "Pull yourself together, for God's sake! A Christian has to trust in God."

"Is he — still — alive?"

"He's alive! He's alive! Of course, he is!" the first to speak rushed to answer. "Help us get him into bed."

And now began the difficult task of getting the bruised body inside. His workmates tried carefully and anxiously to help the poor man, but unfortunately skill and agility worked against their emotions. Luckily the injured man was unconscious. After they got the patient into bed, the workers left one after the other; the only one who stayed was the one who had first brought her the news. He started to explain what had happened, but Karlīne seemed not to be listening or was not aware of what was happening.

"And so — our landowner was also still there; he promised to send a doctor tomorrow — oh yes! — and he said to put cold wet cloths on his head." The worker stood there for a while, and hearing no response, turned towards the door. "If you need a man's advice, Karlīne, you know where to find me." He opened the door slowly and left. "He will not survive," he said to himself as he left.

"Wake up, if only I could wake up!" Karlīne whispered, rubbing her forehead. It all seemed like a horrible dream, and she didn't know where to start, what to do. His injured chest started to rise slowly; his head moved imperceptibly. She remembered the man telling her about the wet cloths. She quickly grabbed Krišītis' 'fancy' shirt, ripped it up, ran to the well, and after a short while the ice-cold cloth was cooling the poor man's burning forehead. "Live! Live!" Karlīne whispered trembling with joy. "Oh Lord! Lord!" The patient breathing quickened and shortened. Karlīne could not change the cold compresses quickly enough.

This continued for a couple of hours. Karlīne was getting ready to run to the well for cold water again when the patient suddenly pulled the compress off his forehead, opened his eyes and in a clear voice he asked: "Where is the boy?" Karlīne ran to the boy's bed. "Krišītis, wake up! Your father wants to see you." The child jumped out of bed, scared. His mother brought him to the bedside, he held on tight to his mother's neck, frightened and half asleep, crying. "Here is your son, Ansis, do you want to see him?" But the patient was already deep in a sleep from which he would not awaken.

January's snowstorms covered the new grave with a thick blanket, and the chatter about the horrific event died down. His beloved image lived on in only one heart, in countless ways, as a dream of happiness and youth.

Karlīne didn't have the leisure of crying and feeling sorry for herself, as she had to provide for herself and her son. During the summer she worked in the fields around the manor for a wage, in the winter she spun and knitted for the wealthy ladies of the manor, who if they wanted to have nicer clothes or linens, knew enough to appreciate Karlīne's fine spinning. But one had to wonder why Karlīne didn't offer her son as a shepherd, he was old enough. The wives became restless: would she raise him to be a gentleman: this child should have been herding a long while ago already, to earn his way. But the chatter was even louder when they heard that Karlīne had gone to the sexton to ask if he would take her son in at the school. Good Lord, who had heard of this! Learning to write, who needed that! They all knew nothing good would come of it! Perhaps a landowner's or a supervisor's or a miller's son, but a servant's — a widow's child! Even though the wives chattered and gossiped freely and some discussed with Karlīne in a roundabout way the 'paths of sin' and 'disappearing forever', which sometimes happened with those who were 'educated', still around Martin's Day Kriss enrolled in school with the sexton. At first, he wanted to start after the winter, so he could 'immerse himself in the readings', but later, when

Krišs returned home from school with one commendation after another, Karlīne's strength doubled, and — to everyone's surprise — Krišs completed the sexton's school along with the Lielmanis owner's sons.

Krišs was confirmed on Palm Sunday. As was tradition, after the sermon the minister called each of the confirmands' names. As he went along the long row, he stopped, coughed and continued in a louder voice: "Krišjānis Ragaiss. I must also mention, dear parishioners, that of all the children, Krišjānis Ragaiss was the first to learn the commandments, as well as the other lessons of faith and responses and I mention this to the congregation, so this may encourage other parents to teach their children the Lord's wisdom and follow the way of the Lord."

It was so quiet in the church you could have heard a leaf fall. The minister meant well with these words, but unfortunately, they did not fall into the hearts of angels.

The landowners' wives turned arrogantly away with anger and hatred in their hearts. The minister would always announce and praise the best student, but the student was usually one of the landowners' children.

Only one heart was bursting with love and pride; the mother's eyes saw nothing in the whole church but her slender son kneeling at the altar.

The next day Karlīne went with her son to the manor. She would ask the lord of the manor if he would take her son to work as a gardener or in the stalls, or as a huntsman. What luck it would be to get into the manor and in a good job! What do people at the manor have to worry about? If you work hard and please the lord, you will have bread to eat.

"I believe I know you," the lord of the manor looked at Karlīne, "are you not the widow of Ragaiss, who died so horribly here?"

"Oh! So, the gentleman still remembers me!" Karlīne said happily. "I have come to ask you, sir, if you would take my son into service — he is grown now — he was confirmed yesterday. He has gone to school, he can write in German, he studied with the sexton." She pushed Krišs forward, quietly urging him to kiss the lord's hand.

He observed the blond boy with pleasure. *"Nun, was für einen Dienst möchtest du denn haben?"* (So, what kind of a job would you like to have?) The boy blushed up to his ears. Where was all of his German vocabulary? *"Mir — mir — ich weiss nicht,"* (Me — me — I don't know) he stammered. The lord smiled and handed him a book. *"Kannst du das lesen?"* (Can you read this?) Well, of course, he could read it. He read quickly and confidently, though he didn't understand what he was reading. The lord appeared to be satisfied. He then asked him to write and calculate and then, after a moment of consideration, said to Karlīne: "I want to keep him. My granary supervisor is quite old and his writing and calculations are not what they used to be. Krišs can be his assistant — that will be good!" He turned to Krišs with a serious face: "But clean hands and a clean heart, boy! Otherwise…" and didn't complete his threat. "Not my boy, not my boy!" Karlīne exclaimed hurriedly and fell to kissing the lord's hand. "I have raised him well; he will not touch anything that is not his."

"I hope not," the lord said as he got up. They were dismissed. They were so happy, they felt neither hungry nor tired. What would Karlīne's heart say, if we could translate? "Is there any son in the district like my Krišs? Who was just yesterday praised by the minister in front of the whole congregation? And who has always been top of his class? And whom did the lord of the manor speak with in German and ask to read some passages? And who has worked with all her heart and soul to ensure he would become this person, better and smarter than all the rest? Yes, who was that?" Slowly, but confidently the snobbish little devil opened the door to Karlīne's heart, where it found a pleasant and well-prepared home.

Krišjānis Ragaiss quickly adapted to his new life. In just a year he was almost solely responsible for all the riches of the granary, and the old supervisor was there in an honorary position, 'to watch over the keys'. When he died four years later, Krišs became the manager not only of the granary, but also of the keys and was given a place to live on the estate — two large rooms and a garden.

Karlīne's first years at the manor were as lovely as a fairytale. Why was the 'supervisor', as she was sometimes called, not invited and honoured! And Krišs ensured his mother was able to appear at events in style. She always had a silk scarf and a shawl that rustled. Karlīne enjoyed appearing where there were people, either at a party or in church. Now, where she lived so close to church, she attended out of habit. In her heart she was no longer driven to church as in the past. She knew she had to praise God for all she had received, but had she also not been good and devout, and had Krišs not been the most upright boy in the district? It was only right and fair that after so much hardship the warmth of the sun and happiness was shining on them once more.

Krišjānis Ragaiss was no longer just some boy. There

was a new brewer and miller at the manor, both Prussian. He befriended them, and the manor clerk — a dairy farmer's son — joined them as a fourth. He was one of Kriss' classmates in the sexton's school. Kriss liked his new community; some were called gentlemen, including him. In the evenings, if they had time, they liked to go to Kriss' home. His mother would make tea and the young men would play cards. They would converse in German, which Kriss was good at now. His mother enjoyed listening to the foreign language at first, but she tired of it after a while, even the card games no longer interested her, so she would leave the young men and spend lonely evenings in the other room sitting at the spinning wheel, where she lost herself in memories of her youth.

Even the card players got tired of the same old games.

"Do you know what," Vahtels the clerk said one evening — his real name was Paipala — "when I went to school in Jelgava," he liked to talk about his school days in Jelgava, "my landlady had a son, a damn fine man! He knew all kinds of tricks. He had once worked for a wealthy man as a valet, and he showed us how these men played for money. I'm telling you! You could win thousands in the blink of an eye!"

"How crazy," the brewer added.

"Can you show us how this game works?" the miller asked. "There are many different games, I know them all very well — well, shall we try?"

"What nonsense!" Kriss declared. "That's not a game for us."

"You're sorry to part with a few coins?"

"Sorry! Sorry or not, can I make more? You know I'm not paid in cash. You all earn more in one month than I earn in a year. But if you want to play for grain and potatoes, I'm in," he finished laughing. "Well, can you not convert those into money? You won't die over a couple of coins, and if you have none, I can lend you some." Vahtels was winding him up, jingling coins in his sack. Vahtels dealt the cards. Kriss protested less. It all seemed very innocent. They played.

The rooster had already crowed a second time when the young men left. They parted ways, quickly and quietly saying: "Until tomorrow night?"

The devil was given one finger, and he took the whole hand. There was no longer any resistance.

"Son, you look so pale and exhausted!" Kriss' mother said to him about a week later. "It must be from all the card games in the evenings. You should give that up now. I don't like this devil's game at all."

"Go on, what nonsense! Who doesn't play cards nowadays! We can't live like monks." Kriss left, slamming the door behind him. "How Kriss has changed, he is nothing like my son!" Karlīne sighed. Kriss had truly lost his cheerful nature. He went to work serious and ill-tempered. What had he worked for all year! All of his earnings ended up in Vahtels' hands in just a week. "But I really am going to stop now!" he declared. "He won't reel me in any more, I won't be playing with them tonight — let him find another fool!" But a little while later, he was already thinking: "What's lost is lost, it's not worth feeling sorry about it! Surely, I will win it back!" Determined, he returned home. When his evening guests had gathered, Kriss hastened to tell them he was no longer going to play, he was tired of it.

"Tired of it!" Vahtels mocked him. "You don't have this,

you see," he said, rubbing his fingertips together.

"What business is it of yours?" Krišs exclaimed, upset. "Do I owe you anything?"

"Now, now, don't be angry! If you have no money on hand — you know — I would be happy to…"

"You know, if I were you, I would play," the brewer also started in, "he has taken so much from you, are you going to let him keep it?"

"Well, of course!" the miller agreed. "Now you just have to take him apart. What fool loses courage right at the start!" Krišs conceded. And that's how it went word for word, until Krišs once again thought: "This will be the last time. Let's play one more time this evening!" When they parted that night, Krišs had won back a good portion of his losses. Now, of course, he couldn't leave it that way; now, of course, he had to win all of it back.

A week later he had already borrowed and lost a second year's wages from Vahtels.

Karlīne watched her son with growing concern and unrest. She spoke with him, questioned him, but she got no answers; he just brushed her off with curt replies to leave him alone, there was nothing wrong. How could there be nothing wrong, when he never laughed any more, and did not eat!

It had been a week since they last played cards. His mother thought this may have been at his request and that Krišs was now stewing about it; her heart skipped a beat thinking he may have actually done this to make her happy. "I'm sure this moodiness will pass!"

But in fact, the game had disbanded because the brewer had a lot of work now and the miller was sent away by the lord to the other manor.

One evening, Vahtels came over. "You must want money, yes?" Krišs asked him quickly. "Forget about the money, am I asking for it?"

He sat down next to him and spoke to him about this and that, not even noticing how guarded Krišs was. "I was at the Siena manor yesterday," he started again, "and I drove past Ķepuri, you know the houses there, on the edge of the main road? But now they have built an extension onto it, I tell you! Imposing, like a castle!"

"I didn't even know that Ķepurs was so wealthy, he has small fields and they are not well cared for," Krišs said with surprise. "Well, why is his father-in-law a forest ranger then? The man has enough trees in the forest!"

"Oh, so he built the extension with his lord's trees?"

"Not with his lord's trees, but with his lord's money; the old man shuffles off to the city at night with a few beams and returns with money."

"For heaven's sake! Does anyone else know about this?"

"Perhaps, but who wants to get their fingers burnt, and — his lord will not go poor over those few beams."

"Ptui!" Krišs spat.

Vahtels remained quietly seated, took a pipe out of his sack and lit it. "Yes — not everyone is a fool!"

Vahtels left. Krišs went to bed, but he couldn't let it go, he couldn't fall asleep. When he finally did fall asleep, he had a dream: Ķepurs was standing on the roof of his new house counting money; one shiny coin fell out of his hands and slid down. Ķepurs leaned forward — his foot slid, and he fell off the high roof.

Krišs was startled awake. "Ptui!" he spat.

The next day he met Vahtels by the granary. They exchanged a few words, and were already parting when Vahtels suddenly remembered:

"I wanted to ask you something! Do you happen to know someone who would sell a portion of wheat, I have a good buyer, a Jew from Jelgava, he promises a good price, there is apparently a shortage!"

"No," Krišs replied with surprise, "how would I know anyone? Maybe Kārklēns is selling, he apparently had a good harvest."

"Well, if you don't know, you don't know, I was just asking! What a fool!" he grumbled as he walked away. Krišs watched him walk away for a long time, finally understood, and wiped his brow, which was drenched with sweat.

The next evening Vahtels returned to Krišs. Krišs sat at the table, barely acknowledging Vahtels' greeting. Vahtels put his hand on Krišs' shoulder: "Listen! Now I really am in need, I don't know whom to turn to, it would be good if you could repay me now, you hear?"

Krišs went pale.

"But you know I have nothing; I have nothing right now. Where would I get it? You told me you have enough money right now."

"Yes, I said that once, but now I need it for all sorts of reasons — could you perhaps get it from your lord?"

"Where do you get these ideas? More likely…"

"Well — more likely?" Vahtels bent down, and Krišs lifted his eyes to see Vahtels glaring back at him. He could feel Vahtels' hot breath on his face. "Don't be a fool!" Vahtels

53

whispered. "You have the keys! One lot from the granary and it's done!"

"What are you talking about?" Krišs wanted to shake him off. "You want me to steal from my lord?"

"Yes, your lord will probably be upset about those few lots! Do you think the foremen don't take from him? Of course, they do! Who in their right mind would be so foolish to die of hunger when there is a full bowl in front of them? Do you think it's a sin to scatter a fistful of rye for the pigeons? And one lot? That's a big deal! Was this year's rich harvest all your lord's hard work? If God has provided, we should also partake."

"And when — and when — we get caught?" Krišs stammered, and he was ashamed about it.

"Well! You have to be smart about that! Who's going to catch you? Nonsense! Don't you worry about that. You just have to unlock the granary. I will handle the rest. You will just have to rearrange the piles and even things out, and — and — you think the foremen don't do the same?" — "They don't? Of course, they do!" Krišs thinks he's convinced about everything the foremen do.

Vahtels' tongue was like a well-greased pulley. Krišs was half listening in disbelief — he believed everything was so easy, almost a joke, a trivial thing — just this one time…

"Now you can prove that you also have a pretty smart head on your shoulders."

"I — could put it off." Krišs said, as if responding from a distance.

"What is there to put off? It has to happen tomorrow night. My vendor is here; the night is dark, I will get the guard drunk, he's an old friend. So, I'll expect an answer tomorrow, yes or no! And if you won't do it — understand! — I need the money — and…" Kriss waved him off, impatiently.

It was a dark night in late November. Around midnight two dark figures left the supervisor's lodging and crept over to the granary. At the door of the granary one of them took out a big key from under his arm, stuck the key into the lock and started to carefully turn it. Chink! — came the sound from the first turn. The man waited a moment and continued to turn the key. The heavy oak doors opened slowly. The man stepped back and crouched by a tree that was a few feet from the granary. His partner motioned, and like bats several more dark figures appeared. Little lanterns glowed like wolfs' eyes, and very soon the shadowy figures disappeared with heavy sacks. That repeated again and then once more. Somewhere further down the way was the sound of a squeaky wagon and the snorting of horses.

All of a sudden, Kriss heard a short, sharp whistle, the thieves rushed out of the granary door and disappeared like a flash of lightning: the dark doorway stood open like a gaping hole in the night, like an open grave. Someone pushed into him. "Run!" he heard Vahtels' voice. On the other side he heard loud voices: "Thieves, thieves!" He heard the sound of gunshot. Kriss ran away. But in which direction? "Thief, thief!" rang in his ears — and "Forever, forever!" — echoed his conscience. Out of habit his feet led him back home. His mother ran out the door towards him: "Kriss, what's happened? Were you there? Let me look at you! Say something! Standing there speechless! Heathens! How can they break open a door with two locks!" Karlīne spoke quickly and ran nervously up to her son, who was standing in the middle of the room looking confused. "Well, go on, go on!" she urged him. Kriss looked into her eyes. "The granary door was open, Mother."

"What are you saying? You forgot to lock it — unlucky thing!" Karlīne was shaking him. Kriss trembled: his chest was burning like fire. "I — unlocked it — myself!" he stammered.

"You? You were in the granaries tonight? Kriss!" A sense of horror unleashed in a loud, unnatural scream. "You were with the thieves?"

"Don't say anything, don't say anything," Kriss whispered. Outside came the sound of many voices; the room was soon full of people. "Granary supervisor! Come with us! The lord is looking for you. There were thieves in the granary!"

As if coming to her senses, Karlīne looked around at everyone standing there; then with a fiery look in her eyes, she turned towards Kriss and loudly declared: "So! You have come for him? Here he stands, the thief!"

"Mother! Have mercy!" Kriss cried out in pain. The door to the room was wide open, and the candlelight barely shone on the people standing outside.

"What? Could this be? The supervisor himself! Nonsense! She must be joking! The thieves have frightened her!" The people were talking over one another.

"My God, my God!" Karlīne grabbed her head, asking herself what she had done. She fell moaning onto the bed. Silence fell over the room.

Kriss turned to the crowd and in a weak subdued voice, like someone who is dying, he said: "Tie me up, I am the thief!" Everyone stepped back, unsure what to do. Then one of the older workers approached him: "Come along then, supervisor!

You will not try to escape even if you are not tied up."

And Kriss, separated from everything familiar to him, went into the dark starless night towards his dark future.

It turned out, the theft had been rather large. The thieves were highly experienced and had left no clues. Interrogating Kriss was of little help. He didn't know any of the thieves, except for Vahtels, who had soon disappeared. Although Kriss had told the absolute truth, no one really believed him. The lord of the manor, in particular, ensured he would be transferred to the remand prison in Jelgava as soon as possible. He was more upset about Kriss than anything else. Perhaps he felt guilty that he had trusted a young person with such great responsibility; he always said he had up to this point been too good towards people and now he no longer trusted anyone, he saw everyone as liars and thieves.

Kriss was taken to Jelgava. The workers who were taking him left in the night. Kriss acted like he didn't care, but when they drove past his lodging, he grabbed the hand of the man sitting next to him and asked: "Could we just — stop here?"

"We aren't allowed!" the worker replied. "And also," he continued warily," it would make no difference, she is unconscious." Kriss sighed deeply, but didn't respond. They reached their sad destination in silence.

Karlīne was having nightmares. During the day, one or another of the workers' wives arrived to care for her, but no one wanted to stay with the sick woman during the night. Old Trīņus lived in the servants' home, where she received food from the parish. The old woman was very mistrustful; nobody could do or say anything to please her, and people always teased and annoyed her. One day a servant's wife returned home from the manor and muttered: "What's she doing there, crouched down behind the stove, couldn't she go to the manor to take care of the woman, at least she would be doing a good deed!"

"Isn't she smart!" Trīņus growled back. "Is this woman my sister? Let the women from Lielmanis go; they are done begging for food and drink for now. And look, now it's time to look down on the poor once again!" Trīņus continued to grumble for a while longer, but the next day, she rose early, put on her shoes, tied a few things up in a bundle and went to the manor. There she settled in with the ailing woman and, if someone else came to care for her, Karlīne quickly explained that Trīņus was already there and would be staying. It was also not a great burden to take care of her. She gave her something to drink and covered her with the blanket when she would kick it off in a feverish sweat; when she was having bad dreams, Trīņus made the sign of the cross: "Lord God! Protect us from harm!" The ailing woman ate nothing, but Trīņus thought this perfectly logical: "She is not long for this earth, so why waste food."

But Karlīne returned to the living. One day Trīņus came into the room to find her sitting up in bed, no feverish flush in her cheeks.

"Well, supervisor's wife! Now you really are back on your feet!"

"Don't call me the supervisor's wife!" the sick woman replied with a weak voice, and a little later: "Is he — already — gone?" Not waiting for an answer, she fell back onto the bed and closed her eyes.

Trīņus also appeared not to have heard a word. She started

building a fire, as now the care for the woman could really begin, that is — feeding her. She offered something to Karlīne almost every hour. "Now you just have to eat," she urged her, "to regain your strength. God saved you from your illness! You weren't getting up, yes, you weren't getting up — that's what I thought, and see, you pulled through!" And so, the ever-grumpy old lady kept busy caring tenderly for Karlīne, who only knew her by name. Even she started to grow roses of love in her heart for Trīņus, they were just covered over and hidden by the sharp thorns of her daily life.

A week later, Karlīne started to get up and move about.

"You no longer need me, I can go home now," Trīņus said. "Yes, you may go, and — thank you for taking care of me!" But her thanks sounded cool and indifferent. Trīņus, as it turned out, was not expecting any thanks, and extended her hand to the woman: "If you ever need me again, I would be happy to help where I can!"

"Thank you!"

That's how they parted.

Just before Christmas the lord of the manor sent word to Karlīne that she could stay in her lodging until St. George's Day, but she will need to find another place after that.

Spring arrived. One day, Karlīne received word that she was to see the lord of the manor. She listened, her knees trembling, anticipating the lord's news. He was stern as ever and stared coldly at the woman as she entered the room. But upon seeing the shrunken figure, her pale face and eyes full of fear, a chill ran over him and he didn't know where to start.

"Sit down," he invited her nicely. Karlīne remained standing. "I must inform you," he began after a moment of silent suffering, "that your son has been sentenced — to — Siberia."

"To Siberia!" Karlīne repeated in a strange, barely audible voice.

"To twenty years."

Karlīne turned and walked towards the door. "Do you not want to hear any more?" he asked with restrained compassion.

"What else?"

"Three weeks from today he will be sent away from Riga along with others. In exactly three weeks."

On a beautiful Sunday in May many parishioners had gathered at the N. manor church. The word of God was seldom heard now. The former leader of the church had died and ministers from neighbouring churches came to N. manor's church very rarely.

Today's visiting minister was a wonderful speaker. His words knocked at the door of the heart like iron hammers, you could tell he knew how to tug on the heart strings. But after his sermon, and after he had mentioned all the dead and christened in the congregation, then came the most important part. The minister put all of his books over to one side, grabbed the edge of the pulpit with both hands and stood straight and stern. The church fell silent as a grave.

"And now, dear congregation, I must mention one of the lost lambs of your herd..." And then — as a warning to other Christian souls about Satan's spells — he read Krišs Ragaiss' verdict and sentence: "Sent to Siberia for twenty years!"

Suppressed whispers filled the church. All heads turned towards the door. There — in the very last pew — Karlīne stood staring with unflinching eyes at the minister. She would have looked dead, were her head not shaking slightly. She stood in the very last pew. The place where she used to sit in the Lielmanis pews by the pulpit stood empty — on this day, no one had dared to sit there.

After the service, many parishioners remained standing amongst the graves, they couldn't leave. The clusters of people were all talking about Karlīne. They knew she had been in Riga to see her son. She had been away for three weeks. But had she found him, had she seen him, talked to him? Each could imagine as they wished, Karlīne was the kind of person whom no one dared to approach.

There was again a suppressed chatter amongst the people. Karlīne walked past them. Without looking at anyone, without seeing anyone, as if feeling the ground with her feet, she walked through the crowd, which stepped back quietly and stood silently watching until Karlīne disappeared over the hill. Karlīne had become odd.

Through the blooming fields of spring and the colourful splendour of summer, the yellow mists of autumn and the sparkling clear winter, a beggar-woman wandered, poor, but still neatly dressed. Wherever she entered, people grew silent. One winter afternoon, the servants' hall was full of people, chattering — Karlīne comes in, without greeting anyone, not saying a word, but stands at the door and waits. A child brings her a stool and remains there with her. The room falls silent, carts rattle, someone joins the child and stands there, waiting. Karlīne starts to sing.

Karlīne sings her song with a sorrowful, heavy melody, as if soaked in tears. She sings about an innocent child, a handsome young man, a man lost in and consumed by crime, a heartbroken sufferer. The longer she sings, the greater the silence in the room. Her song is like a deep spring looking for a heart. Every verse starts with the refrain: "Oh Krišjānīt, oh, Krišjānīt, you bear such great sorrow!"

"She has added new verses again!"

"Yes, I hadn't heard this one before."

"It's wonderful how she creates and changes them."

"Let's see if a normal person could do that," the crowd whispers and marvels at her.

When Karlīne finishes, she sits quietly. She doesn't recite any other verses or prayers, nor does she pray herself. If she is given anything, she quietly thanks them and gets up to leave. Regardless of the weather, Karlīne walks; no one has ever heard of her staying overnight somewhere.

Karlīne walks along the road hunched over, but with quick, youthful steps. She doesn't look right, nor left. The road is lonely, the fields are quiet, it starts to rain. Everyone is rushing home. Karlīne follows a path which leads into the pine forest. Perhaps her home is beyond the forest?

Twilight begins to deepen in the forest. Karlīne sits on a wet stump. All around her tall, rain-soaked pines are shedding tears. Karlīne, a grey shawl over her head, hugging her knees, unaware she is swaying back and forth, sings softly: "Oh, Krišjānīt, oh, Krišjānīt, you bear such great sorrow!"

MOTHER'S SORROW (1912)
ANNA RŪMANE ĶENIŅA (1877–1950)
TRANSLATED BY MĀRA ROZĪTIS

In memory of Maija
You sparkled in the sunlight like a dewdrop
then sank in the ocean of eternity.

I

"Mamma, which child do you like best?" asks Lita.

"My dear child, you know very well that you are all loved equally."

"Yes, I know, but the face, whose face do you like best?" Lita persists.

"I'm not sure, I'll have to think about it," I answer, trying to avoid the question, "you each have your own beauty."

"But I know."

"Who then?"

"Maija."

"And why is that?"

"Maija has the rosiest cheeks."

Lita is right. She is observant and has noticed how

everyone, be they a visitor or a passer-by on the street, pays particular attention to Maija, on account of her rosy cheeks. So crimson, so suffused with lifeblood, it seemed they were fit to burst, and golden brown hair that weaves around her head in silky tresses and the smile of big blue eyes and even whiter teeth in response to every pleasant word.

At the outset of 1905, Maija is the youngest of my three children, two daughters and a son. We had just celebrated her second birthday.

She is a strong and sturdy infant, agile, intelligent and in constant motion, always active; Maija can't rest for a single moment. In her search for more outlets for her unbounded energy, Maija often gets up to all kinds of mischief. Coming across a bowl full of water, she has washed herself and all her clothes, until there is water dripping and streams flowing everywhere; another time, the earth from the potted rubber tree has been piled into her pram, and the pram pushed hither and thither until earth is scattered all over the place. But the biggest battles with Maija are about books with pictures. "Pich, pich," Maija obstinately persists with her plea to be allowed to leaf through the picture books. Permission was often granted to Margis, easily given to Lita, but not to Maija. Her fidgety fingers always tore the pages as she turned them, and so consent to this pleasure was rarely given, and only under supervision. But every prohibition is at the same time the sweetest inducement.

One afternoon old Anna, the children's nursemaid, who had swaddled and coddled Maija almost from birth and was still proud of her little darling, runs in desperation from room to room — Maija is gone! I go to her assistance. We call and shout — not a sound, no trace of her. Now Margis offers to help, as he is well aquainted with his sister's psychology and habits. After rushing from the nursery to the parlour, he lifts up the covering of the couch with a resolute gesture and look, there, Maija is underneath the couch, spreadeagled on top of a secretly taken volume of Art Nouveau. She is staring at us with eyes ablaze, like a cornered forest creature. Then, quickly extracting herself from her uncomfortable position she trots off nimbly, straight to the punishment corner, without even waiting for my order, because she has learnt that in this corner each transgression finally comes to an end.

Whenever she is on her way to or from this corner she never forgets to ask for forgiveness and never bears a grudge. Throwing her arms around my neck, she declares, "Me love mamma," and with that, all has been said. And if ever Margis or Lita were the guilty ones, and they should be the ones asking for Maija's forgiveness, nevertheless it is Maija, not understanding the moral subtleties of this formality, who is the first to go to them with, "Me love Maga, me love Kika," although she had just now been yelling at them in despair.

Now, as her language skills are steadily improving, these two closest of her companions are referred to more clearly as "Malgis" and "Ita". You never hear Maija crying, if she is angry or in pain, she screams at the top of her voice but after a moment stops and laughs, and all her pain or agitation vanishes.

It is easy to tease Maija because she opens her trusting heart to anyone, confident in the goodwill of adults. This trusting nature sometimes results in Maija being more fearless than the older children.

At Christmas time, when snow-covered Father Christmas came into the room, with his big bearded face, fir branches, and a sack on his shoulder, Lita and Margis were afraid to approach him, although he promised them all kinds of bounty, and offered them beautiful Christmas presents. The first to boldly step up to him was Maija, and it was only after she had returned to her place, unmolested by the strange man and bearing many acquisitions, that Margis and Lita summoned up the courage to go forward for their share of the spoils. But Maija was also easily scared by ill will. You only have to pull a face and glower at her, and her great courage deflates, and with eyes wide, she calls: "Flai, flai!" as she steps back. At those times Margis reassures his little sister, "Don't be afraid, Maija, it's only a joke, see, I'm not scared," as he confronts the menace with manly valour.

Margeris is four years old. A somewhat pale, serious, fair-haired boy. Slow-moving and with an enquiring mind. He wants to understand everything completely and so is never fobbed off by slapdash explanations. His 'whys' come slowly, after much thought, and he is satisfied by only a well-considered answer. When he understands the reasons and reasoning that underlie each prohibition or command, he will comply immediately. Otherwise, he holds his own council, and thinks his own thoughts. And if the resulting activity is, according to grown-ups, some piece of mischief, for which he must suffer punishment, then Margis will first investigate, why it is considered mischief, and after understanding that fully, will submit in silence to the appropriate punishment, without attempting to explain or justify his actions. He suffers every sadness and every bruise without complaint, and only a flushed cheek will hint that something untoward has happened to him. And if the suffering is very great, a few slow tears will roll down his cheeks. Ready to climb and run and explore the world in a variety of ways, he never seeks to show off any achievement but is always self-contained and humble. He carries much love in his heart, but only rarely does he express it, in a shy touch or a word.

Maija and Margis enjoy a particular bond. At times they are the greatest of friends, at others the most bitter of enemies. Margis always needs Maija for his vehicle and boat games, either as a passenger, sailor or conductor, and he is the one who always tries to relieve her of any fine object that has appeared in her hands, either by force or cunning. If force is used, then Maija's piercing screams soon summon a helper or rescuer, but if cunning is employed, then the desired object easily changes hands. "Look Maija, I'll give you this, that's a whole lot nicer if you give me what's in your hand!" And Maija's trusting hand will open and Margis will have achieved his wish.

At other times, when Margis has overturned all the chairs in a line and created a train, that travels without delay from St Petersburg to New York and back to Riga, then Maija is seated in the second carriage, right behind the driver.

"Here's your ticket, Maija, we'll take this train to St Petersburg." And they set off, whistling, buzzing and ringing bells. But not long after, with a few rearrangements, the line of carriages has turned into a ship, taking both passengers to Moscow.

But the discord is not always the fault of Margis, little Maija can also be unrestrained. At times when Margis has, with great difficulty and overcoming numerous technical problems, constructed a house with a high tower, which still needs a decorative touch here and there, then Maija appears and with an unexpected push, Margis' house has been demolished. Now it would be Margis' turn to scream, but with masterful control, he does not do so, he just stamps his foot, frowns, and in a raised voice, admonishes, "Maija!" Without waiting for any further development of this episode, Maija has already hurried into the punishment corner. If I happen to be in the vicinity of such an episode, and Maija's actions demand a somewhat sterner reaction, I ask, "Which hand was the guilty one, Maija?" then without another word, Maija extends one or the other of her chubby hands, as if to say, let mamma's judgement fall if it must. Meanwhile, Margis has recovered his composure, has forgiven Maija in his heart and now, with deep friendship restored, a new adventure is being prepared.

My eldest, Lita, is a bright, slim six-year old, blonde-haired, rosy-cheeked, with a somewhat wide nose and yellow braids. She rarely takes part in these games of Margis and Maija. She prefers to be with adults, sitting quietly to the side and listening attentively to their conversation. She never interrupts, but if she happens to be addressed by someone in the company she becomes agitated and blushes to the tips of her ears. She answers quickly, in the hope that the conversation will soon end. In this respect, she has great admiration for her brother, who can speak to strangers as well as to his own family, with the same, slow self-confidence, each answer well thought out before it is given.

Otherwise, Lita feels more sensible and grown-up than the 'little ones'. She achieved mastery of the alphabet at an early age and spends a lot of time reading folksongs and tales. She looks on the games and mischief of the 'littlies' with a grown-up eye, as she herself had never consciously instigated any mischief. If she had accidentally broken a dish, then her consternation and tears had been hard to assuage, because of her extreme sensitivity. Speaking to her, one must be very careful not to use either a harsh or pitiful voice. Harshness hurts and pity saddens her. In each case, she will burst into tears and salty streams will flow down her cheeks as she rushes to another room, to cry out the sorrow in her heart. When she was Maija's age, she would cry her eyes out about a dirty smudge on her finger or clothes and at the age of four there was not a greater source of sorrow than my exclamation, "Oh, poor Daddy" — this 'poor', according to her, was the description of the worst calamity, and her heart would overflow in commiseration. I am still not allowed to sing the song, *"When I was small, I did not see,"* for as soon as I begin, Lita has run up to me, imploring in a trembling voice, "Mamma, please don't sing that song!" Where does this extreme sensitivity come from? Did I instill it in her then, in her first year of life, there in that distant rural school, when the autumn winds howled outside, all those empty evening hours when I sat, with my infant in my lap in the darkest corner of the room, surrendering to the melancholy of autumn? When I whispered all my heartache in her ears too young to understand? When I saw all my disappointments held in her little hands? The little one sat in my lap so quietly, and listened so intently as if understanding that the heart will be wounded by the first steps taken into real life by hope-filled youth.

Or perhaps it was her father who cultivated the child's

sensitivity, by overflooding her still immature imagination with the melancholic poetry of our folk songs.

A year ago she would illustrate each of her amusements with a self-written verse in the manner of a folk song. I particularly remember these verses:

Leaves of gold fall from the trees,
Weaving in a golden crown.
A maiden comes and bows down low,
To take the crown of gold.
On my golden steed I ride,
And see my bride to be,
On her head a golden crown,
On my steed, a blanket gold.

However, over time, Lita's sense and sensibility grew while her sensitivity decreased, or else sank deep into the waters of unconsciousness, and only occasionally was there a faint suggestion of the mystical in the child's imagination. As once, while I was working in the next room, I heard Lita leading a game in the nursery. It was an enactment of a funeral and Maija had to lie down as the deceased. But Maija's character was unsuited to this role, she was up every minute, which led to this role being reassigned to Lita's doll. Quickly, but with feeling, Lita spoke these words: "Goodbye, Christian child, a sweet angel will sleep by your side. He will weave golden wreathes for you and put them on your breast, and he will weave a crown of death around your bed." To make it sound even more solemn, Margis had to repeat each phrase. He performed this duty responsibly, but he was left unmoved by this mystical game. Lita continued: "And black, black pines will grow on the mound of your grave but its silver flowers —

will never bloom." To calm her fervent soul Lita liked nothing better than our family's evening hours.

In the twilight the living room looked even larger, every object seemed to be alive and breathing, the lanterns of distant streets shone in the windows and Atis, the father of my children, is quietly playing the piano. The four of us are crowded in the rocking chair: Lita, as the eldest, is next to me and both Maija and Margis are on my lap. I quietly tell my little ones the story of Tom Thumb, but Lita keeps interrupting, "But mamma, that's not right," for I am forced to enlist the help of my imagination to compensate for my poor memory, and Lita cannot accept such violence being done to a much-loved story. When the story is told, we start to sing our folksongs. Lita knows the words of each verse better than I do, and keeps a firm hold on the melody, Margis follows our lead, always a beat behind and Maija harmonises with aaa and iii, sung in either a higher or lower pitch. Although our voices are so diverse, and the vocalisation is quite unexpected, the earnest warmth of the evening levels out the sounds and unites them in a single naive harmony. The first to grow impatient with this evening idyll is always Maija. Suddenly she wriggles and slips out of my lap because she can't sit still for so long. Every nerve, every muscle wants to keep moving, doing, living. Her active mind can't be constrained by the cosy comfort of the evening. She has already grabbed hold of her pram and started running so that all the house thunders with the clatter of its wheels. It's time to get up and light the lamps.

The most enthusiastic running takes place at dinner time when everyone is seated at the long table in the dining room. Margis and Maija have already eaten in their room and as they await their bedtime they begin to run full pelt around those still sitting at the table, Margis leading and Maija chasing him, her fat little legs thumping like pistons. If anyone pays the runners the attention they seek and tries to catch them, then the glee of both runners is unbounded, and with growing elation they rush even faster and yell even louder, until for the sake of peace Anna must be summoned and both heroes must travel to the Land of Sleep. They don't want to go, they beg to stay up a little longer, but the little longer soon passes, and they must be off. One after the other they are washed and put to bed, Maija, Margis, and last of all, Lita. But their heads are still buzzing. Lita is particular in upholding the tradition begun in the first year of her life, according to which I must reserve a half-hour, to spend with the children, before they fall asleep. If I sit on the edge of Maija's bed I must take the hands of Lita and Margis, and they will hold mine tightly. And then I have to sing a lullaby about 'baby bears' or 'little Ansis'. Both Margis and Lita love to fall asleep to the sounds of a soft lullaby, but when I think they're asleep and try to leave the room silently, then one or the other, sensing my intention, in a voice muffled by sleep, as if coming from another world, would plead, "Mamma, don't go!" Only Maija doesn't rate this kind of sending to sleep highly. When Maija feels sleepy, the feeling overtakes her completely. Then she declares, "Wan sleep," turns onto her side and falls asleep immediately, all by herself.

The climax of our family joy comes on Sunday mornings. While we, the adults, are still in bed stretching our limbs that are still stiff from a working week and giving in to laziness, the children wake up one by one and following Sunday tradition, barefoot and still in their nightgowns, tiptoe from their room to ours, and creep into our beds, snuggling up like baby chicks.

Play fights, laughter, kisses, and whoops of joy! Ears ringing with the children's excited cries, eyes full of the sight of their happy faces and lightning-quick movements, the vigorous stamping of little feet in our laps — there is nothing dearer in the world than one's own children! I'd willingly lay down my life at a moment's notice for any one of my dear ones.

II

It was late March when Margis suddenly fell ill. He was hot and all his skin was red. I inspected him closely and found a small wound with dry threads of his woollen socks stuck to it just below his knee. It turned out that he had injured himself falling from a chair a few days previously, but as usual, his manly reticence had prevented him from drawing attention to it, nor had the maid noticed it. I think that it may have led to an infection of the blood. The doctor that we consulted also thinks that his illness is caused by this infection, and he advises us to seek the advice of another doctor who specialises in the treatment of wounds. The child's temperature continues to rise, the second doctor arrives, inspects the leg and says that the injury, although nasty, cannot be the cause of the fever. We inspect the boy carefully and discover a red rash on his chest and back. Margis has scarlet fever. Scarlatina, the deadly scourge of young children! My body trembles, it will now be a life or death struggle! Thinking hard and with feverish hands, I set the nursery in order for Margis' convalescence, and both girls are put into another room. But three days later

Lina awakes with the same red rashes that Margis had, and her bed, together with its patient, travels back to the nursery. Maija is left alone outside, sad that she is not allowed in. "Me wan mamma, me wan bloder, me wan iter," she wails outside the door, but the door opens only for the doctor, who comes twice a day to check on the children. I closely observe each of his looks, every movement he makes, it is hard to speak but I conclude that the illness has taken a serious turn. Once, after he has left, I hear my mother weeping behind the closed parlour door. She has come to help me take care of the patients. Atis tries to console her, but his own voice is despondent. I don't cry, because what I feel is anger, rather than pity, despairing anger at this evil disease. I am like the owner of a valuable object, who has unexpectedly been set upon by a thief. We stand face to face. There is nowhere to run or hide, no, here in this narrow room we have to engage in the final battle. If I will be victorious, I will regain the whole world; if he wins, the world will be worthless to me. We take each other's measure and weigh up each other's strengths. Each movement is contained in a consciously peaceful rhythm, nerves are wakeful and on guard, I'm level-headed and clear-sighted. The heart holds an unfaltering awareness: to survive, not to tire, right is on my side, he is a thief and a robber, I must succeed.

To protect the children's inflamed eyes, dark fabric covers the windows. The air hangs heavy with sickness and exhaustion, and circulates lethargically from the gasping breath of wounded lives. Every mote of dust, every shadow in this dimly lit room is subject to my will. My undiminished will, that has only one object: to pull my children from the jaws of this fierce illness.

But it has bitten hard into those tiny lives. Margis also suffers from his infected leg. The injury is in a tender spot, just above the bone and cannot be easily healed.

The cleaning and scraping of peeling skin is difficult for the feverish child to bear. While the doctor performs the painful procedure, I hold Margis tightly and try to ease the sharp pain by all possible means, with kind and loving words and promises. I try to cheer the child up with jokes, he tries to laugh along with me, but we both shed tears, because his suffering is so evident, although, as is his wont, Margis bears it all without screaming. Only when the pain is most extreme, when his whole body is shaking and he can no longer bear it, he starts to berate the doctor: "Why are you pressing that stone so hard into my leg? I'll throw you in the deepest river, lock you in chains and send you to Siberia, you, you..." By threatening the doctor with these diverse punishments he tries to confuse his pain. When the doctor has completed his work, and the pain eases, all his malice vanishes, and he is happy to believe me when I say that the doctor wants only the best for him.

Lita's condition has a different complication — her throat is so inflamed that the doctor has to swab it with a long brush that has been soaked in brown antiseptic liquid. Although this treatment isn't a tenth as painful as the treatment Margis receives for his leg, Lita is a delicate child and she begins to fret and worry from early morning — how long until the doctor will come? And when the doctor finally comes, she pleads in a trembling voice: "Mamma, mamma, where are you going? Don't go!... stay with me, hold my hands, so he can heal me quickly, quickly." And I hold my second feverish child in my arms, while the doctor completes his work.

Nights and days pass, uncounted and unrecognised in their passing. There is no light, no darkness, only a twilight of sickness and pain. There is no world and no time, there is only the clock with its slowly moving black fingers that tell me when each powder is to be administered, when temperatures are to be taken.

What is time to me, what is the world? My life is concentrated within these four walls, and its force rises and falls with the breathing of my children, at times vigorous, at others feeble and weak.

The peace of sleep has become a stranger to me, as my children's feverish nightmares whirl ceaselessly in my head. When I close my eyes, they creep out of my brain and flitter along the walls and taunt me, like tiny devils. How can I sleep, how can I calm down while I haven't smothered them one by one and cast them away? And sometimes mystical omens and signs muddle my mind.

In the dressing room of the country church after her christening, didn't Lita roll off the bench, despite everyone standing around and watching over her? Couldn't that have been an omen, as the old women had anxiously foretold?

And couldn't it have been Death rather than the New Century, who stretched out his arms and blessed the few days-old-baby Margis? I remember full well that wonderful apparition that I saw so clearly, just as the new century had begun. It was late evening. I had laid down, but was still awake, with eyes open and thoughts wandering. Next to me, my baby son was sleeping sweetly after being fed. A small blue nightlamp shone its dim light in our room, leaving the corners in deep shadow.

And then I saw how the door opens slowly and in steps a tall top-hatted gentleman, dressed all in black and stooping a little.

I'm not at all afraid, although he is a stranger to me, and a voice from somewhere says that he is the New Century.

His expression is sober and serious, and in accord with his status, each movement is restrained. His bearing is that of an aristocrat fostered by an age-old noble house and lineage.

His shoulders slightly sloping, as if from great fatigue, head a little bowed, a high forehead, filled with thoughts, a pale face but eyes alight with delight and insight. With slow steps he approaches Margis and leans over him as if blessing him, and then just as silently leaves, the door closes behind him.

I was awake, and with my conscious mind I observed him leave as a slight tremor passed over me. My heart was pounding and I could feel my soul like a living being, bold, uplifted, for it had come face to face with Fate in the depths of the Unknown. From that time, whenever I imagined the children's futures, I translated this vision as a sign of the expansion of my son's soul and his coming achievements in the far distant future.

But now, I must reconsider — who knows, perhaps my vision was of Death, who had hurried to set his seal on the brow of my son, but in order to lead me astray had come disguised as an aristocrat?

Superstition, you might say. I became obstinate with everyone who made fun of me about my omens, dreams and visions. Yes, I do believe in omens and visions. I believe in all that I feel alive in myself, that can only be fathomed through belief. In that sense all religion is mere superstition.

Should I be satisfied with only those things I can see, hear, smell, feel, taste?

I believe that I belong to the Transcendent World, I believe in my hidden connection to its majesty, I believe in what I sense within myself, without fully understanding it.

And how is it possible, that the thought born of my mind, or the glimmer of a sensation would lie outside this, our most wonderful World? Did not its Guiding Spirit create the very essence of us, are we not, together with all of our lives' trifles, a part of this Spirit?!

Where does the boundary lie between life's trifles and its great events? Does not a tiny, tiny drizzle bring a plague upon the whole of humanity and cut down its paragons?

And the nondescript chronicle of our days! And the histories of our centuries, don't they also vanish in eternity like a single drop of water in the ocean? In the absolute being of the world, everything, each and every thing has the same value.

Those were the arguments I had, in the silence of each night, with myself and my imagined opponents. For I would not want to give in to doubt and would rather be clear in my mind and hope.

But don't we have a clearer view of the face of Fate in the darkness of misfortune? Oh, these ponderous thoughts have no end!

If omens are to be believed, then Maija should be the one who leaves this world first; she was the one who came into this world so unwillingly, it was only by a supreme effort that we rescued her to our everlasting joy. But now she is healthy and energetic and delightful, and her little voice rings like little silver bells through my distress, when she runs to the door and calls out happily: "Love mamma, love bruvver, love itter!" The light of her dear words and her liveliness shines into our twilit room, and a sweet freshness mitigates the bitterness in my heart.

Maija has understood now, that visiting us is impossible, she no longer pleads at our door, so after affirming her love for us, she runs off again, pram wheels rattling, fat little legs pounding. Only once did we suffer a short painful moment. The maid did not respond to the bell, so I opened the kitchen door, to call her, and suddenly Maija appeared, rushing towards me, with eyes alight and calling at the top of her voice: "Mamma, mamma!"

How I wish I could have scooped her up in my arms, but how could I, if she had inhaled the most minute amount of this disease by being in my proximity, it would thrust her into the same agony that her brother and sister now suffer. I blow her a kiss and quickly slam the door shut. Maija is left outside weeping profusely and crying out: "Me wan mamma." Even her grandmother cannot console her.

Then Maija accompanies her grandmother to the country because nine days have passed, she is still healthy, she is out of danger of contracting the disease.

The clock continues its remorseless lonely ticking, and my mind its endless struggle.

Margis would have survived the scarlet fever, his leg is improving, but his kidneys begin to fail, and the boy is lethargic and grows more yellow with each day.

Lita's course of the disease also takes a turn for the worse and her condition deteriorates. The unresponsive girl tosses and turns with her fever dreams. Oh, how close the enemy has crept! How hot is his breath, how heavily he lays his hand on my shoulders! It is hard to remain calm, while confused thoughts whirl in my head, and my hand trembles like a starving beggar's when I try to measure out the medicine.

The doctor now comes many times a day. He says: "If the fever increases during the day, then prepare a bath and call me immediately."

Horror walks through our room in an ice-cold cloak.

The child is unconscious!

I keep a constant watch on the thermometer — the silver thread continues to creep up. The bath is prepared, the doctor must be called. But look there, can I believe my eyes? The shiny silver column has fallen a little, and the child's breathing is calming down. No bath, no doctor is needed, the fever is abating!

Half-conscious I kiss the child's hands and weep at her burning hot feet.

The next day the doctor informs me, that in these evening hours Lita's life had been weighed in the scales of Fate, should she be left to me or given to Death as a tasty morsel. I give thanks to you, almighty Fate, for your merciful ruling! See, I prostrate myself and press my brow into the ashes your foot has made!

***

From this day on everything grows lighter around us. The children recover slowly, oh so slowly, but they do recover. I take the dark fabric from the window and put up a lighter one.

Outside, the first days of spring have arrived, and we hear the sparrows chirping. The chatter of my patients dances around me, then they request bedtime stories. Margis is the first one to sit up. Despite his sunken cheeks and yellow pallor, he begins his block building on the cover of a thick book. Lita has little strength, she lies with her raw-boned face turned towards Margis and follows his movements with staring, tired eyes. I begin to leaf through some books.

Holy week arrives. Not only the doctor but also Atis visits. He is on holiday from work and so does not have to fear transferring the disease to someone he may have contact with. We begin to wait for Easter in a much happier frame of mind.

On Easter Sunday I take down the fabric covering the window and let the sun shine into our sickroom. And what a wonder! A rooster stands perched at the foot of Lita's bed with a pile of colourful Easter eggs he has laid, and a hare was leaning over Margis, together with a similar pile of eggs. There's much excitement, happiness and many questions. How had they come into the room, and will they continue to lay the same pink and blue eggs every day? "No, this rooster and this hare only lay their eggs on Easter morning and after all their hard work they will have to rest until next Easter. Take care of them, so they can accomplish the same wonder next Easter!" The hare and rooster are petted reverently by both children.

The doctor has arrived for the last time to inspect his patients. Neither Margis nor Lita have any reason to fear him now and they welcome him with friendly greetings.

Unexpectedly, Margis solemnly presents the most beautiful of his Easter eggs to the doctor, intuitively recognising the psychological significance of this gift. The doctor is genuinely touched by the child's innocent recognition of his efforts, and with a laugh he asks: "Aren't you going to threaten me with drowning any more?"

"No, no," answers Margis in all seriousness, firmly convinced that the doctor could be forgiven his earlier abuse.

After Easter we left the room of our ordeal to be disinfected and set off in a closed carriage, still fearing the sun and wind, to another flat on the outskirts of the town, where we had decided to spend some time until we had recuperated. We were now comfortably installed in three light and spacious half-empty rooms.

With weakened limbs and unsteady steps, my children begin to walk again. It is as if they had returned from some distant shores, where they had forgotten the customs of this land and had to learn them anew. At first tentatively, then with increasing freedom, they begin to walk once more on life's wonderful earth.

Sunday morning. Atis has come to visit, and we open the doors for our children to go outside. Open-mouthed, like tiny chicks that have crept from the warm shelter of their mother's wing, that's how my children look out into the sunshine. Leaves are budding on the trees, the heads of white flowers are peeping from the bright green grass and can be plucked. The children are quite intoxicated with the delights of spring and begin to chatter and laugh, and hop around without restraint.

A few more days and their period of convalescence is over, we have religiously taken a warm bath every evening to wash our sickness ravaged bodies, so now no remains of the illness can be found anywhere.

And so May arrives. I set my mind to my usual everyday tasks and we decide to take our recovered patients to visit their grandparents in the country, so they can recover their strength completely in the fresh invigorating air of the countryside.

When the four of us arrive at the gates of the garden, the first to come towards us is Maija in a short red dress, with a worn red hat atop her braids and holding a thick slice of bread smothered in butter and sprinkled with chives. Her eyes open wide on catching sight of the unexpected guests, and light up with happiness; her butter smeared cheeks shining. Oh, Maija, how sweet it is to lift your agile, healthy body high in the air and kiss your shiny cheeks! And Maija's joy at seeing us again is indescribable. She does not let me go, and dadda and sister must also be kissed. Grandfather comes up with a rolling gait from the corner of the garden, pipe in mouth. Greeting Margis and Lita, he laughs in his good-natured way: "Oh my bumblers, pretending to be sick, were you?" Grandmother approaches from the verandah and brushing away tears and with heart melting in joy, she presses the children close to her breast. Even the nursemaid Anna has hurried over, tearfully relieving the new arrivals of their coats.

We go inside. I have brought Maija's things that have to be unpacked. There's a swing to be hung in a doorway, a white dress that I sewed as the children began to recover and my hand was not needed there all the time; there's also a pair of shiny shoes and simple leather slippers. They must be tried on to see if they still fit her growing feet after all this time.

But what's this, why are Maija's feet so fat and heavy? Oh, my goodness, the child's dress has no pockets, so all the eggs that she has saved, have been stuffed into her socks. Both feet rattle. I haven't yet managed to retrieve all the eggs before Maija has leaped out of my lap and hurried over to Margis: " 'S mine, 's Maijas!" Margis has found his old hobby horse in the corner and is getting ready for a ride, but this horse has now been passed down to Maija for her use, which has led to this dispute over ownership.

When grandmother seriously explains the situation to Maija, that this toy had indeed once belonged to Margis, then Maija gives up her objections, because she always knows when her battles will succeed or fail. And if success is not assured, she will turn her back on the unobtainable object and turn her attention to another activity, otherwise, she will scream until she has obtained what she considers to be justice.

After this upset, Maija leads me into the garden with her round brown hand, summoning the others to follow. This garden is Maija's whole huge world. Excitedly she runs up to each of us, pulling us this way and that, wanting to show us and tell us all about the treasures here: here is a gravel pile that grandfather has had put in the sunniest spot just for her, there are the dandelions lifting their proud yellow heads under the apple trees, there's a flowering gooseberry bush. "Bellies, bellies!" she aims to cheer us with the wisdom learned from her grandmother about berries that will be savoured in summer.

The day is warm and sunny, a few sprays of cherry blossom hang against the blue sky. With Maija leading the way, my children weave in and out between the bushes, humming like May bugs and happily reliving memories of all the wonderful experiences, that are, from their early childhood, connected to this well-known and much-loved garden, as magical as only experiences in early childhood can be. When the sun begins to set, the whole family returns inside where bustling and chatter reach a crescendo. The little ones reel and rattle on, while we adults have so much to say. We unburden our hearts as if we were sailors who had finally reached a safe harbour after the trials and tribulations of a storm at sea.

When it is dinner time, Maija climbs firmly into my lap and wants to be fed by her mamma, a spoonful at a time. Then it's time for her to go to bed, but the overexcited child can't fall asleep. I sing about Little Ansis, about the mouse, but Maija just keeps kicking and grumbling, eyes shining in the dark. Margis sleeps in the next room, but Lita has also been put in grandmother's room, next to Maija. I tell the girls not to snuggle up too close, but after a while I see — both heads lie next to each other and hand in hand both girls are hugging and kissing, as Maija loves her elder sister so much. I feel a sharp pain in my heart — they shouldn't be doing this — and I part the girls, only to calm myself with the thought that Lita has recovered and the illness has passed.

Early next morning Atis and I have to leave for work. My children are still sound asleep, with flushed cheeks, tousled heads, and arms and legs spread in all directions. I stroke my dear ones, kiss them lightly, and whisper a wish under my breath, for their happiness and health, in the house of their forebears, in the flower-scented garden, in the care of their grandparents.

III

During the second week, I receive a telegram saying that Maija has fallen ill. I become afraid and weep but in my heart

I cannot believe in the possibility of death until the very last breath is drawn, as I did not believe in it then, long ago. How could it be, why do such things happen, isn't there any justice in the world?

On Saturday morning we set off for the country house, to the children. Little Maija, who has been put to bed on the living room couch, greets us with outstretched arms. Happily, she hugs us repeatedly saying: "Me love mamma, me love dadda!" — "Sweetheart, let us go outside." But Maija shakes her head — no.

"What's the matter with my little lark?" The child doesn't rightly know where the problem lies, but she points to head: "Ouch in head."

Her forehead does not feel warm, but her body is covered with a red rash.

My mother explains, "On Wednesday I was telling Lita how I had noticed as I was dressing her, that Maija had felt cold and on Thursday, when I returned from the market I saw that she was red all over, with a red brow and nose . I kept her inside all day, although she had an appetite and she kept on playing. On Friday afternoon I called the doctor and he told us it was scarlet fever. Then I hurried to send the news to you. During the night Maija had turned black and blue from the illness and Anna had been sent to fetch the doctor as quickly as possible. He only arrived the next afternoon. We pressed him with all our despairing questions. But he was jovial and cheerful. Her temperature had fallen a degree to 39°C, her throat was clear. He prescribed eardrops, to protect her ears from infection, and wrote another for a possible kidney infection and boric acid to swab inside her mouth. He couldn't tell if it was a serious form of the illness but encouraged us to hope for the best. I mentioned that her hands and feet felt cold compared to the rest of her body. After feeling them he declared that they were warm enough. He couldn't return before Monday, because on Sunday he'll be visiting his family. If there is a turn for the worse, we should get in touch with his colleague and then he left." Our minds are somewhat set at ease by this news, and Atis prepares to return home. He wants me to accompany him, her grandmother could nurse Maija just as well as I could.

But I stay there.

How could I leave my youngest child in my mother's hands, when I had nursed both older ones until they had recovered.

Once more I'll sit for six weeks by my dear infant, supporting her through the worst moments of the fever. That's what I decide and that's what we all hope for.

Atis leaves by himself.

I make up a softer, whiter bed for her, braid her dishevelled hair into four plaits to keep her head cool, brush away bits of gravel from her temple, line up all the medicine bottles in order on a small table within easy reach, and sit myself down next to the patient, keeping an eye on the passing hours and her needs.

The bouts of fever return and she becomes delirious. She calls, " 'ranges, 'ranges," wanting one of the oranges that I had brought, but she was not allowed to have any. Then she calls out to her playmates — "Ena" (Erna) and "Afed" (Alfred) and demands that they give back what they had taken from her. In between, as if she has come to her senses, she asks: "Where dadda?" "He has gone back to Riga, child."

87

But my answer remains beyond her understanding and after some time she asks again: "Where dadda?"

Then she calms down. On top of the covers, Maijas hands lay together as if in prayer, may this adversity retreat from this poor innocent child.

Thinking she is asleep, I start to get up to stretch my legs, but Maija senses every one of my movements and raises her little hand to bid me stay.

Occasionally she wants her grandmother and her weak voice calls in her sleep, "Ganny, ganny." Grandmother comes. The child opens her eyes, sees her and is satisfied, then lets her eyelids close again. But in her sickness she does not ask for her brother or sister. It is as if she instinctively senses that they would have little understanding of her distress. She is disturbed by their happiness and loud voices whenever they run up to her sickbed.

The child is obedient and lets herself be cared for. She does not struggle or grumble when she has to take her medicine or have her mouth wiped. Though unwilling, she still takes the liquids that are proffered and submissively opens her mouth to have it swabbed. When it is done, she looks at me and pleads: "No more!"

"No, no more my little lark, no more now, later my dear little girl will let me wash her mouth again." The child nods, closes her eyes and calms down.

It is evening. Maija's temperature creeps up, it's now 40°C. Her lips are dry and peeling, so I keep offering sips of a refreshing drink, but she repeatedly opens her mouth wide as if wanting to throw up. How hard it is for the child.

Her hands and feet are still cold, my mother and I try to

warm them in our hands.

As night falls, we feel that the burning fever is not abating, so we decide to send for the designated doctor. He arrives after midnight. He seemed young and inexperienced but he performs a thorough examination of Maija. He tells us not to worry about the retching, it is a common symptom of scarlet fever, but he found her heartbeat to be irregular.

He leaves with a promise to return the next morning.

Anna fetches the new medicine to improve her heart function — four powders to be given every two hours.

It is very late and my mother falls asleep. I remain awake and lay down next to my child, warming her hands in mine and drawing her legs close to me.

A shaded lamp on the table, the persistent ticking of the old clock, and my father's occasional snore from the next room.

Maija is unconscious, eyes half-closed, and her breathing is rapid, so rapid.

I think about a preposterous letter that some schoolchildren had brought to me a few days ago on behalf of their parents, who wondered how they should react to it.

The letter began by calling upon God, as if in prayer, but the prayer itself was brief. What followed was a long and absurd instruction to immediately transcribe the message in nine letters and send them to one's acquaintances. This message will travel around the whole world and speak to everyone in it. But if the instructions in this letter are not followed, then beware, for on the third day disaster will befall your whole family. Several examples follow, someone's daughter was crippled, another's wife died unexpectedly, etc.

Quite in a panic, the schoolchildren explain that many parents had received such a letter and do not know whether to believe the threats expressed in it or not. I was troubled somewhat by the letter's audacity, but every driveller can't be believed, even if God himself is invoked. I told the children that their parents should ignore letters like this — it is just some rogue trying to dupe simpletons, but are we going to be those simpletons?! It ended with us laughing about the writer's clever concoction.

Now, feeling the sick child's hot breath, my thoughts waver. Could such willpower exist, that reaches across the whole world, and could such a person exist with that willpower, a person capable of mocking the world and poisoning all life in it with his evil intent and wickedness?! And my child now has to die because I refused to believe in such evil?! My God, my God — have you forsaken me and left me in the power of this evil?!

Towards morning my mother awakens, I close my eyes and sink into a nightmarish sleep for a few hours. I do battle with a phantom that embodies the power of evil, but I am weakened, I am like a plaything in its hands, and laughing malevolently it rips me to shreds and casts me aside.

When I finally awaken, I find that Maija is no better, although illnesses usually give their sufferers slight respite in the morning hours. Her temperature is 40.1°C. Her eyes are half-open but she is insensible.

Yesterday afternoon she had still managed to say 'Wan dlick' in a tremulous voice, but now she cannot even do that, although she repeatedly opens and closes her parched mouth.

When I offer her a cup of water, her little hands try to reach for it, but her head falls back and all her limbs are limp.

Once, Maija's eyes open wide, the glassy stare is gone, and with a sensible expression she turns to me and feebly reaches out. I know, Maija, what it is you wish to say — love mamma; you'd like to hug her but you can't any more, this ordeal has sapped the very last of your reserves of strength.

When I have kissed your weary hands, then your eyes seem to be searching for something else. I understand this wordless wish of my child and call for my mother, to whom Maija reaches out with her little hands and sensible gaze. Her grandmother bends over her little darling but Maija has slipped back into unconsciousness.

At that moment, Maija, you still loved us, your little heart had not yet withdrawn from our hearts and that was its final farewell.

The doctor arrived at about eleven, listens to Maija's heart, and says that its beating has strengthened. 'But…' he continues by saying something vague about brain function and then falls silent. He says no more but sits as if deep in thought. Then he rises and prepares to leave.

"The powders are finished — what now?" I ask.

"Nothing more is necessary — a bath if her temperature does not fall." Weeping, grandmother speaks up and says that she feels that the child isn't long for this world, there are white patches around her nose. The doctor doesn't reply, but I feel my anger rising at such talk. If I could even entertain such thoughts, I would have fallen to my knees at the feet of the doctor, and with arms around his knees I would have pleaded with him as my Saviour, to save my child's life.

But bidding him farewell I just said, "That can never happen, that my child should die."

He did not answer, just left, as if ashamed. About what? About his impotence?

The hiccups have eased, but the fever has increased, and consciousness does not return. The child lies still, sunken, glassy eyes half-closed. Perhaps she is only resting, perhaps she is at ease.

Now and again, Lita and Margis run up to Maija. Like startled birds, with eyes full of fear, they regard their sister's weakened state, and with the easily expressed pity of the innocent, bow their heads, but outside the sun shines again and birds twitter.

In the next room, I hear the assembled neighbours discussing Maija's illness. Each of them has their own opinion, each has a long story about what happened to one or another of their acquaintances, what that one said, what the other one did. What impertinence — outright gossiping in a house of sorrow! Then I hear Anna's tale about what had occurred to her with Maija. She had woken up one night and gone to see if Maija hadn't kicked off her bedcovers. But when she'd looked, Maija was not there. Unbelievable. Where could the child have got to in the middle of the night? Anna had searched all over, under the bed, on the couch, the child was nowhere to be found! Had she been spirited away? She'd gone to wake up grandmother to tell her that Maija had disappeared. They lit the lights and looked all over, but Maija was nowhere to be found. But then suddenly, it was as if scales had fallen from their eyes and they both saw Maija fast asleep in her own bed. What kind of blindness had struck them both at the same time, and wasn't it a sign from God, that they would lose Maija forever?

"Yes, that's right. She's not long for this world," was the

conclusion that closed the conversation.

A wave of fury rose up inside of me; how can they say things like that? But I bit my tongue and kept my peace. What could I say — Maija is so, so...

I remember a dream I had before Maija fell ill; I lost my front tooth. Isn't that a sign, according to the old ones, that a near relative will die?

Oh, God!

And another memory of a seemingly insignificant incident from New Year's Eve. We were a large company thinking about how to pass the time until midnight and we decided to hold a séance to ask the spirits about how many years we had left to live. When we asked about Maija, the table did not levitate at all. We laughed at the spirit's obstinacy and continued with our fun.

This memory burns through my brain like a hot needle.

Oh my God, deliver me from the fatuity of doubt.

That afternoon Maija looked at us for the last time with an expression of awareness. Just looked, at me and at her grandmother. She no longer raised her hands, perhaps she couldn't, perhaps she didn't need to. She just bid farewell to the living. To those living ones who had been the closest, the dearest in her short life. Looked upon them for the last time. Then a glassy brightness covered her eyes and they saw no more. She saw nothing more here, never again.

But at that moment realisation had not yet dawned on me. I put her in the bath, and when consciousness did not return and her temperature did not fall, I dressed and set off for town to search for more doctors. It was about six in the evening. I went from one to the other, wherever I knew of a doctor in our small town. None were home, neither the first, the second, nor the third. Of course, it is Sunday and the weather is beautiful. My wagon rumbles desperately through the quiet, empty streets. People that pass by look at me questioningly: why ever is that horse being driven so hard? And I have to give up my search, what if something happens to my child while I am scurrying around here? I turn the horse once more to the door of the doctor who had come that morning and write him a note to come immediately, for the child's condition is worsening.

When I return, upset with my pointless journey, Maija lies there as she had been lying before, motionless, her glassy eyes half-open.

Through these half-open, unseeing eyes I feel that a foreign evil power has gripped my child and is observing me. It looks at me with a scornful and indifferent sneer. I want to close those eyes, but the lids are stiff and can't be moved. Let them be, what was I thinking, as if she were a corpse.

All of a sudden it seems that Maija could be conscious. Leaning over her face I ask her: "Do you love me, Maija? Shall we both go outside soon?"

As I ask I think to myself: if Maija nods her little head, it will be a sign, that she will live. How could she not agree and not nod?!

But Maija turns away.

Did she not understand, or does she no longer care about living, or was it the answer of fate to my questions, Maija herself unaware of the meaning of her dismissal of me.

But I refuse to believe in this suggestion and laugh at myself for faltering.

Maija's hands and feet grow colder, although her body

temperature stays high. Does her blood no longer flow to her hands and feet?

I hold her hands tightly in mine and we put a heated brick wrapped in a damp cloth on her feet. It seems the child is responding to its warmth.

I spoon water into her parched mouth — she senses it and swallows.

Eating dinner in the evening, I hear Margis and Lita laughing in the next room. I get up to go to them but suddenly Maija seems to call. I run to her — "What is it, sweetheart?"

But she lies unconscious. Did she call me, did she feel that I was leaving her, or was it only my own agitation. What was it that sounded in my head in the voice of my child?!

I sit down again next to the child and my thoughts fluctuate between hope and doubt.

Maija's teeth grind twice with a jarring sound. "A sign of dying," said my mother.

I can't stand such talk. I answer angrily: "Haven't you ever heard the children grind their teeth in their sleep?"

Mother doesn't argue, just weeps.

One by one everyone goes to bed.

I continue to sit.

A strange numbness has taken over my brain and my emotions are blunted.

I pick up a book and attempt to read. I can't. I understand nothing.

It's midnight. I take Maija's temperature — 40.5°C.

I wake her to take a bath. I lay down next to my child, completely exhausted.

Then the words of that evil curse begin to dance in my head

again. Perhaps I should get up and write those nine letters… nine letters. But to whom should I address them? Yes, I could write to all those unbelievers, like me, who did not believe in the power of the curse. Let them see what happens when you do not believe and laugh instead at the occult!

But I cannot get up. Oh dear, I can't get up.

I feel myself gently slipping into sleep.

I am unaware that a half-hour has passed, and Anna is waking me up to tell me that the water has been warmed for the bath.

I hear Anna waking my mother too and saying that the child will soon die.

I do not want to hear such talk and begin to get everything ready for the bath.

My mind is clear and light again. I stand by the head of my child and speak to her life force. I speak under my breath, but I pour all my willpower into my words.

"You must awaken, you must recover, you must arise, you must live.

That is what I want.

I want.

If you have weakened, take my strength, take my blood, take my life!"

Then I speak to the water.

"Water, I beseech you, share your strength. Envelop my child, refresh her, ease her weakness, revive her spirit."

We slip Maija into the bath carefully, so she is not startled by the water.

She is flaccid, like a new-born babe, and shows no reaction.

When we have floated her in the water for a short spell, we wrap her in blankets and carefully dry her. I take her temperature — 39°C.

My child will be saved!

But five minutes later it is 40.5°C again!

No matter, but please, don't let it rise!

They say that infants can withstand a temperature of up to 42°C, if it stays below that I can still fight for her life and still hope!

Maija is calm, unconscious. My God, why are her hands and feet still so cold? And her breathing so quiet, barely perceptible?!

I feel her pulse — so faint.

But now — her breath does not pass through her nose.

Her nose is cold.

Her mouth occasionally opens to draw a breath, her jaw moves slightly.

I hear a voice from somewhere, "It is the end."

I quickly try to feel a pulse, at her wrists, at her ankles — there's nothing.

Her heartbeats are intermittent and low.

Maija's breath is dying.

Now I realise: it is the end.

I want to grab hold of my child and run with her, far away from this vale of tears. I would run so fast. But I cannot.

It is forbidden, I can not. The Other, who has taken my child in its arms, is cold and forbidding. It compels homage and I am barred from touching the inert child with my restless hands.

I run outside in anguished exhaustion.

The edge of the eastern sky is growing light, a few stars hang above the dark tree branches.

I'm cold.

I tremble.

I fall to my knees:

"Heaven, earth, distant world! Help me, this poor speck of dust!... Help me!... Save my child! Stars — my last hope — come to my aid!

You have power and might — I beseech you, I reach out to you in despair and hope. World! Power! Omnipotence! And you Earth, Earth!

Look upon me, I prostrate myself on your black breast: give me your eternal elixir of life!

Do not keep it from my poor child!

My child — your child!

Heavens, Earth, World! — Help me!"

People are moving along the road beyond the garden.

I cease my calling and get up.

Then I begin again:

"And you, spirit of evil, who has cast your curse over my child — look, I prostrate myself to you! I recognise your almightiness and bow down before you!

If you need a sacrifice, take me. Take me a thousand times over. Or if it is a child's life you thirst after, take Margis or Lita instead of Maija!

No, no — I love them too! But take me, take my life. Take your revenge on me, persecute and torture me. Only let my child be set free from your curse.

Destroy me!"

There is no answer from anywhere.

Everything stays as it was, cold, silent and insensitive. It's laughable.

Suddenly the agony stopped, the trembling ceased. I no longer wished to wail or pray. What does that mean? Is the crisis over, has my child come back to life?

Or else ————

My heart knows that screaming would be in vain.

I still stand there for a moment, listening to the rumble of distant wagons and I feel the wind blowing through my hair.

I go back inside.

I approach Maija — is she —?

My mother is crying, Anna is crying.

Anna is the first to speak: "She is no more, little Maija is no more!"

"When did she die?" I ask, in a cold fury.

"Just now — a few minutes ago."

I fall to my knees next to my child's body.

Then I get up to go outside!

My heart is breaking!

There is a pond beyond the garden. Let us go Maija, let us go together into the Celestial City.

They hold me tight. They lock all the doors. All three are against me and they are stronger than I am.

I fall to the floor.

I am aware of falling — I want to fall! I scream.

I am aware of screaming — I want to scream!

They try to lift me up.

Get away! Leave me!

Let me fall, let me scream, let me smash everything to pieces!

But what can a tiny mite, a speck of dust accomplish?!

My body's thrashing is futile, nothing is smashed or broken or razed to the ground.

Everything stays as it was, every single thing.

The clock keeps ticking away steadily.

Only Maija's life is no more.

My father stops the clock and begins to sing a death lament at the head of Maija's bed.

"Stop. I do not want that. It's a mockery!" He falls silent.

I lean over my child: my warm, dear child with half-opened eyes, but there is no pulsing life in any part of her.

Then I come to my senses. I realise that I have to put another place in order for my Maija.

I will do it all myself.

There is an empty bed on the verandah, I lay a clean sheet on it. The deceased are usually washed — but what is the point of hauling her around, she has already been bathed twice today.

I loosen the four braids from yesterday and part her hair so it lies on both sides of her head.

I squeeze her eyelids down a little, but I don't close her eyes completely — why force the dear eyes that do not want to close.

I take off her nightgown, put on a clean dress, lay my dearest on the verandah bed, and cover her legs with a clean sheet.

I light a candle at the head of the bed, place twigs of greenery around the bed and white lilies that Lita has plucked by her head.

The outer door of the verandah stays open.

Light has dawned. The air is atremble with the songs of

larks, but my little lark has fallen silent.

Never again will that little mouth smile, or scowl, or sing "Loverly lozes," (roses)!

A cold and frozen tranquillity.

Very soon the last warmth evaporates from Maija's body. I stroke her forehead, cheeks — they are as cold as stone at dawn.

A strange tumult crowds my soul — is that really my Maija who lies here so cold.

Yes, it really is Maija.

But why did I have to put her out here in the cold?

Wait child, I'll take you and hold you, I'll warm you, I am warm enough for both of us. Lie here on my breast forever.

What suffering! What a comedy this human life is!

No, that's all nonsense. The skylarks are singing outside, the morning is dawning, but there is no Maija. Why? I don't understand. I rest my head next to her — no, I cannot understand. What's to be done — there's nothing. I'll have to awaken the older children, so they can see what happened to Maija. Lita says nothing, Margis cries, neither of them understands what has actually happened. Soon they are asleep again.

I'll have to send a telegram to Atis and my brother. So. What else?

I lean over Maija — no, no, she can not be warmed again. Her body is stiffening. I can do nothing. All-powerful free will — how absurd, how utterly ridiculous! A human being is but a mite, a speck of dust!

I'm cold. I pull the day bed next to Maija's resting place and lay down on it, pulling fur coats over me, for I am shaking with the cold and I can't stop.

But then I start up with a fearful thought.

Heavens! In the night, when I was battling with the dark forces of death and called for assistance, I did not call on God! Is that why God did not come to my assistance? But isn't God the life force, the whole living world? And did I not prostrate myself to God himself, falling to my knees in front of all His creation?! Is God only the name of God?!

My God, my God — did you judge me, your insignificant creation whose mind was clouded by despair?

But it could be, that you pay me no mind at all, that your concern is only for Yourself, your own Self, your own will, your own might! As the saying goes, you love those most, that you take so young.

If that is so, then you loved my Maija very much.

You had need of a little angel and you chose my child, ignoring my pain.

You, the most Almighty, and me, the one you toyed with.

How could I have done battle with You, the Almighty! who has no mercy for his desperate subjects?

I sink into a nightmare and struggle with no end of fiends. Later I get up, dress warmly and sit on the bed by Maija.

Without any thoughts, without any emotion, the odd hot tear rolls down my cheeks, my throat constricts, my hands form fists.

The older children are up and call for me. I go but must return again, I cannot leave my smallest one all alone. I go to and fro.

I begin to wait for Atis.

He comes, bringing a whole heap of roses.

He falls to his knees by Maija: "My little girl! Maija! Dear child!" Both of us burst into tears. We lay the roses around Maija, and recount to each other how Maija sickened, how she died — so lightly, so softly, without raising a finger.

Her soul was not sad to leave the Earth, it did not fight Death, it rose up and flew away and left behind a cold little body for us.

Yes, the doctor must still be paid and I must think of everything Maija still needs before we lay her in the ground.

Atis and I go into town. I grasp his hand because my steps falter and my eyes are constantly flooded by tears.

We look for a coffin for Maija, but can't find one that we want — smooth and simple, we have to buy one with gold fittings and frilled ribbons.

We purchase a large silk shroud, arrange for a photographer to come to our Maija, order a post carriage to take the child to the city of her birth, send a telegram for a place to be set aside for Maija in the family plot in Riga, and then we return to the house of our sorrow.

I don't want to put my child in a funeral shroud. I dress her in her white dress and the shiny shoes I had bought for her on Saturday. With those on, she will now step into her grave.

The photographer comes. We arrange a place for Maija on a bench under the ash tree in the garden. Atis carries the child out and we set her down, as if asleep on a white sheet — her head a little to one side, her little hands lying freely at her sides.

We lay sprays of cherry blossom around her and gently scatter white petals over her.

Wasn't Maija herself that white blossom, plucked too

early, never to come to fruition.

Brought to rest she now lies in her garden, where she knows every pathway, where she watched every bud open and bloom appear.

At rest, but her eyes are sunken, their expression unfamiliar, bluish eyeballs turned towards us with deep indifference.

And the ready smile has vanished from her lips, giving Maija such a serious appearance that she never, never had while she was bubbling with life.

The photograph is taken. Now we lay her in the coffin — I am pleased that it is comfortable — we lay the white shroud over her legs, scattering white blossoms over her, place a red rose by her head and a white one on her breast.

We close the coffin.

The carriage has arrived. We dress, say our farewells, lift the coffin into the carriage, and take our seats on either side of Maija.

Maija will be taken to a place where I can visit her grave every day.

The carriage moves swiftly along the dusty road.

It is a hot summer's day.

Everything is suffused and growing, except Maija…

The tears will never end. Streams flow down my cheeks and onto the child's white coffin.

Atis tries to find some words to console me. But what can he say — his own mind is a tangle of sorrows. Atis says that my soul will be all the richer for these sorrows.

Riches! I want no riches. Neither worldly nor spiritual. I only want my living child. Let my soul be empty, let it know only one thing, love for one's children.

And you? Wouldn't you sacrifice your all, to regain Maija?!

See, you would. I was right. How is such injustice possible?

The horses stop. The coachman gives them water.

We lift the coffin lid. Maija is lying there, head to one side. Sleeping a sleep so deep, a sleep from which she will never awaken.

The carriage wheels are turning again and raise clouds of dust that follow the carriage.

The city. People crowding the streets — all alive. Only Maija was not allowed to live. Everyone else is allowed to, that crippled beggar over there, and there, that drunkard with saliva dribbling down his chin and that blind old woman, and that sickly infant, all of them, but not Maija…

The cemetery. The sun is setting. There are still patches of light on the pathway that has been scattered with sawdust and pine needles.

Birds sing.

Bells peal.

Four men in black carry my child in her coffin to the cemetery chapel.

Atis and I follow, two destitute paupers!

They bring the coffin inside, place it on a long black table then leave.

Grey high vaulted walls.

Twilight.

Behind Maija's head there are some potted palms, and in the gloom beyond them, two more coffins covered in flowers. This is where I will have to leave my child. This is the first time she will have to sleep alone, in a strange place without her family. Her small soul will be very much afraid.

Come little soul, I entreat you, come home with me. Let the extinguished flesh rest here, but you come. It's cold here, damp and dark — I will warm you, I will cradle you.

We scatter white cherry blossom, dandelion flowers, and small sprigs of green on the black table. They were all dear to Maija, perhaps the dandelion was her favourite because it was the brightest, so we put a dandelion on the coffin lid, at the end where her head lies.

But we do not close the coffin lid completely, in a silent, secret hope — what if she awoke again.

We set roses around the resting place of the child's white coffin, and then it is time to leave.

The two high iron doors bang behind us, the key turns with a grating sound.

We still stand, leaning against the door, we know we must leave.

That night Maija's soul comes to me in her former body. I cradle my Maija, suffused with sleep, her limbs warm and soft and her eyes slowly open wider and wider.

The next morning I wake early and hurry to my child. On the way, I buy posies and garlands of forget-me-nots. But I am not allowed to enter the chapel, for health reasons. To prevent the sickness from spreading.

But do I not belong to the people in need of protection? Is there no mercy for me in any place?

I lie down on the stone steps by the doors, my heart is in pain and pounding fit to burst. What have I to do with other people?

If they consider me a hazard, then I will no longer approach them. Just open the heavy doors and let me in. I can stay inside, there is no need for me to come back out, I do not need humanity!

Atis comes. He knows the proper words to use and we are let in. Maija has not moved. Her face looks quite fresh, but brown patches have appeared on her arms and hands.

We have invited the doctor to come — perhaps Maija is just paralysed. He looks at her closely, no, there is nothing to hope for after the infectious disease, and the brown patches — they are a sure sign of death.

We will bury our child after midday, now we still adorn her coffin with my forget-me-not garlands and we attach roses to the coffin lid. Then we go to meet the older children and their grandmother at the station.

They arrive. The children's eyes dart in all directions, their grandmother has tied black ribbons around their hats and they know they must control their agitation.

Our friend, S. has come with us to lay Maija in her grave. We lift the coffin lid again and in turn, we bid farewell to the little sleeper. I take my leave too — never to meet again. I stroke my child's body, brush my cheek along her lips, kiss her forehead and eyes. Then Atis closes the coffin, never to open it again.

I don't want strangers to carry my child on her last journey, so we carry the coffin ourselves. My mother and I, Atis and S. The mourners are Margis and Lita. Each of them carries a large flower bouquet. We walk slowly along the pathway covered in conifer needles. The bells toll.

Maija's grave has been dug next to a large tree. A deep,

deep hole spread with evergreen branches. S. talks of a little dewdrop that sparkled in the sunshine for a moment, then sank into the ocean of eternity.

A few voices sing.

Now the coffin is lowered into the grave.

A child asks his mother, "How will that little girl be able to climb out of that deep hole?" And Margis cries out: "Never, we will never see Maija again."

I crouch down by the edge of the grave. There, deep in the earth is my Maija, the light of my life, my little Maija!

Flowers and soil are thrown on her little white house.

One after the other your family scatters soil over you, my child.

It falls with a thud on the lid of your coffin!

I desperately want to scream but I must control myself because there are strangers here looking at me with a cool curiosity.

Then I take some soil, Maija, and I throw it over you, three handfuls, one after the other. With these handfuls, I cast my happiness, my love and all my hopes to be buried down there next to you, my child.

The hole has been filled with earth, a mound is made, then covered in conifer sprigs and decorated with flowers.

The strangers leave.

I still have one request. Come to me each night Maija, come and be warmed by me, lie on my breast, don't forsake me, my dear soul, don't forget your mother.

We leave. The children are impatient to go. We eat and drink among strangers in a garden. Once, I can't remember about what, we even laugh. The fiend in us is always alive.

And that is what makes a mockery of our soul's most sacred moments.

We take my mother and the children back to the station.

Night comes with its ordeals. Frenzied storms whirl in my mind. I thrash my limbs against the unfeeling wall. Atis holds me back as if I had palsy. When I finally fall asleep towards morning Maija comes to me in a dream, sad, tired and wilted.

Life in this vale of sorrows grows unbearable.

I spend the days at her graveside, at night I continually call to her as my despair is hard to control in the dark.

It is decided, that it would be best for me to travel somewhere far away from the place of my sorrow and so I travel to Finland.

IV

by Lake Saimaa, 30th June

"Dearest!

Thank you for sending me here to Finland. Everyone, whose life has dried up, should come and water their parched soul in Finland. The nature of this country is like a sip of water from a cool clean mountain spring when the noonday sun is high and treetops burn red. It is such a pity that your work prevented you from joining me here. I imagine how your business must have you rushing around in dusty streets, hot from the sun and with tired shoulders. And how you sit in a friendless room in the evenings, alone with your worrisome burden and sorrowful heart.

While I sail around on Finland's clear blue lakes surrounded by beauty.

My sorrowful mind is consoled by Finland's dreamlike clarity.

This land is like a virgin maiden in the early morning, lightly veiled in light blue dreams.

Some of her places are gentle, dreamy as if she was demurely preserving her modesty with a slight tremor of her hardly green young leaves by silent bays. In other places she is cheerful and merry with white birch trunks that sway in the wind and birch leaves so supple and so brightly green as if they had just been washed by dew.

And in another spot she is quiet and sad with dark firs by still waters, and sinking into herself knows all the secrets of life. And over there she is proud, harsh and unapproachable, rising up high along a bare grey cliff face that in its immovable splendour casts a shadow over the water.

At the rapids at Imatra and Rauha the waters of this land swirl in an overabundance of boundless strength and are thrown up as foam, high in the air — the racing water rises, tumbles, hisses in its struggle, the air thunders with its deep hard breath, but a silvery veil rises over the ferocity of the battle and with a red smile drifts up and away over the forest treetops.

The sun shines all day, gentle and delightful, with its light falling brightly over the forests and cliffs. But all these streams of light converge mournfully in the beautiful lakes and swirl down to the very depths as shining eddies.

It is midnight as I write this, sitting on a pier that stretches far into Lake Saimaa.

Not far away, sunk in a deep sleep, lies the boat that will sail away with me tomorrow at four.

Do you know, it never gets dark here at night, I can write and read easily.

Not long ago the great ball of the sun reddened at the edge of the sky and its reflection stretched shimmering over the darkened water like a column of fire.

Then the cheek of the moon with its pale light rose over the cliff top, and at sunset, one can already sense the faint stirring of dawn.

The lake is still and vast, the calls of fishermen can be heard from far away. They have lit fires in their boats and sail to and fro throwing out their nets. The conifer forests along the shore are black and motionless and daylight is extinguished on all the small green islands. But they still tinkle softly, sleepily.

Cows, that are put out to pasture on these islands all summer, doze as they chew their cud.

As they shift in their sleep, the tongues of the cowbells jangle and waves of this chiming fly slowly over the wide water like silvery sprites and disappear in the pale distance.

It is so, so beautiful here, my dearest, and the tears that I brush away in the purity of this land, under its sky of peace, no longer burn my heart, but instead refresh it.

You know, of course, that I have forgotten nothing. Each moment I am reminded of my sorrow and walking on my way I must often turn aside to subdue the upsurge of my pain.

But here, in my dreams, I have often had the good fortune of hugging my child, alive and healthy.

When I awake afterward, it seems that all I have to do is summon my strength and shake off my misfortune like a dress I have outworn and on my return home, Maija will once again run towards me calling happily: 'Me love mamma!'

However, earlier this afternoon by the Punkaharju ridge it was especially painful.

I had sat down by myself under a gnarled fir tree on a grey boulder by the lake.

Both forest and water were permeated by the heat of the sun, and sunk into a deep sleep. Not a leaf, not the seam of a wavelet moved.

A single bird twittered overhead, her chicks in a nest.

Suddenly all my memories of Maija arose at once in my heart, and I couldn't stop weeping like a banshee. A row of handkerchiefs for my tears was drying in the sun, whichever one dried was immediately drenched by my tears again, dried again and once again drenched by my tears.

Don't call me naive, or confused or arrogant — I am as I am, it is good and honest so. You know that I trust my emotions more than my reason, for my emotions have never misled me, while I have often been led astray by my reason.

You must know that as I am writing this letter to you, now and again a moist sheen brightens my eyes.

The same sheen that appears each evening when I finish writing a letter to Maija. I want to believe, that this is Maija's soul smiling at me, and the reason that I can now see her clearly is that tears washed my eyes clean when I wept so bitterly.

You won't laugh at me, I can reveal everything that I feel because I know you are my sorrows' kin and share them.

The night grows ever more sublime. In a wonderful confluence, the pale moonlight has merged with the evening's warm twilight and the freshness of the early morning. I will not creep into my cabin but instead, now that I have told you of all that I have seen and felt, I will devote myself to reading Dante.

On this trip, I have spent much of the time with him.

It is good to read the literature of masters in fateful times. Their great vision can mend pain-tattered souls, their virtue can cleanse emotions that have been muddied by despair.

And lifted by their strict rhythm, life can renew itself and once more continue within the boundaries of its term.

I often send postcards with greetings to my older children, I hope that they are happy and flourishing in the garden of my father's house.

We will meet again soon.

Yours.

My child, my dearest Maija, our little sister!

To forget you I travelled far away from your little grave, and to stop thinking of you I went to look at the sights of foreign places. But how can I stop thinking of you and why should I forget you?!

You were my little lark, that sang the whole day long without pause, you were the tiny soul of early spring. Its burgeoning life. Its fresh breeze. Its blue flower. But my little flower opened its blue petals for but a short time, smiled at the sun, then bent low to the earth and gently slipped underground again.

Did you have enough of the world? So soon? But I did not have enough of you.

Not at all.

I want your soft warm hands to clasp me, I want Maija to hug me close and say: 'Me love mamma' in her clear, determined voice.

I want to stroke your supple and healthy body early each morning and late in the evenings when you wriggle around in

113

bed in your short nightshirt.

I want to kiss your swift little legs, that found it so hard to stop moving in the evening under the tight covers as well as your little gravel-soiled hands, that froze in death with tiny creases that you had worked into them by your digging in the earth the whole day long.

I want to stroke your sharp red cheeks and white brow and gold silken hair.

I need your happy liveliness that washed over me and everyone else that you glanced at with the light of joy from the blue windows of your soul.

Where is it now, child, this joyful liveliness of yours?

I watched as your shining eyes sunk and closed. I saw the light of your blue eyes go out as they looked at us with a deepening apathy. And your mouth as it closed, tight and grim.

Is that why you had to look so serious, my little bird, because you had solved the greatest mystery — the mystery of life and death?

Oh my! Whoever has solved this mystery will never laugh again, will never cry, will only close their eyes and in grim apathy become inert and cease to be.

Was it so, my child?

And now, my dear lively little dumblehead, you are just as wise as all the world's great thinkers and practitioners, who have struggled with this self-same mystery their whole lives only to solve it on their deathbeds.

I know Maija, that by departing, you have lost nothing, for life never offers as much as it promises in its earliest years. You have seen and enjoyed all the best of life and you have been innocently mindful of all that you have seen and enjoyed.

You saw the sun, you saw the grass creeping out of the earth towards it, you saw leaves unfurling and blossoms opening, 'Look, look glanmamma, look flower!... an see, see, glanmamma, bellies, bellies...' How you celebrated and praised your discoveries!

And I showed you the moon and the stars in the evening and the white sky at noon. And you waded through the green grasses, plucking handfuls of dandelions and catching butterflies. And at home, you built and dug tunnels in the gravel pile...

Dear little Maija, you have experienced the purest, the most beautiful that life offers, and dark and immoral thoughts have not wandered into your soul, nor has deception or bitter disappointment soured your heart. The berries are not always sweet, and sometimes they are taken by sparrows.

Nor have you lost anything, Maija, we have, those you left behind.

We laid down our joy together with you in your grave.

Your proximity drove away miserable and wicked thoughts and sadness melted in your embrace.

Let your memory now be my refuge and the wellspring of my vitality. In memory of you, I will be reborn each day, my soul cleansed — you who have been my life's greatest joy and deepest pain.

Your mother.

A few more words, dear Maija!

I thank you with all my heart, that even being so far away, your little soul has found the way to my dreams, for every night I still hold you. Or perhaps, carried in my thoughts, it follows me everywhere? If I knew for sure I would not need to weep so much. For the fear eats away at me that your little body grows more distant and a stranger to me — I cannot forget how deep in the ground it was laid. There are times when I cannot say my dear words to you, my child, for it seems they scatter over the earth and cannot reach you. Could you not give me a sign that your soul is close by and waits for my words and caresses. When I return home, I will have presents from these far shores for your brother and sister, who will run to greet me, but also for you, my dear heart. What will they be? I will not say, but soon you will see me come to visit your place with presents for you...

Dear Maija, a great radiance passed over my head, like a lucent star. Was that your soul, my sweetest child, that shone down on me? Was that the sign I just begged for?!

May you have sweet and hallowed dreams, my child!"

10th July

"My child, my dearest Maija, my beautiful departed bird! — see now, I am once again prostrate on the conifer needles on your grave and I kiss the flowering forget-me-nots, the pansies and the white rose that we planted here, my tears fall on the wilted lily of the valley posy, small flower heads drooping sadly on the fir branches. Your dear friends, Mathilda and Alma have placed those proud and majestic lilies at your head.

And I have brought along the big rubber tree, whose soil you always loaded into your little pram.

I cannot conceive the joys of your existence now, but it could be that your former games are still dear to your spirit. That's why I brought you a handful of dappled pebbles, the loveliest ones that I could find on the sands of Lake Saimaa, those I will place at your feet.

One more small present — this pair of Finnish slippers, so walking along heaven's white uneven pathways is easier. I'll tie them to the rubber tree's branches. And this shiny little spade I'll press in here by its roots.

Now, my dear child, I will come again every day to be with you!

A little bird has flown down to sit by your head, one with a yellow breast and proud little crest, he's chirping and calling, then he gives a final sad cry and flies away.

Was that your soul, little Maija?! And were the white butterflies and bees and wasps that had nestled in your flowers and are now humming and buzzing around my head, are they your warm greetings to me, my child? It's been two nights since I saw you, my heart!

Where has your little soul wandered? It couldn't have forgotten its mother. I will wait for you tonight and fervently hope you will come to me again. Curious black-clad women have gathered here behind me, trying to overhear the words I am saying to you.

They are probably laughing at me because they do not know that although death has the power to take a child from its mother, it has not the power to take her soul, and its cruel scissors cannot cut the bonds of understanding and closeness that bind us. Or that I am not alone in my lament, I am not alone in my faith.

I feel that sad young woman over there who hides her mournful eyes behind her veil and leaves the cemetery with lingering steps, I feel that she would understand me because she too has buried her joy deep underground.

Have your cherry blossoms already wilted, Maija?

And you, with your little alabaster legs?! Oh Maija, place your hands over my eyes!

Can you feel that my tears are not as scalding as those I shed then in those first nights when your light by my side was doused?

But the tears of my sorrow still fall so heavily, so painfully, while the heart they have bridled abides only with you, my child. There is no forgetting, no end to this overwhelming grief.

The closer life's end draws, the greater and darker their shadow grows until it engulfs all rays of light.

Oh, Maija! My time will come when my soul too will be untethered from life's warmth.

A big black coffin will be buried next to your little white one. My cold mortal remains and unstirring spirit will lie in the big black one.

The same trees will sigh above us, birds will twitter in their branches, butterflies will sway gently with the funeral flowers, everything will bud and leaf and play in the sun over us, only the white crosses will be unmoving in their solemnity as they mutely stand guard over the stillness of the graves in the kingdom of death. Then our souls, Maija, united in perpetuity, will fly high above life and death.

Until that time, my child, this little place of yours with its grass-covered grave and sandy path and four yew trees standing sentinel — let this place be my sanctuary.

Here I will come with my daily worries and troubles, some petty, some more serious, here I will come to lay them to rest in that sorrow, the deepest in this world — a mother's sorrow for her child.

Next to you, I will lay all my small disappointments and frustrations and after I have cleansed my soul in the memory of my great sorrow, I will always return to my life with a purified and peaceful heart.

Maija, my little girl, your soul is now more clear-sighted and virtuous than mine, which is still entangled in the delusions of this world.

I pray to you.

May you be your family's guardian angel. Let your innocent hand lead us along the pathway of clarity, let your hallowed soul protect us from all thoughts of wickedness.

My child, it will be so.

I say Amen."

***

When I had finished speaking to my dearest departed one, the sun was beginning to set.

As I sit on the bench next to her grave my thoughts turn to the dark knots that bind life and death together.

Suddenly I feel my Maija seated in my lap. Sitting upright she leans against my breast.

I know, her body lies buried under the earth, but it is her soul that has come to embrace me. If I close my eyes, I see how the light evening breeze gently lifts her curls that glow golden in the light of the setting sun.

All my nerve endings feel her body leaning against mine.

This miracle, this quiet joy of sweet love, it does not surprise me at all.

Both of us continue to sit, silently. The forgetfulness of dreams in my mind, and the deepest sense of contentment in my whole being. The evening is late and Maija seems to have fallen asleep on my breast.

The guard comes to tell me I must leave.

I must get up slowly and carefully take my sleeping child in my arms. She seems to awaken and hugs me tighter. My dear, dear little sweetling! When we come to the cemetery chapel Maija deliberately slips from my arms and placing her little fist in my hand, begins to walk next to me with tiny steps.

I walk slowly, ever so slowly and I feel the closer we approach the cemetery gates, the slower and heavier my child's steps grow and the feeling of love turns to sorrow.

At these gates, we must part.

I kiss her brow. I feel her embodiment grow dimmer and drained of colour and then I see it slowly rise and drift away, with a flitter of its white dress, to its last resting place.

Atis calls these manifestations visual fallacies and a result of my nervous exhaustion.

I don't know why I had the good fortune on this occasion to see my child not only in a dream but when I am wide awake and to feel her so intensely with all my wakeful nerves. I had the good fortune to experience this. And whoever has been smiled upon thus by good fortune, does not seek to look for the reasons. I know only that I must thank God for bestowing upon me this ability to be able, at these wonderful moments, to stand on the boundary between Life and Death and to apprehend both Kingdoms!

Now I no longer doubt, that my evening prayer at my child's grave will be answered — Maija's soul will always be here with us as a guardian angel.

Let God help us understand her signs that point the way to good works and to heed her warnings about evil intentions!

Maija, we will always be united and I fervently hope that we will often embrace each other, just as we did this evening.

Honeymoon Trip (1925)
Angelika Gailīte (1884–1975)
Translated by Ieva Lešinska

Having found out from newspapers that Elza Zīlītis had been engaged to Valdis Zirnis, son of an industrialist, Rigans were mighty surprised. They had already written off Elza, who was, at twenty-seven, an old maid, whereas young Zirnis was coveted for a husband even by seventeen-year-olds. Among the ladies, where interest in the family lives of others was particularly keen and often supplemented by creative imagination, this startling news was thoroughly reviewed and discussed.

Well, who was she really? Daughter of landlord Zīlītis — there were thousands of those in Riga! Old Zīlītis was neither a banker nor a political party leader. The cream of society did not frequent his house and Elza was not invited to participate in any philanthropic organisations where people meet and where it's so wonderful to do good deeds and show oneself. Some ladies, who were in the know, told others that Elza in fact avoided going out much and spent her free time either reading or sitting at the piano, but would never play for others.

And that she dressed like a nun. And this woman would now be the lady of the spacious Zirnis house! One of these ladies knew all about young Zirnis' love adventures, while another had information about his more serious involvements.

Despite all these signs to the contrary, the wedding between Miss Zīlītis and the budding industrialist Zirnis did take place. And society ladies had to grudgingly appreciate the sophisticated taste that had gone into arranging it. If one wanted to be truthful, it could not be denied that Elza did not really look like a spinster. She looked rather bashfully virginal in her white exquisiteness. Some ladies had already succumbed to her string of real pearls.

That same evening, the young couple went on their honeymoon trip, creating new material for the imagination of the social circles, which could not stop discussing it. And it was not entirely without reason as we will see from the ensuing string of complications.

Elza indeed seemed like a little dove that had chosen a lifelong union with a hawk. Presently, however, she was in the grips of a newly awakened passion, which she took for love. And her partner was so swept away by this unusual play of feelings that, following the rather varied gallery of ladies which he had let roll through his life, he felt that he had found the best wife in this strange person. Intoxicated by their sensations, they passed through Berlin without Zirnis having any desire to visit those starlets in whose company he had so often had a good time, even as they emptied his pockets. He could not expect any additional loans from his strict father, so, being a good calculator, he had decided to marry well: to get a wife whose dowry would help to fill these financial gaps and whose presence would not interfere with his life. Based on these calculations, he had chosen the quiet Miss Zīlītis. Skilled in the arts of love, he had played his cards so well that he had managed to ignite passion in this reticent maiden who, for almost ten years after her mother's death, had not heard a gentle word or felt someone touch her lovingly. Her father was too Puritan for that.

Yet Zirnis had overrated his own abilities as a cold Lovelace, and as we have already pointed out, the game seemed to turn into reality because of the dreamy passion radiating from his bride.

Dresden seems to be built for dreaming. Situated on the banks of the Elbe, with its blue line of mountains on the horizon, it seems to be a veritable Florence of the north. The old churches, the noble palaces, and public buildings with their green bronze roofs lend the city a painterly aspect.

Having arrived in Dresden from the hustle and bustle of Berlin, the Zirnis couple were awakened in the morning by birdsong coming in through the open windows. Gardens and greenery were all around. Nature and art combine to present a beautiful contemporary idyll.

Both for business and pleasure, Zirnis had rushed through all of Western Europe's famous art collections, albeit mostly because it was something that was *done*. Right after graduating from school, Elza had accompanied her consumptive mother to the South. There she had managed to acquaint herself with Renaissance art, and Botticelli's *Madonnas* had held the most attraction for her. Later, after she had seen some reproductions and from what she remembered, she also got interested in Raphael because of his profoundly harmonious approach. Here, in Dresden, people tended to linger most in a small, remote room with a single painting — Raphael's *Madonna Sixtina*. In her simple nobility she seemed to rise above the earth and bring about the presence of the divine. Viewing the *Madonna*, travellers tended to suddenly go quiet. Accompanied by his wife, Zirnis too viewed paintings seriously for the first time. But self-inspection or delving into art for any length of time was not in his character, so he was happy when on a sunny day they could just sit on the shady Brühl's Terrace. After a hearty breakfast, the travellers took a boat trip on the Elbe to see Dresden's surroundings. Having walked around Loschwitz where Poruks once drew inspiration for his life's work, they crossed the river to Weisser Hirsch. She had never seen anything like it before. The apple-trees were in full bloom and roses were twining around gates and up the walls of houses. Zirnis was looking to buy a bouquet of roses for Elza, but she said she was happier just to see them grow in such extraordinary splendour.

The next morning the couple had decided to go to the mountains to see the so-called Switzerland of Saxony. Leafing through the newspaper as they were having their morning coffee, Zirnis cast a sudden glance at his wife:

"Aren't you a Wagnerian? They are showing *Lohengrin* at the opera tonight."

Elza looked at him as if just waking up.

"We absolutely must hear it in this musical city," she said with determination that Zirnis had never encountered from her before. She suggested going to the closest mountains, so that they could be back by evening. And, of course, they first had to purchase tickets for the performance.

And so it happened.

All along the way Elza seemed to pay no attention to the surrounding nature. She was equally indifferent to the beautiful palaces on the banks of the Elbe. Only the gentle, yet refreshing forest air in the mountains and the view that opened from the Bastei Cliffs to the Elbe and the surrounding mountains seemed to open her soul to nature. Zirnis found this change in his wife surprising but wrote it off to female caprice.

A sensitive person tends to enter the Dresden Opera, that keeper of the best musical traditions where the orchestra, soloists and the choir become a harmonious one, as a sanctuary.

With the first familiar sounds, Elza herself became a taut string, ready to respond to the slightest vibration. But when Lohengrin arrived in a boat pulled by a swan, she felt that this messenger of clarity, who had been her imaginary friend throughout her youth, was even now untying her from everyday life. She felt a sudden stab in her heart. Could she rise to his call any more? She had become unfaithful to him by sacrificing herself to earthly passion. Just like that Elsa on stage, she was not worthy of her Lohengrin. She painfully averted her gaze from the bright and divine being and turned to her husband. He too was busy watching: his gaze seemed to be drawn to the round shoulders and deep décolleté in the next box. He had no idea what Elza was experiencing.

The light in Elza's eyes dimmed. It was if a bolt of lightning had struck her: this man whose wife she had become was a complete stranger to her. That which she revered, that for which she had lived until recently, that which lifted her and made her spirit soar was distant and indifferent to him. Her awakening from the giddiness of passion was painful. It wasn't love that had tied her to this Lovelace. She wanted to return to her loneliness, to the quiet house of her father. Yet she lacked the courage even to say it, let alone leave by herself. Never before had she taken action on her own. She had only known how to dream.

Dresden, with which she had fallen in love at first sight, now became intolerable to her. She wanted to go somewhere, to move. If it was impossible to go alone, then at least they should go away somewhere!

Zirnis saw the sudden change but could not figure out the reason for it. He would have liked to spend some time in the local dance halls — he too experienced a reversal to his old desires — but in Munich there would be even more of those. And so they went southwest.

Munich was famous as an artistic city where not only German but other European artists could find education and shelter for their Bohemian ways. The Bavarian capital with its public buildings, squares, and monuments was an embodied testimony to the great taste of its rulers.

Wandering through the city governed by the spirits of Richard Wagner and that royal dreamer, Ludwig the Second, Elza felt at home in their company, which was really her only one until she met her husband. Since the fateful Lohengrin evening in Dresden her passion for him had burned out. It was replaced by her spiritual love for Lohengrin, that fighter for light that she fully associated with Ludwig the Second.

Her husband often left her alone in the evening, returning only at dawn. So they each followed their own path, from which they had been temporarily sidetracked by their initial passion.

Elza wanted to visit Ludwig's palaces near Munich, on which he had spent his aesthetic imagination and the state coffers alike giving rise to a conspiracy against him and bringing about his tragic death. Yet the palaces — Linderhof surrounded by flowers and greenery, Neuschwanstein at the top of a cliff — remained as an eternal fairy-tale monument.

But first Elza wanted to visit Ludwig's last, unfinished palace on Herrenchiemsee. Zirnis did not go along on the daytrip to the island.

They were travelling in the southwesterly direction, toward the Alps. Already from the train one could see the silhouettes of the mountains on the southern horizon. Even though the mountain range was still barely visible, Elza found the view extraordinarily beautiful.

She had not compared the train schedule with the steamer boat tours on the lake, so it turned out that she would have to wait a whole hour for the next one. But Elza didn't want to wait. She had looked at the map and knew that the palace was situated slightly obliquely to the Sternburg wharf. That would mean walking around the western end of the lake, not more than five or six kilometres. She asked the newspaper seller if the palace was accessible on foot. "Why not?" The woman replied. About a three-quarters-of-an-hour walk.

That was nothing! That meant that she would get there before the boat. And during her seaside summers she had often covered even larger distances. It was impossible to get lost, because the palace was on the very edge of the lake. So she set out.

But the gravel path soon ended in a wild thicket. A young man, apparently an artist, was coming toward her carrying a box of paints. She asked how far the palace was. The artist gave her frail figure the once-over, and with a true Munich humour, replied: "Madam, from here one reaches the palace in an hour, an hour and a half, or even two hours!"

Elza thanked him and continued on her way, even though she was startled by the news. She had been walking for close to thirty minutes and now she's told that at least an hour's walk remains! The newspaper woman must have only taken the boat.

After a lock there was a stand of reeds so high that she almost disappeared among them. The path was wet and soon so were her feet, but she didn't want to walk too far off the lake for fear of losing her way. Something rustled in the bushes — had she perhaps startled a bird or an animal? Elza suddenly felt afraid: what if someone were to attack her? But the air was so gentle and the sky so blue that she forgot about her fears and continued on. Quite tired, her feet soaked, she finally ended up on a gravel path. To the left of it was a fenced-in park where workers were busy stacking hay. She thought that she had reached her destination — she had been walking for more than an hour after all. But how can they tend to a royal park by cutting hay and stacking it right there! When she inquired as to where Ludwig's palace was, she got the reply that she should continue walking. Eventually she would reach a driveway that would lead her to the palace.

So there must be still quite a walk ahead of her. And so it was. On the left there was a string of parks with villas. Some of them bore signs of disrepair, others, in the hands of the newly rich, were all spruced up.

Finally she had reached her destination — after two full

hours! While along the way she had felt very tired, as soon as she entered this smallest of the Bavarian king's palaces, which Ludwig had inherited from his father and in which he had spent his happy youth and the terrible last hours of his life, Elza entered a strange state of mind: she no longer felt herself. The tiny rooms, the simplicity was in great contrast to the splendour of the Chiemsee palace. And this intimacy was imbued with Ludwig's love of Wagner. In a small dining room, whose windows opened to the lake, Lohengrin's swan in Meissen porcelain stood in place of a vase. In a polygonal turret room were pedestals with the characters of all of Wagner's operas. Another room featured paintings illustrating various heroic legends. In between, there were inscriptions in old Gothic letters: aphorisms and folk verse.

Elza read: *Whoever feels no pain in love,*
Feels never any love in love.

Any lover would understand it. And so did Elza, who suffered from her infidelity to this dream lover. He did not punish her, however, he rewarded her with the presence of his spirit.

Finally the guide led the visitors to the bedroom. "Looks like the house of a Latvian country minister in the late nineteenth century," Elza thought. It was a very simple brown wooden bed with large and small pillows covered in light blue silk. A sign read: *Do not touch!* There were yellowish water marks on the pillows. The guide explained: "The king was put in this bed when he was pulled out of the water. These marks are from his wet hair and clothes." As soon as the guide turned away, Elza quickly passed her hand over the place on the pillow where his beautiful locks had once lain.

The excursion was over. The guide led out the visitors only to let in new ones — the cramped premises accommodated only a few people at a time.

In a daze, Elza walked down the well-maintained paths of the royal garden. She had read that a chapel had been built opposite the place where Ludwig's body was found. The park was expansive. Along the path there were benches here and there.

Not far from the water's edge, Elza noticed a metal cross in the water.

"So this is where it is!" she whispered, dropping to her knees.

She only came to when she heard some voices approaching. Getting to her feet she looked at the shore. There was a nicely kept knoll. On top of it was a chapel and a little lower, a cross with St Ludwig's statue and an eternal wreath at its foot.

While the strangers examined all these objects with great curiosity, Elza walked deeper into the park. After six when the park was closed, she returned to the cross. It seemed to be beckoning to her. It was the love of her youth, her only love. She had been unfaithful to it, taking a passing passion for love. She had paid for it with great suffering after the cruel awakening in Dresden. But now she wanted a union with her faraway dream friend who had been so alone in both his mirth and misery. Elza felt that Lohengrin was calling her. She waded into the water, going deeper, ever deeper, and as she reached the cross, she dived down as if into the arms of a lover. Where her head had sunk, bubbles rose to the surface, refracting the setting sun and looking like diamonds on the crown of the bride the dream king had found in death.

Zirnis waited for his wife for a couple of days, and knowing that she had very little money with her so she couldn't go far on her own, went to the police. A few days later she was found in the Starnbergersee, just deeper than where she sank. The body had changed so much that Zirnis had it cremated. The urn was buried in the land of Ludwig the Second. After all, Zirnis was hardly a sentimental man who'd be inclined to carry around a suitcase containing someone's remains. After this unpleasantness, Zirnis toured some more around the Alps and then went back north. In Berlin, he made up for lost time and in Riga heard many nice condolences. Then he got involved with his father's business, of which one day he would be the sole owner. Once the official time of mourning came to a close, Zirnis started looking for a new wife that would make a suitable spouse and would not cause any problems. He didn't have to look far. For the life of him, Zirnis couldn't understand what had ever driven him into that crazy marriage a year previously.

The only person to whom Elza had had a connection, her father, quietly passed that same year. He had left his rather substantial property to found an orphanage. That is how this family came to an end, and soon no one would even gossip about them.

Process (1927)
Alija Baumane (1891-1941)
Translated by Ieva Lešinska

There had been a change: schools were now mixed, with students of both sexes studying together. The subjects were clearer and more lively, the school year was different, and the language of instruction was now Latvian. The students had grown up during the years of great historic events; they had developed in various, sometimes unpredictable and undesirable ways.

At the very beginning of the autumn semester, Miss Ore noticed two students whom she was not teaching, they were in a lower grade and were not yet learning chemistry. The boys were brothers. The younger one was slightly taller, ganglier, with blonder hair and a pensive look on his face. The other boy's face, with its triumphant bright eyes and dark hair over the pale, determined brow seemed familiar to the teacher. Miss Ore had been working at the school since before the revolution, having started here as a young chemist while still a student at the University of St Petersburg. She had very thick blonde hair then and an attractive, albeit not very healthy face. The older female gymnasium students fell immediately in love with her. Now that the relationships between teachers and students were freer, they asked Miss Ore to end her single existence and get married. Her long-time suitor was a highly placed state official who was as fat and rough as she was slender and pretty.

Trying to remember of whom the dark-haired boy reminded her and musing about various old events in the school's life, Miss Ore got a worrisome hunch. The next morning she went up to the two boys: "Was your mother's maiden name perhaps Marga Sala?" "We don't know," the paler boy replied distractedly. The other one furrowed his brow and after thinking awhile, said: "Yes, her name was Marga. She died a long time ago." The boys were well-developed and responsive, but they didn't have much to say. What they did say didn't seem to be the information the teacher was after.

A little later, Miss Ore talked to one of the teachers. "These are the sons of engineer Aivess Dzintars," he said. "I know their father. His name is quite popular now — he is our new and great entrepreneur." "Oh, so it's that same Dzintars?" "Yes. He gained his fame already in Russia, building railroads, developing and carrying out various projects. I'm not sure we have another great technical talent. But as tends to happen to great men, in their personal life, one tragedy is followed by another." Miss Ore's colleague gave her a short synopsis: "A few years ago, his wife died. It seems they had shared a great passion. At that time Dzintars had been working with exaggerated, supernatural inspiration and energy to earn money for her treatment. She had gone to Italy and Egypt. When, on the way back she died, he became mentally ill. Having spent a few months in modern, excellent psychiatric sanatoriums, he recovered. Now that he is back here and is using his talent and energy to lead great construction projects, he is beginning to lose balance again. He told me that he is still mourning his spouse and often experiencing strange states of mind, fearing the future…" "What a sad story," Miss Ore observed. "It may very well happen that our talented Dzintars will have to undergo serious psychiatric treatment."

Miss Ore felt depressed after this conversation and she kept thinking about the two boys whom she never saw again. A few days later, her colleague made a casual comment: "It turns out that Aivess Dzintars's wife was a student here in her day." Now Miss Ore no longer had any doubts. At home in her apartment she rummaged through old papers and remembered what her mother had told her. She, who had never experienced love, now read notes that had been taken from city to city and partially lost. They had to do with expelling the student Marga Sala from the gymnasium shortly before her finals.

***

Most female students in the senior class were around nineteen, but one was around twenty-three. The stuck-up Gaiga Sēliete and the daughter of wholesaler Vīndedzis were the youngest; Gaiga was not yet fifteen. The final exams were about a week earlier. It was not all that frightening; the results were quite predictable based on their performance through the year — one could neither place great hopes on nor become anxious about last-minute accidents. Yet it was simply unbearable that spring was throwing the days dripping with honey at them, and that they had to stay in the city and just dream about the blooming apple trees in the countryside. In the lower grades it was not felt so keenly, but growing up, the young women experienced the sweet torment of spring with ever greater intensity. They were full of unfulfilled desires, their minds languishing. They would kick their books, read poetry, and went for group walks on the sun-warmed streets at night. They tried to do something mindless, crazy, and irreversible, and felt happy about it. For the last week they would whisper or write messages to one another in class. During breaks, the entire class was tight like a ball of yarn — there was something secretive and passionate going on; they called out, they blushed, and they smirked, getting more excited by the minute. Only Gaiga Sēliete didn't know what was going on. Class representative Lonija Greizais, who wore her thin hair up like a housewife and whose velvet collar pushed up her chin, walked around kicking her long, ugly dress and looking insulted. Her whole demeanor suggested pettiness and narrow-mindedness. A few years ago, Lonija Greizais had left sixth grade. This year, pressed by practical need, she came back to take the graduation exams, and being the oldest, did not really behave like a student. Her friend Dilbe was a careless creature who laughed a lot. The two of them would go from girl to girl talking to them separately and as a group. Helping with the smirking and laughing, they were followed by Emma Zābalniek and Bonventura Galiņš, who were of a subservient character. "Someone is trying to turn our gymnasium into a love factory!" someone called out.

After classes, a secret meeting was supposed to be held in the classroom. Gaiga Sēliete was the only one surprised to be told not to leave and pricked her ears to find out what was going on. Marga Sala, a dark-haired, fresh-faced girl was standing next to her desk. Then she sat down because everyone was staring at her. Lonija Greizais got behind the lectern with Dilbe at her side. "Everyone here knows what we are about to discuss —"

"Not me," Gaiga interrupted. "Gaiga Sēliete is too young; we didn't want to explain it to her. Let her find out as much as she can from this meeting. Now everything will be out in the open and we'll each make a promise not to say a word about it." Dilbe, with her lazy eye, looked distracted and excited at the same time. She asked Bonaventura Galiņš and Emma Zābalniek to join her at the lectern, and they immediately did so, obedient like soldiers. Greizais continued in strict and rapid-fire tones: "Something quite impossible has happened. The honour of our gymnasium has been muddied. We have to suffer for one student. If a student behaves not like a student but as a street woman, then she alone should bear responsibility for it. Neither I nor any of you deserve to be considered anything like her! I invite this student to leave our establishment without taking the graduation exams. For we should not subject our teachers and others to her lack of virtue."

Marga Sala stood up. Her fresh face had even more colour in it. She straightened her slender body and started, "Dear girls —" But Lonija Greizais interrupted her: "Don't forget that there are some older than you!" "And we are embarrassed by your behaviour!" Dilbe said smirking. Galiņš and Zābalniek were prompting her; she was not very sharp. "May I say a few words before I go?" Marga Sala asked. "Please," merchant Vīndedzis' daughter said. "Please," Lonija Greizais repeated mockingly and left the lectern along with her toadies. Yet the lectern remained empty.

Gaiga Sēliete exchanged a few words with Vīndedzis. It turned out that Sala had talked to all her classmates except Gaiga. She had asked them to defend her, not to go along with Lonija Greizais. Those who didn't know her thought that Gaiga was rich and very spoiled. Marga Sala liked Gaiga's appearance and pluck, her slightly tragic misbehaviour toward teachers and her leadership spirit. Sēliete had transferred from another school, she was considered gifted, but here she was not a very good student and was not friends with anyone. The girls knew that her brother was a composer and had heard that her family was not rich. Marga was afraid that Gaiga Sēliete would not understand the seriousness of her situation, that she would be cold and arrogant, and lead the others. So she had asked them not to tell Gaiga anything.

"If I have to go soon, if I can no longer be here, I will not hold it against you. But I beg you, girls," Marga Sala said from her desk. "I beg you, please let me graduate from the gymnasium. It is very important. My husband is not very rich and I will have to make money too to help to support our family. When the baby comes…" "Quiet! That's enough! It's like a slap in the face… how can such words be pronounced in between the walls of an educational establishment!" Lonija Greizais was shaking as if in a fever and biting her lips. "Let her continue!" Gaiga Sēliete and Vīndedzis called out. Some other girls joined in. "In this day and age, I am nothing without a diploma. If I don't graduate, you know very well that I will make very little. And I'll have nowhere to go… in a few days, the graduation exams will begin, they will last for a couple of weeks. No one knows anything. I will have taken care of the formalities and they will be of great support to me in the life that will begin outside these walls. You are students, pure and happy. Almost all of you are still children. But I am already living a life. Another life, a great, incredibly beautiful and sad life... I don't feel guilty. I know that which cannot be given away and is wonderful as life itself..." "Stop digressing. You should have simply stated the motives in support of your silly request not to be expelled from the gymnasium." Lonija Greizais sounded upset. "I did so." "Anything else?" "I have nothing more to say." Lonija Greizais, tripping over her long dress, rushed to the lectern. "If you graduate together with her you will all be considered strumpets! Don't you think that people will find out that this school shelters fallen women? Your career will be over, gymnasium or no gymnasium, if you do not immediately demand that she be expelled!" Lonija's sentences were awkward, but the girls were silent and agreed with her. "I am against the expulsion!" Gaiga Sēliete stood up. No one joined her. Marga Sala suddenly rushed up to Gaiga and dropped to her knees in front of her. Then she quickly got to her feet, and without looking at anyone, left the classroom. A moment later, Gaiga Sēliete, Vīndedzis, and another girl followed suit. The rest remained and waited for the headmistress. The headmistress knew about the meeting and had stated that she had no doubt regarding her girls and the decision they would make.

A few weeks earlier, Lonija Greizais had noticed that Marga Sala's attractive, medium height body had changed. She had praised Marga for having gained weight. Marga's face seemed to have become translucent and her smile even more beautiful. Lonija didn't think much of it but the next day told Dilbe and other girls that Sala seemed to be as if lit from the inside. So everyone started paying attention. Finally, she decided to talk to her, and Sala, feeling happy and excited, told her: "It's a good thing that the exams are about to begin: I will graduate and get married right away." Lonija Greizais decided that there was too much naivete or cheek in this. She immediately went to the headmistress.

When the headmistress entered the classroom she was excited yet full of concern; her large frame seemed to be even straighter. "My dear students, I am grateful. You have shown that you are conscientious and of noble spirit. This was an unexpected mishap and I don't even know what resonance it may have. I should talk to you some more about contemporary morality, but I don't want you to suffer because of one bad apple. So now I only have this to say: you know how private schools, Latvian schools are regarded. Just a tiny speck of dust and we are considered the worst arsonists and rabblerousers, so we are just one step away from being closed down. I feel so refreshed by your unanimous, heartfelt decision regarding that lost soul! I will not say much, you understand, girls…" The headmistress asked Lonija Greizais, Dilbe, and Bonventura Galiņš to come up to her and kissed each of them on the forehead.

After the expulsion, they tried not to talk about Marga Sala, but the desire to know was great. In particular, the chemistry teacher couldn't find peace; she reproached the girls for not telling her, for she could have helped Sala. After the incident she felt great malaise and wanted to leave the school. Marga Sala disappeared from view completely. It was said that she lived far off in the suburbs but even there she could not be found. Her defender, Gaiga Sēliete, behaved rather arrogantly and derisively towards her classmates. The exams were taking place, and teachers seemed to give her better grades than she was trying for. They kept repeating that Sēliete had deliberately thrown away the gold medal for which she would have otherwise qualified. Some girls, however, thought that she was not all that talented after all, just full of hot air.

After her expulsion from the gymnasium, misfortunes poured over Marga Sala as if from an open sack. She was an orphan, but her parents had left her a substantial inheritance. Her uncle had raised her. The expulsion made everyone pay attention: Marga's family and others only then found out about her relationship with the student Aivess Dzintars. Marga had a while to wait to be of age, she had not been confirmed, and the family accused Dzintars of being a fortune hunter. After marriage, the husband became the manager of the property. "All right, I will prove that I don't need her money. We'll just not get married." Aivess Dzintars was a very talented engineering student who was working to survive and living with his mother and two grown sisters. Marga's guardians said that he was only after his wife's money, hoping to provide a comfortable life for himself and using her innocent youth for his own gain. "He seduced her to ensure her hand in marriage and get to her inheritance, for Dzintars's mother has only a decrepit shack and a vegetable patch." "Marga believes in me and will love me regardless of the lifestyle I could offer her," Aivess said. Yet the family was up in arms about the girl's immoral behaviour, forcing her to move from town to town until coming of age. After her son was born, her uncle tried to marry her off to some respectable man and take her away from the crazy Dzintars. Aivess worked long hours, but they barely got by. When Marga finally was able to claim her inheritance, he didn't want to touch it. At that time they were in Russia, in a northern city where engineer Dzintars was employed. The World War was taking place, but Marga's husband was involved in great technological undertakings. When the course of their life was finally improving, it turned out that during their first difficult years Marga had contracted consumption. She did not worry because she had always been so full of life. But Aivess was afraid, and they started moving from one doctor-recommended country to the next. Yet the end came very soon.

Miss Ore read the notes about her favorite student and behind these fragments tried to see the love of this pure, tortured soul. The world was just jealous of sweet perfection! Yet this perfection made darkness and people's cruelty melt away. Miss Ore knew that Marga Sala did not seek revenge against anyone.

It said in her notes: *"Es waren zwei Königskinder, Die liebten einander so sehr..."* ("They were two royal children, who loved each other so much...")

HELĒNA (1942)
MIRDZA BENDRUPE (1910-1995)
TRANSLATED BY LAURA ADLERS

It happened in the autumn of 1935. At the time I was still a student in the Faculty of Architecture. In the spring, our pleasant but strict professor, for whom construction was the God of all art forms, urged me not to waste away the gift of the summer months and complete an internship or prepare my portfolio and measurements in good time for autumn, when they will be necessary for my exams. Because I had spent much of the winter and spring working on the construction of a large building and my studies had fallen behind, I decided not to do an internship and instead devote my summer to my studies. But the summer lured me to the countryside, and when I recovered from the mild inebriation of the speckled pastures and the babbling brooks, you see, it was already nearing the end of August, and my student's conscience was scolding me, asking me where my drawings and measurements were, where were my sketches and portfolio? I had none of these things. My drafting set, sketch books and pencils lay idle gathering dust somewhere on the shelves and drawers of my long-forgotten apartment in Riga. And as that same conscience continued to torment me, and would not leave me be, one morning I put on my shoes and by dusk of that same day I stepped off the train onto the platform at the Riga station. Tired, dusty and dizzy from the noise, I pushed my way into the crowd, from which I had grown completely unaccustomed over the summer.

When I got to my apartment, I cleaned up after the day's travels, and was immediately drawn to my pencils, drafting set and paper, which I only managed to get organised that evening, so when I woke in the morning they were already handy.

As I lay in bed, I thought for a while about where I needed to go and what I should draw first, but a heavy sleep came swiftly over me and wouldn't allow me to make a firm decision, so I left it until morning. I had a restless sleep. In one dream I saw a naked woman engraved in stone, her fingers plucking the strings of a *kokle*. But the strangest thing was there was a sound from the *kokle* strings, though they did not vibrate — the sound was deep, which is actually not usual for a *kokle*, and a sorrowful passion, which cut through my heart like a knife, made me cry out in my sleep. And then I noticed that the stone hand of the woman that made the *kokle* sing was bleeding — dark drops of blood dripping into the sand from the greyish stone hand. And the voice of someone I couldn't see whispered in my ear:

"The daily bread of love is suffering. Love takes our blood for its sad and passionate song." Startled awake with the strange spirit of the dream still fresh in my mind, I stared into the darkness, confused, for a long time.

I still remembered the dream the next day and a melancholic unrest kept me home until the evening. But as evening approached, I realised I couldn't spend another day resting, I had to hurry up with my drawings and portfolio. "First I will measure an old monument," I decided, "a gravestone." Determined, I left the house in my trench coat — it was a very hot day, there could be a storm — and my pencils and a small sketch book had sunken deep into the coat pockets. I thought the best collection of gravestones would be in the Big Cemetery on Miera Street, so I set out in this direction. After the dusty heat of the street, the cemetery was damp and cool. I don't like cemeteries, nor the air in them. Feeling the shadow of the oldest tree in the cemetery heavy on my shoulder, I soon also felt that light pressure on my chest that I always associate with intense dislike. "The roots of these bushes and trees are saturated in the juices and soil of decomposed bodies," I thought, and my dislike grew and multiplied. The damp cool of the cemetery was not refreshing. Fighting the desire to leave immediately, I stood on the cemetery path and thought: "Perhaps they're all still here, though we thought they were gone? Perhaps their light, their hunger still clings to the earth and life?"

I walked on slowly, trying to take a deep breath, but whether I imagined it or it really was so, the air still felt so stale and heavy, that my lungs took it in reluctantly. Walking through sun and shade I looked at many graves — old ones and new ones, tidy ones and untidy ones, and I found that I was uneasy not just about the cemetery air, but also about what I saw before me. So much ugliness and excess created by people for the final resting places of their dearly departed. I wanted to see in their places noble simplicity, immaculate tidiness, peace, inconspicuous and restrained sorrow. But here in all their glory were these wondrous twisted, stretched, ornament-laden crosses, which no longer even resembled crosses and which were missing the tranquillity of clean lines, here were the absurd tin wreaths, daubed with many different colours, laying in glass cases with or without, paper flowers or rotten ribbons.

The sun was setting in the west. I wandered around the cemetery, ill-tempered and restless. I was looking at a gravestone when I turned my head to the side and was so startled that my breath caught painfully in my throat — just a few steps away from me, the face of a very still woman was looking right at me. A dull, pale face with a harsh red mouth was watching me with wide-open dark eyes. In the next tense moment I saw the woman in her entirety — straight, dressed in dark bluish clothes, her arms at her sides, she was standing by a grave, the only thing between us was a chain around this grave, in the corners were four low stone posts.

I was the first to break our state of shock, but in its place, in order to distance myself, I asked, without even considering what I was saying, so quietly that I was practically whispering: "What are you doing here?" "The same as you," she whispered back just as quietly and gave a pale smile. "Did I frighten you?" "No, I... wasn't expecting..." She came out onto the path beside me. I noticed her pale face was covered in freckles and her eyes had dark purple circles around them. I still did not move and stood without taking my eyes off her. We stood this way for a few moments, looking at each other. "Let's go," she said, "Are you leaving?" I didn't know what to say, I quietly started to walk with her. As I already said, my lungs did not like the cemetery air, I inhaled as little as possible, and the shallow breathing caused me to become dizzy easily, my eyesight became blurred, and it sounded like my ears were full of ocean waves.

We walked on slowly at the same pace, still not uttering a word. We walked this way through the cemetery and finally left it, and without exchanging any further words, as if this was self-explanatory, we continued together along Miera Street to Brivibas Street and onward into the Old Town. By this time the sun had set and the sky was slowly clouding over. In the thick and clear glass of a shop window on Kalku Street I noticed my reflection next to the young woman's silhouette and looked at the woman herself, in shock and disbelief. She didn't turn towards me, but continued to walk with me, as if we had an unspoken agreement about our final destination and direction, our pace unbroken by any intersections, we went straight ahead towards the Daugava River.

On the pontoon bridge I looked briefly over the railing into the water, on which the dull reflection of the red sky was rocking. I looked at the woman and saw her red lips moving, as if she were whispering to herself, the expression on her face one of deep longing. "Water," she said this one word in her slightly hoarse and quiet voice, and said nothing more, but that one word was expressed with a sound similar to someone who was dying of thirst, who talks about water as if it were a miracle, the greatest craving, a matter of life and death. "Yes, water," I replied a little unsure, our eyes met, but they quickly turned away and we continued on our way. The evening was quiet, so quiet, not even the wind was blowing on the bridge, and it usually follows pedestrians crossing from the Old Town to Pardaugava and back again. The dull sky, woven with clouds, gradually lost the reflection of the red sunset. A sweltering heat lay over the city, the people and the waters of the Daugava River. "What's your name?" I asked abruptly. She answered, unsurprised and without hesitation: "Helēna. Helēna Jasinska." I told her my name, she repeated it quietly, and we fell silent once again. We had crossed the bridge and were heading towards Arkadija. I started to speak. I told Helēna about my summer in the countryside, about the gravestone that I was to have drawn in the cemetery, about my studies and my life. Helēna listened attentively but said nothing. I didn't ask her any questions. At one point, I mentioned that my brothers and sister had all died at young ages, and she said: "That's terrible."

By that point we had gone past Arkadija, and our walk continued through the quiet, narrow and winding streets of Tornakalns. The windows of the sunken homes in the gardens lay open. We rarely met another person in the twilight, which grew ever deeper and darker. One narrow street ended at a field overgrown with grass. We threw ourselves down onto the grass. Helēna sat across from me, her shoulders lowered a bit, and looked me in the eyes, her naked elbows resting on her knees. Her facial features were still visible in the dull light of nightfall, they were calm, even, but something in the lines of her neck and shoulders, of her whole being, showed an acute inner tension, something which could best be compared to the inner stress of someone who was overpowered by unquenchable thirst. I didn't know this, I felt it. Then she slid with her whole body into the thick grass, her hand grabbed a swathe of flowers and grass, now pale in the twilight, and stiffened in this movement. "The earth smells," she said barely audibly, and these words from her mouth again had the same deep meaning and sound of longing as those I had heard earlier on the bridge, when she spoke about water. We got up and continued walking.

There are autumn nights with threatening stormy skies, which in the end do not become storms. The air is so hot, so humid, so heavy, that not a leaf moves in the trees, and blades of grass lie flat on the ground. It was just such a night, the air was just like this as we continued on our silent walk together, as if in a trance. My ears were nervously aware of every sound, as often happens in deep silence, but there was nothing to hear, there was not even the sound of other people's footsteps nearby, as if we were walking in a dead city. Not darkness, but a strange greyness lay around us. Looking over at Helēna, I caught a glimpse of her face, a narrow, pale expanse, heartbreakingly helpless against the dull half-darkness that surrounded us. Sometimes our feet tripped on uneven stones on the path, sometimes they sank in sand, and I reached out and gently grabbed Helēna's arm above the elbow and didn't let go. Through the thin fabric I could feel the coolness of her skin, a coolness which is associated more with flowers and water. I had long ago lost track of which streets and which part of Tornakalns we were in, it was Helēna who was deciding the direction of our night walk. Helēna suddenly stopped by a garden on the edge of a cobbled street. "I live here." She reached over the low gate to open the latch on the other side and went in. I followed her through the gate without hesitation. All around us was a garden, we were standing on a path on either side of which could be seen the dark heads of trees. At the end of the path, deep in the garden, I could see the contours of a building with a high roof.

"There's a bench," said Helēna, taking my hand and leading me there, "if you are in no hurry —" "No," I replied and sat down beside her, only now feeling how tired I was. And it was so hot. I got up, took off my coat and threw it onto the back of the bench. Something must have fallen out of the coat pocket, I heard it land in the grass, but forgot about it immediately. After all, this only happens once in a lifetime, to feel this so completely for a person — where your nerves, every drop of blood, every feeling and thought connects together to ignite and spark. You're holding another person's hand, but it's not another person — it's you yourself, an inseparable part, the thing that completes your life.

Your confused and naive sobs of longing in early youth, your sadness, which called out but heard no response, the weakness within you, which had sought refuge — all this is satisfied in that moment, everything is set right. And you know there is no doubt you will ever lose this spark again. At that moment even death is just a leap, and passion — a sacrifice and service, that purifies and does not overwhelm. Your soul and your spirit are also burning — you are saved, so pure and calm even in passion, that while your hands hold your magnificent prize, you are invincible, immortal, powerful.

"I was searching for you," I said very quietly," I just didn't know it. Water didn't refresh me, bread didn't fill me, even the birdsong was not terribly brilliant — it was you who was missing." "I am here," she answered, but I continued: "I was not who I should be. Now I know that I'm actually much stronger, I know more, and I'm also better. Because you..." "I am with you," she replied a second time. It could have been two hours past midnight when Helēna freed her thin arm from around my shoulders. "I must go…" "You say that so hopelessly, Helēna." "I must go," she whispered barely audibly, pressed her mouth against mine and got up. I also got up. She put both hands on my shoulders, trying to look me in the face, kissed me once more and disappeared into the dark out of view. I took my coat from the back of the bench and went to the street. I stopped for a moment. The silent, deep night. I looked in one direction, then the other — an abyss, absolutely nothing. Not even a light. Not even a lonely barking dog. I became sad. Just like Helēna, I was disconnected from security and peace. Without a thought, I turned around and left down the street. I didn't actually know where I was, so I turned at the first intersection. Then the second and third. I walked around, love-struck and aimless. I arrived home as the sun was rising, I fell into bed with my clothes on and slept until noon. Upon waking, I ate in a hurry, washed my face and hands and left the house to return to Helēna. I was impatient and restless. While I slept, a storm had passed through the city, now the weather was pleasant and the air was clean, so I headed to Pardaugava on foot. I followed the same route along which Helēna and I had walked the previous night. But beyond Arkadija I suddenly had a thought that was so unpleasant I shivered — I didn't know the street where Helēna lived, nor the house number. Desperate and stunned I started to wander from one street to the next. It seemed that at any time soon I would find and recognise the street and garden I was looking for. I searched in vain until late into the night. Early in the morning of the second day I was already back in Pardaugava to continue my search. On the third and fourth days as well. On the evening of the fifth day, I found the place I was looking for. Completely unexpectedly, when I had lost all hope and was heading home. At first, I couldn't believe my eyes, then I ran to the gates. Yes — the same gates, beyond them the garden path, the house with the steep roof. I reached out and pushed the gates, they were bolted from the inside. Then I leaned over the gates and pushed open the latch from the other side, as Helēna had done the other night. At that moment, when the gates opened, a thought shot into my head: "Stupid, infatuated fool — you could have just gone to the address registry! What will Helēna think of you now?"

I looked around me — this is where we stood that night, there is the bench. I hurried towards the house. The surrounding garden was overgrown, the grass and bushes uncut, there were broadleaf thistles growing under the old apple trees. On the path where I was walking, grass was growing in separate clusters. As I approached the house, I was surprised — the windows were locked. As I moved closer to the door, I noticed there was even grass growing and some fine bent grass swaying on the threshold. It was likely this door was not in use and I had to find another. I went around the house. I didn't find another door. I returned to the first one and knocked loudly. No one answered, there wasn't a sound from behind the locked windows. A horrible feeling came over me. To rid myself of this feeling, I looked at the house — it was an old wooden house, painted green at one time. Olive green paint had decayed and become grey. Some of the window shutters had boards nailed across them on the outside. The steep tile roof, the walls, the windows — the whole house left the impression that no one had lived there for quite some time.

Perplexed, I returned to the bench — is this even the same garden? I felt it was. I looked behind the back of the bench — something white was sticking out from amongst the nettles and the tall dandelion stems. I bent down and picked up my own sketchbook. It had probably fallen out that night when I threw my coat over the back of the bench. I was overcome by a growing feeling of melancholy and fear. I had to find answers.

With big steps I returned to the house, I went around to the back and walked further into the garden and shuddered with joy — there right by the fence an old man in a blue sweater was stooped over a vegetable garden. I approached him. The old man said nothing when he saw me and looked at me with his pale blue eyes. "May I see — does Miss Helēna Jasinska live here?" The old man was unclear in his slurred reply: "No-o." The old man had a difficult time speaking. I questioned him for a long time — he had to repeat every word several times before I understood him — I heard things that my mind was unable to process. Apparently, no one had lived in this house for twelve years. No, the owners were not Jasinskis, they were called Brikmanis. And they were abroad. He lived nearby in the neighbourhood and came here just to watch over the house. He had planted for himself a vegetable garden. I thanked him and in a hot fever of impatience I practically ran away. The next morning, I went straight to the address registry. I filled out the application — I could only complete the person's first name and surname. What else did I know about Helēna? After an hour and a quarter of searching I was told: "We don't have anyone by that name."

"No one?"

"No."

"But how is that possible?"

"That I don't know," answered the unfriendly, thin girl, who was holding my application in her hands.

"But that surname... perhaps her family"

"There is only one Jasinskis. A clergyman, a Catholic priest. Aloizijs Jasinskis. No family."

Stunned into silence I lowered my head and went on my way. People around me were looking at each other a bit surprised, sneering. Despair was written all over my face, for all to marvel at. I returned once more to Pardaugava. I thought I should perhaps speak with someone who lived next to the enchanted house. It was awkward to intrude on people with such an unusual question. I no longer remember how I did it, but I did manage to visit five apartments in the buildings beside the abandoned house, but no one in these apartments knew anything about Helēna Jasinska, nor about the Brikmanis family, the owners of the house. A caretaker of one of the neighbouring buildings made a suggestion: "Go, son, across the street, where an old lady lives in the attic apartment. She has lived there for many many years. She is a bit blind and deaf, it won't be easy for you, but she talks a lot — maybe you will have some luck. The woman's name is Degiene."

I thanked her and went to see Degiene. Degiene lived in a flat much like a pigeon coop, built into the roof. I marvelled at the builder's odd imagination. I yanked on the bell at the door for a long time — no one answered. I tried to push on the door handle — the door wasn't even locked. I went in. I closed the door loudly, so she would hear and not be startled. I was confronted by a strong smell. The narrow room was warm from the sun. It smelled of marsh tea, clove, and calamus root. The room had yellow unpainted wooden walls and a few things in the room — a cupboard, a bed, a table and a couple of stools were right there in front of me, but there was nobody there. I didn't know if I should stay or go. The old lady had probably gone somewhere, maybe she was sitting in the garden, warming herself in the sun. Without even thinking, I sat down on a stool and waited. The strong smell of marsh tea was making me dizzy. Yes, in one corner on a shelf there lay many handfuls of dried herbs. Whom were these dried flowers and herbs for? I really don't know if I had fallen asleep sitting on the stool like that or if I had even lost consciousness — I was already so exhausted and hadn't had a good night's sleep in days. A gentle noise shook me awake — when I opened my eyes, I saw an old woman in a black lace kerchief, sitting on the bed, singing softly. I rubbed my eyes, but I was completely dazed and drowsy. I got up and started to stammer something about disturbing her, waiting and Helēna. The old lady didn't look at me, she sat curled up with her arms around her knees singing. Her broad, dark eyes looked towards me without seeing me. I listened perplexed to the words of the song.

"Angel of death, your sickle lies at the root of the lilies."

"What is she singing," I thought, "maybe I'm still asleep and dreaming?"

No, I saw everything, I understood everything, but the stinging, strange mood of the dream wouldn't leave me.

"The lilies grow pale and ask…"

"Mrs. Degis," I said, then remembered the old lady's deafness, walked over to her and went up close to her. Only now did she look up at me with her dark eyes.

"Hello, son. What do you want?"

"Mrs. Degis," I spoke as loudly as I could, leaning forward slightly, "I am looking for Helēna, Helēna Jasinska."

"Helēna Jasinska," the old lady repeated thoughtfully, "Jasinska… wait, dear, Helēna Jasinska is dead. It must be ten years already. I remember." I laughed and tried to control the shivers that came over me. "Dead? That can't be!"

I leaned in even closer and yelled even louder: "I met her not too long ago."

"You met her? But she is already —" the old lady looked at me. She looked for a long time, then looked away and said:

"I don't know, son, I don't remember. I am so old. Perhaps she hasn't died. I don't remember, I don't remember anything." She reached out her hand and gingerly stroked my shoulder. My head was spinning in the marsh tea infused air. And this old lady was demented or imagining things. And she was surrounded by the cemetery air. Her eyes looked through and past living people and onto the faces of the dead. Dead — Helēna?! Without saying goodbye, I broke into a sweat and ran outside, without closing the door behind me. The lady was probably crazy, how could that nice caretaker send me to such a person? I drank in the clean outdoor air in big gulps and tried to drive away the nightmarish and melancholic mood. I have done everything humanly possible to find Helēna or traces of her. I have collected all possible information from every possible place. And it has all been for nothing. I have run along the street after a figure which reminded me from a distance of Helēna's figure, I have jumped off a moving tram when I thought I had seen her face in a crowd on the street. I have looked under so many hats adorned with flowers and veils, stood at gallery, theatre, concert hall entrances, when people started to gather there. Many times I have walked around Pardaugava and the cemetery on Miera Street, I have sat for many hours on the little wooden bench in the garden of the house in Pardaugava. And all of it, absolutely all of it has been for nothing. Helēna has disappeared from my life, as if she was swallowed up by the unyielding grey abyss that I saw that night as I left her and looked around beyond the garden gates.

Foreigners (1964)
Ilze Šķipsna (1928-1981)
Originally written in English

Biruta was a Latvian girl who came to Texas at the age of
eighteen as a displaced person sponsored by a church group
that had collected enough money to give a female foreign
student a year at its own small-town junior college, which
closed down the following summer and sent its eighty-six
students looking for new schools and other mentors.

During that year, Biruta had learned English and grown
another, final inch: in September, late at night, she got off the
bus in Austin, dry-throated with the dust of eight hours of
unfamiliar, round-about roads, and carried her suitcase to the
station café. It was a dim place, musty with slow window fans
and deserted. An abandoned newspaper lay scattered on a table
and Biruta picked it up and studied ads for rooms with kitchen
facilities, weighing them against her summer wages which
she had counted twice the night before when she had finished
wiping the last spoon and hung the frayed drying cloths on the
dark lines behind the drug store for the last time. She was glad
the summer was over but didn't regret it. Some summer, she

158

thought, she would do harder things — pick cotton or shear sheep or whatever, because she wanted to know the country where she had come to live as its own people knew it; to look out of a bus window and know what the crops were and how they felt to the touch, and where the cattle went when they were not grazing on the pasture; to feel the mood of each town through which she passed and imagine what kind of places people went home to and maybe chat with them a little without being asked right away where she came from and why.

People, bus, country; cedars and scrub oaks and other, nameless trees, scattered in more space than was comfortable to know, washed in deep light with flat, hot edges — Biruta still kept the day before her eyes while time was moving toward midnight. Of the city spread out around her she had seen only the lights and she knew no one here except the waitress who was now reading behind the counter and waiting to close up. Biruta liked looking at her and being in the café; she always had held onto pauses in the rush of events, and this was a big pause. Her dutiful sponsors already belonged to the past and she was on her own, free to sit in a café and free to do whatever she wanted. She now had a multitude of freedoms which she had never had before, not in endless German and Austrian camps and cafes during the war and after when thousands of displaced persons were killing time in such places for lack of other places to go and things to do.

Biruta spent the night at the bus station, moving from the coffee shop to the waiting room and from one bench to another, mixing with the crowds when a bus arrived and returning to her suitcase afterwards. Occasionally, she caught a glimpse of a prim face in the window of a passing bus and repulsed the vision of humiliated horror on the face of her dormitory mother or Sunday school teacher, glad she had left *them* behind along with the unwanted, white-gloved hypocrisy into which a well-regulated, well-mannered campus life had trapped her. She slumped comfortably in her seat, stuffed her hands into the deep pockets of her dress, content to be wrinkled and dusty, and secure in her ability to sit through a night in a waiting room without behind bored.

In the morning, she shoved her suitcase into a locker and went out on Congress Avenue with her hands free and the early light shining in her face. The Capitol looked like its picture in the *Texas Almanac* and Biruta walked through the rotunda, stepping lightly on the Seal of Texas in the centre of the floor to gaze up at the high dome, excited at being in a tall building again and in a real town, and the day fresh and early. From the north steps she could see the University of Texas campus and walked toward it with a measured step, as though she had been getting ready for this day all her life.

***

Too restless to stick to his matrix algebras and problems in statistics, Hayden had driven cheerlessly in empty Thanksgiving streets for an hour, sorry he had not gone home to Houston for the holidays and suddenly aching with an emptiness which his conscious mind, crowded with too many axioms and postulates, had been hiding from him. Finally, he let the old car drift out to Manor Road and Cousin Mary (he suspected her of being no relation at all, but had never bothered to find out) who was not expecting him. He arrived too late for dinner — Cousin Mary, a grey, shrunken person with a bird-like nose and a face the colour of nicotine stains on the fingers of a chain smoker, had just cleared the table of food and was stacking seldom-used china and heavy silver, collected years ago when she had first come to the university looking for her man.

"If I'd known…" she sputtered when she saw Hayden, throwing a nervous glance over her shoulder at the girl who was standing in the dining room. "If you'd let me know…"

"Don't," Hayden said, thinking he meant for Cousin Mary not to get so excited and fuss about a meal for him, but finding that he had said it to the girl. It was not what he had meant to say to her, he wanted to say 'don't draw up and away so'. She was tall with blonde hair that was straight except for turned-up, shaggy ends. Her face was both long and wide, with much room for thoughts and feelings to show, but Hayden had seen them being erased while Cousin Mary fluttered around him, and he wanted them back.

"We call her Bee at the office, bless her heart," Cousin Mary was saying as she steered them into the living room, square and crowded with old chairs and four yellow-shaded floor lamps silently aging in the corners. Hayden went straight for the green sofa, his favourite place since childhood visits, and Cousin Mary smiled at him with pride and approval.

"What a treat for two lonesome gals," she said. "I've just been telling Bee about the Thanksgivings we used to have when Grandfather Thomas was alive — it's downright heartbreaking to think that the family hasn't been together since his funeral."

"Funerals are perfect for family reunions," Hayden said,

"but what a bore for Bee."

"Oh no," Bee said quickly and carefully, "I love to listen."

Hayden smiled at her — her eyes were serious and eager and he felt them on his face as he traded family tales with Cousin Mary, speaking just a little more vividly, with a bit more flair than he usually did to describe grandfather's barbecue pits and the time he had filled his barn with a hundred relatives who did not know each other, or how, when grandmother had broken her back, he lost his head and bought himself a new saddle with the hospital money. Cousin Mary's favourite tales were about Hayden himself and what a stubborn child he had been, locking his own parents out of the house because he had been left at home for some misdeed, keeping them on the street for an hour of arguments, threats and supplications before he would open the door; or that he had almost stayed in England forever after the war and would not tell anything about it except how beautiful the sunsets were at sea.

Hayden laughed — and then suddenly it did not seem funny to him and he wanted to take Bee away. It was late and they said goodbye to Cousin Mary and walked into an unexpected fog, soft and damp against their faces and streaked with blurred, slowly moving lights. Hayden drove through the streets silently, feeling that the fog made everything seem closer and at the same time divided them away from the rest of the world. Red taillights dilated and contracted in front of them and swirls of blue and green neon floated in upon them from the side streets.

"Almost like Trafalgar Square," he said to Bee and she looked at him blankly.

"I wouldn't know," she said. "Am I supposed to?"

"No, not at all," Hayden said quickly and suddenly wondered how it would feel to kiss her, and when.

***

In the spring, on a Sunday afternoon, Cousin Mary summoned Hayden unexpectedly, received him with a painful sternness and began speaking before he had seated himself.

"Bee's a foreigner," she announced, "and foreigners may be fascinating, but there's no point in marrying them. If you do, you'll come to grief."

Hayden threw back his head and laughed.

"Look at yourself," Cousin Mary snapped, "the perfect Apollo with less sense than God promised a billy goat eating green apples. What are you doing all day up at the university if you can't find a nice American girl who would be a credit to the family?"

"Bee's a nice girl," he said and looked out, remembering that the window was the reason he had liked to sit on the sofa as a child.

"As though you knew anything about her! She's worked at the telephone company since fall and *nobody* knows anything except that she's running around with you instead of attending her classes, and buying dime-store earrings by the dozens like any hometown girl which she isn't. Where are her parents?"

"Some place in Germany," Hayden said, "they'll be coming over."

"To live on you?"

"Come now, it's really none —"

"You met her in my house." Cousin Mary pressed her temples between the palms of her thin hands and sighed with the weight of self-imposed responsibility, too depressing for an old, lonely woman to bear in silence. "And you'll be the first one to blame me. First fuss you have — she won't complain like a regular wife that you're insensitive and don't love her; she'll accuse you of dropping bombs on top of her and wishing her dead, wait and see!"

"You know I was in the navy," Hayden said.

"That's not the point. God only knows what she was doing in Germany during the war. And what shall I say to your parents?"

Hayden laughed again, louder.

"You can tell them she's one inch Texan," he said. That was what Bee had told him when he teased her for being a stubborn European or a snobbish one. Once or twice he had asked her about Latvia, out of politeness mostly, because he lacked interest in anything but her presence, and Bee had answered him — that it was cold there in the winter with a lot of snow; that all the operas were sung in Latvian before the war; that even the ministers had lied to the Russians and to the Germans when it mattered — but her voice seemed unwilling, as though it were an effort for her to find her way back to a forgotten time and place which had lost all meaning for her. She'd rather listen to Hayden and his ideas about the perfect computer which, now a miracle, now a monster, would slowly but insatiably feed on the world in order to transform it into a perfect mathematical system of formalised facts.

"How ridiculous," Cousin Mary said scornfully, "can't you be reasonable?"

"Haven't *you* been in love?"

She came over and sat down beside Hayden, smoothing out her dress with stiff fingers, her face suddenly solemn. Hayden was relieved, ready to listen to ancient romances in order not to continue the conversation. Cousin Mary leaned so close to him that he could feel the nicotine-covered breath.

"Your children," she whispered, "will have an accent."

Hayden shot up from the sofa and walked to the door. He was angry, but managed to keep his voice casual. "So long," he said, "I've got a date."

He did. He took Bee for a ride in the spring air and later they walked hand in hand down wide streets with budding trees and big houses set back far from the pavements; they looked at the luminous, glaucous sky after the sun had gone down — Bee asked what "glaucous" meant, but Hayden could not really explain it — and laughed in the warmth of the evening and nothing mattered. Wisterias were blooming in front of the house where Bee had a room and as they were sitting on the stone steps of the porch watching the blossoms tremble lightly and then gradually fade into purple dusk, Hayden told Bee that he was going to marry her. He felt her hand stiffen in his; when he no longer could see her face in the shadows of trees and of approaching night, she spoke quietly, as one confessing an early love.

"But I'm a foreigner," she said.

Hayden had expected it.

"Then we're equal," he said, "because I'm a foreigner to you."

It was a gallant thing to say for a man living in the heart of his own country, and Hayden knew it; it was also lovely and right, and Hayden said it with a feeling of a special truth which he himself did not quite understand for some time to come, not until several years later, anyway, after the death of Stalin. That evening, their foreignness drained away and their separate pasts, their families and friends and even their joint future receded beyond the horizon like pale waters in face of the immediacy of the moment and of each new day upon which they lay as upon a sundrenched beach, whole, open to each other and absolutely present.

***

Hayden finished Graduate School a year after they were married and went to work on a government research project the following week. He wished he had more time to recover from the last hectic summer months of school and take Bee to New York to see her parents who had in the meantime reached the United States, and exhausted, settled in New York City along with ten thousand other bewildered Latvians, but his new job could not wait and he soon found himself caught up in the happy buzzes and hums of computer units and the beautiful logic and exciting order of codes and programs. Days were too short, yet he always looked forward to the evenings when he and Bee played and talked together, or sat in the living room each with a book in hand, brought along as an excuse for sitting idly together and as a refuge, should conversation lag and silence breed shyness.

The room was small and the lamplight soft; in winter, Hayden sometimes built a small fire in the shallow fireplace so that they could watch the leaping flames and feel the warmth of the crackling logs spread into the room along with the sensation that they belonged to an ageless community sitting by their fireside, of familiar strangers and quiet readers by the light of a lamp or a candle, the night shut out behind high walls and closed windows, tapping against a pane with a perpetual, leafless branch and withdrawing, while thoughts and thinking itself spread across centuries and continents, perceptible like the warmth of the fireplace though the fire had long since gone out. It seemed that they were a link in a long, vague tradition and it made them feel richer but no less private in their life together, which was young and without many traditions of its own.

On weekends, they sometimes went home to Houston; Bee got along nicely with Hayden's parents (though it wasn't really important to him; he knew, even now, that he would merely keep away if she didn't) after they quit trying to please Bee by hunting out other foreigners for her to meet. Hayden had been puzzled and amused watching Bee turn reticent when meeting a French hair stylist, a vivacious young German secretary, a Belgian missionary couple or other, more enigmatic Europeans, who as soon as they got together, began to nod sage heads in mutual and foregone agreement about the advantages of the European way of life.

"Is it because Europeans don't know much about Latvia either?" Hayden asked once, after an evening of broken conversation with two young, olive-skinned Greek boys who had just arrived in Houston and were still exclaiming over everything with fresh, loud disbelief. Bee had hardly talked to them, spending most of the time discussing dachshunds with Hayden's father who had once known a man to breed them simply because he loved to invent fancy names which he eventually forgot so that he had to read them out of his register and then look to see which dog came, though that did not solve the problem since the dachshunds didn't know their own names and ran up in a body or else ignored the calls altogether.

"No," Bee said with a mock laugh, "it's because I want to be the only attraction."

"The only dog with a fancy name?"

"As long as it can't be a plain one. Though seriously — I don't like world adventurers. Why would anyone leave home if they didn't have to?"

"For a better life," Hayden said thoughtfully. "Is it so strange? But what about Velta? You don't like her, either, and she's a Latvian."

"She's a freak," Bee said, "she'd be a freak if she were Chinese. Or an American." It infuriated Bee to think about Velta, the only other Latvian in Austin whom she had met at the University, floating through hallways on high heels, with platinum hair and a look of suffering femininity on her face which softened or deepened according to the type of man she was talking to, as it had through quick years of facing and mirroring men of various nationalities. She spoke Latvian with a German accent and threw in English words liberally, and Bee was convinced that she came to borrow Latvian newspapers only because she liked Hayden's straight, strong shoulders and intelligent eyes.

The newspapers, wrapped in old sheets of the *Herald Tribune*, were sent each week by Bee's parents. Hayden learned to decipher Ņujorka, Cikaga, Mineāpole and other northern cities which appeared in print, marking the progress of the immigrants. He liked to look at the pictures of Latvian girls in national costumes marching in parades in front of the United Nations building and he listened to Bee translating stories about the immigrant millionaire who had in five years proven once again that the rags-to-riches legend of the New World was not a legend. Most of all, however, he was fascinated by the death announcements — huge blank squares across several columns, edged in black and carrying the name of the deceased in big type across the centre with full names and relationships of the survivors listed in the right-hand corner and perhaps a verse or a Biblical quotation in the left one; sometimes there were two or three such announcements for the same person, placed by more distant relatives and friends as a sign of their own devotion and mourning, often appearing months later and originating in Australia or Argentina or other far off places, reading like a crazy gazetteer of families scattered and divided. Velta claimed to know some of the people, occasionally shedding a tear and clipping an announcement to send to a friend, while Bee herself read the papers with only a casual interest and frequently not at all, letting them go unopened for weeks and months at a time because she was busy studying or reading books prescribed by Hayden when he discovered that she still thought *Uncle Tom's Cabin* was a children's book since someone had read it to her along with *Alice in Wonderland* when she was little; and that she believed that Mayne Reid was a famous American writer even if Hayden had never heard of him, because everybody in Latvia had read his adventure stories, though she could not remember what they were about.

During the Christmas holidays of their second year together Bee went to New York to visit her parents. Hayden could have managed to get a week off in order to go along, but as he watched Bee, suddenly nervous and self-conscious, getting ready for the trip, he felt that she would rather go alone. It bothered him a little that she did not want him to meet her parents and he guessed at the reasons: they spoke little English and were doing manual labour for the immigrant millionaire's construction company and perhaps were no longer the kind of people Bee remembered, and he did not want to make Bee's discovery, already feared, more difficult by his own presence. Still, he was not afraid for her nor for himself, and she returned full of news and unchanged.

When spring came, Bee and Hayden went swimming in the evenings and drove around the countryside on Sunday afternoons, though never very far, because the old car was not reliable and would not, for instance, go up the hill across the low-water bridge in West Austin. They went to sit on the bridge frequently; Hayden loved to watch the water and Bee felt drawn toward that hill by an unclear fascination; she liked to look at the slopes where rough and rocky places alternated with thick, blue-green cedars and long-leaf sumacs and other shrubs which Hayden could not name either. It no longer bothered Bee because whatever Hayden didn't know was not important. It was enough to look at the hill and almost see it quiver in the heat; somewhere, beyond, was the country itself with its silent, spacious secrets which were still hidden from Bee but had lost their weight. She was content with her own place and her own secret.

***

When the twins were born, Bee bubbled with excitement and became frantic trying to name them.

"The dear darlings," she said, holding her baby daughters in the crook of each proud arm, "they need names that both Americans and Latvians can pronounce, ending in a vowel as all feminine names must if you want to decline them properly."

Hayden was of no help beyond conceding that Bee's parents should be able to pronounce the twins' names. Then, a sudden light of recognition crossed Bee's face as she remembered that she had had twin aunts, Marta and Anna, who now emerged from a far-away childhood in dreamlike splendour, their straight backs, kind hands and just hearts untarnished by the ten years during which Bee had not heard anything about them nor given them any thought.

Hayden was disturbed a little — he didn't know why, unless it was the feeling that something had changed in the Bee he knew, that an unexpected though slight movement had taken place, no less hidden from him because it was without intention.

"They'll have all of Texas to grow up in," Bee said dreamily, "and the Texas sky. Names are all I can give them."

"And the Gulf," Hayden said; "they can go fishing in the Gulf." He shifted his eyes and watched the powder-blue hospital walls turn to a foggy, wavy grey in front of him, but the twins began to cry and everybody else laughed, and Hayden's father said he didn't care what their names were, he was going to take them on his boat as soon as they were big enough to fit into life jackets, and Hayden's mother said they were Biblical names anyway, it did not matter how one spelled them, and if his parents had any second thoughts about it, Hayden never found out. Bee asked Cousin Mary to be one of the godmothers, and she and Hayden held their peace. Bee's parents responded enthusiastically — Hayden could see it for himself in the many exclamation points and dashes which suddenly appeared in Mrs. Saule's weekly letters and meant, Bee said, that her self-willed daughter had for once done something worthy of approval. Hayden had never heard of Bee's maiden aunts before but now that they had appeared in his life along with the twins he accepted them, making a vague niche in his mind as one does for family characters from a distant, now dead, time and place.

Bee said that Aunt Marta was — or had been — the head of the entire clan, having presided over it ever since the time when Grandfather Saule had died from overexposure on a hunting trip to the far forest which everybody knew was a tricky and sinister place, and grandmother was paralysed and did not leave her invalid's chair except with Aunt Marta's help, spending most of her time just sitting and smiling at everybody, especially at the children. Aunt Marta kept the family together from then on until the end — which to Bee's mother meant, of course, the last years of the war when they had been separated and when all real and sensible life ended, never to be resumed again as far as she was concerned.

There were no photographs for Hayden to look at, but Bee told him that Aunt Marta was tall and heavy-set and never hurried except with her eyes. Her only failing was the small, curved comb which kept sliding out of her black-and-grey hair because she wore it very short and one never knew whether to tell Aunt Marta that she was about to lose her comb or else wait and pick it up later, because in either case it was a disturbance, particularly when a dozen nieces and nephews were watching for it as they did in the summers when Aunt Marta took them all from Riga to the country where she ruled them according to her own ideas, at the same time running the ancestral farm and upholding its honour in the eyes of the neighbours. The land had actually been let, but the old manor house stood in the centre of its orchards and rose gardens and the wood-shingled roofs could be seen from where the highway passed over Elste's hill and Aunt Marta knew that people slowed their horses to give themselves time to discuss the fortunes of Grandfather Saule in detail. Aunt Marta saw to it that the tenants kept the fences mended and the ditches cleared and that the fields in view were worked carefully and neatly as each season demanded; she required that her Sunday horses be groomed and raring to go so that she could pass anyone she wanted to pass on the road between home and the church six miles away; and she knew how to keep the children in line when they went visiting across the county and was able to look everybody straight in the eye as Grandfather Saule always had. More she could not do, but it kept people from saying anything but the simple fact that old Saule's sons had left the land to become teachers and merchants and such, coming back from the city only for a few weeks each summer to breathe the air of June meadows or listen to August apples falling in the quiet of the morning since they no longer knew how to build a proper rye stack or how to milk a cow. And of course, they came to see the children, more as visitors than as parents, because Aunt Marta was in charge; it was useless to seek refuge with a mere father or mother who simply laughed and declared that Aunt Marta knew what was good for one — after all, she was, among other things a trained nurse and had saved Cousin Olgerts' life when he had scarlet fever and diphtheria at the same time, not counting the lives of countless czarist soldiers in Caucasia where she had almost perished herself during the war, the likes of which, God grant, the children would never see.

One was expected to receive Aunt Marta's just and prudent decisions joyously or else be banned to Aunt Anna's rose garden where she talked to one seriously while pruning and grafting and weeding, with an occasional diversion to memory-tests, nonsense-syllable poems and other games of psychology which she taught at one of the girls' high schools in Riga, until one finally learned that a sullen face was not only unbecoming but also the mark of a darkened soul. Aunt Anna was delicate, devoted and good at heart; nor did Aunt Marta lack love and charity, which sometimes created conflicts within herself and held the entire family suspended in agitation as when part of the family fortune was lost because Biruta's father had refused to go to South Africa and look after it and was about to be ostracised by his brothers and sisters until finally Aunt Marta decided that they should be very thankful that Alfreds was still at home rather than melting away in sun-scorched Johannesburg, which at any rate, was no place to bring up straight and strong Latvian children who belonged to their own people and their own land, even if their fathers had studied in St. Petersburg and were too good to work it with their own hands; besides, it was high time somebody did something about Cousin Yanis who had been overheard speaking French in a city tram which was not to be allowed, because in the first place, he could not yet speak it fluently, and secondly, it was a disgrace when good Latvian boys thought they would be admired for such absurd ostentation.

Hayden listened to Bee's tales and tried, half-heartedly,

to imagine the people and the places; he succeeded in seeing the brown birth mark on the side of Aunt Anna's left knee-cap (Cousin Mary had one on the thigh and it had frightened him long ago when he had first seen her in a new, short bathing suit) and he could just about hear the fine-leaved rustle of a birch grove — there had been birches in England, and the wind blew in all corners of the world — but the whole process was like trying to visualise pages from a battered history book of a country never visited and he gave it up, thinking that perhaps some day, when machine translation would be perfected, he might read some of the Latvian books that the immigrants in New York were busily getting printed and Bee's mother sent down as soon as she had read them. Hayden did, however, keep a surprised, cautious awareness that the human brain was a frightening thing, hiding in itself thoughts and sights and innumerable remembrances which were mute for long years and then suddenly floated up to be relived and reinterpreted and forgotten again as though they had never been. He wondered about the computers eventually knowing much more than anyone knew they knew and perhaps becoming as unpredictable as human memory, but he hoped not.

***

When the twins were almost a year old, Hayden had a chance at a transfer. He speeded home with the news, whistling his way through the five o'clock traffic, and walked around to the back door of the apartment to find Bee in the kitchen.

"How would you like to move to New York?" he called out, watching Bee's face for signs of surprise and delight. The surprise was there — she looked at him wide-eyed and caught her breath. Then, instinctively, she began to empty her face of feeling.

"Wait," he said, catching her arm. "Why not?"

"I don't know," she said, her hands suddenly idle on the edge of the sink. "It's not right. You and the twins belong here."

"What about you? You'd be close to your parents and all the other Latvians."

"That's it," she said quietly. "I came to Texas and married you and this is where I belong, if anywhere."

Hayden leaned against the doorpost and let his hand rub lightly against a chipped place in the old, darkstained wood. It seemed to him that Bee's voice was too even, that she had made decisions by herself long before they were necessary and that the answer had been ready and waiting. His excitement drained away. He rubbed the wood harder, driving a splinter in his finger. It hurt and made him angry and he wanted to go to New York, but not really — something made him think of the relief he had felt, unexpectedly, when he had finally boarded the ship to come home from England and how he had known then that he was not an adventurer.

"We'll buy a house, then," he said, suddenly very happy, "and there'll be plenty of room for your folks to stay when thay come for a visit."

It was a pink brick house in North Austin, white-shuttered and with a nice yard for the twins to romp in and enough space for fruit trees and flower beds and a small kitchen garden which Hayden dug up in the evenings after work and Bee planted with lettuce and radishes and mustard greens that grew up lush and crinkly and delighted Hayden while Bee liked the flowers better and spent sweet hours weeding and fertilising them and breaking up clumps of earth with hands, and watching roses and sunflowers and peonies drink up the water and grow slowly toward the sun, and the twins rolled in the grass beside her and laughed and cried and grew also.

***

It was a hot summer evening when Hayden came home from work and found Bee at the front door excitedly waving a letter at him and shouting incoherently:

"*They* thought that *we* were dead! Can you believe it? *They* have been thinking all these years… and we…"

"Wait," Hayden said and took the letter from Bee's hand, closing the door behind them. The house was in disorder, the twins were hungry and Bee, unable to hold still, was walking around the room in circles. Hayden looked at the envelope which bore a Russian stamp and was postmarked in Riga. It contained a single sheet of paper (cheap, yellow paper in which small particles of wood pulp were clearly visible) covered with a slightly infirm but fluent handwriting on both sides.

"It came in mother's letter this afternoon," Bee said. "It's from Aunt Marta."

"But I thought she was dead," Hayden said.

"I know. Nobody dared to write before Stalin died. Nobody knew anything. But Aunt Marta and Aunt Anna are alive and two of my cousins have been released from Siberia. Somehow, they'd heard that *we* were killed in an air raid in Germany, and they've been burning candles for us and all the other dead ones on All Saint's Day for years."

Bee folded and refolded and smoothed out the letter with careful hands. "Aunt Marta herself wrote this," she said, amazed, "she actually touched this paper and traced these letters and carried the envelope down the street to the mail box. Same old mail box, maybe."

It seemed to Hayden that Bee no longer was in the room with him, that she was struggling toward a place where Aunt Marta and Anna and Latvia and her own childhood existed again, which was almost as impossible and more frightening than trying to grasp the fact of death. He put out his hand to hold her, and she smiled at him distantly, and then fully. Hayden was relieved, but he still felt himself remote from Bee's joy and sorrow; and from the past ties which were closing in around her like an invisible, unbreakable ring around a stone that he had first coveted for its uniqueness, and now he was afraid.

In the next weeks and months, more news arrived from Latvia and became repetitive. The first long paragraph in Aunt Marta's letters was always a ritual offering of rich thanks that Bee and her parent were alive and well. The last paragraphs were devoted to a long and laudatory enumeration of concerts and exhibitions that she and Aunt Anna had attended or read about and were obviously meant for the censors. The middle section contained some camouflaged news: Aunt Anna was still a school teacher and lived in a single small room allotted to her in the old town house now inhabited by four large Russian families; Aunt Marta was registered where she lived in a corner of the old music room, no longer able to climb the stairs, now rotten and unsafe; the roof had been leaking in several places for years and it was, she said, incredible how quickly a good, sturdy house could fall to pieces when small repairs were not made in time; the old fields and gardens had reverted to brush and forest and the cousins would never find the old landmarks if they were to come home some day, which wasn't likely; the maples that had sheltered the house since grandfather's days had been cut down for firewood, and only ghosts of old times came to visit Aunt Marta along with the rain dripping down the dank walls on stormy nights.

At the end of each letter there were always the same greetings, heavy with faraway love and surrendered hope of ever meeting again on this earth; and a final greeting for Hayden whom Aunt Marta never mentioned by name but referred to only as Bee's life's companion. It embarrassed Hayden a little, but he deferred to the old lady's old-fashioned ways and sent his greetings in return when Bee wrote to her which wasn't often since most of the correspondence took place through her parents.

"Why's that?" Hayden asked once when he saw Bee sealing a letter to Riga and putting her mother's name and address on the envelope.

Bee didn't look up. "Just caution," she said. "Some people in New York have had trouble — they've been considered bad security risks for getting too much mail from behind the Iron Curtain. You're working for the government."

Hayden felt himself being engulfed in a cold wave. "How ridiculous," he wanted to exclaim, but didn't, because he already knew that she was right; still, the possibility of suspicion, no matter how unfounded, slowly enraged him and at the same time he was shaken to see Bee dealing with it casually and without involvement, as though nothing mattered but the letters themselves or the photographs that came one day — Bee looked at them and cried, unable to see her once-sparkling aunts in the two old women, shabby in shapeless clothes, puffy-faced and fat with long years of potatoes and bread. Nevertheless, she did insist on showing the pictures and telling the twins that they were the namesakes of the old ugly women. Though not understanding, the baby girls turned sullen and pushed at the photographs with the backs of their chubby, awkward hands, and Hayden felt a short shudder and then was ashamed of it.

***

"It won't be for long, I promise you," Bee said in a voice of supplication though Hayden was sure that she had already made up her mind. "It'll be good for the twins to be in nursery school with other children, and there's not much to do in the yard now until spring."

"If you must," Hayden said slowly. He didn't like the plan, but could not keep Bee from going back to work, though already there was in the air the slight gloom of a hurried life and unattended house, augmented by a weird feeling that he was sharing his home and family with two destitute old women living halfway across the world, two strangers whom he would never meet or know. Their invisible, unfortunate presences floated unheralded through the house, and Hayden did not like it. He felt no deep sympathy but was aware only of a transferred duty to Aunt Marta whom a heart attack had left paralysed and in need of essential, expensive drugs that were not obtainable in Riga but could be sent from the United States, all duties to be paid by sender because the Soviet Union needed dollars. Bee's parents and Hayden needed them also, and Bee went back to work at the telephone company (Cousin Mary knitted her eyebrows and no one told her anything) while Hayden stayed with his computers a little longer each night. There was more money then — enough for the drugs and a food parcel, with some left over to pay for Mrs. Saule's trip to Texas. In the meantime, the twins hated nursery school, and the kitchen garden, in the last warm fall days, spurted forth a vigorous growth of weeds and grass.

On a windy day in early December, Hayden came home to find the cat lying in the middle of the front lawn, the door to the house open and Bee and her mother sitting at the kitchen table in a heavy gloom, dicing carrots with what seemed to him a slow, mechanical anger. There were already far too many diced carrots in the bowl for any ordinary need, but the two women didn't stop. The twins, who had somehow unexpectedly got hold of two aluminum pots, were crawling around the kitchen and banging them about with utter delight and a deafening noise.

Hayden scooped the twins up from the floor and carried them to the living room to play with them a little, but they were furious with him for having interrupted their game and were wrinkling tearful faces and pulling at each other's hair (silky blonde hair which had grown too long and was dirty) and complaining in their own irritating version of English-Latvian baby talk which only Bee's mother, alone with them all day now, could understand. He was glad when they were finally fed and put to bed. Mrs. Saule retired without supper, and Hayden and Bee found themselves alone, sitting across the table from each other a little solemnly in the unaccustomed quiet. The meal was very good, consisting of steaming broth and a chickenroll of some sort — Mrs. Saule was an excellent cook and had more than once apologised to Hayden for not having had a chance to teach Bee to cook, but it was the same kind of ceremonial apology that Bee offered for her mother's perfectly intelligible English and that made Hayden feel oddly inadequate and wonder anew why Bee had not wanted him to meet her parents sooner.

The meal was very good, but neither Bee nor Hayden was eating much.

"Is your mother ill?" Hayden asked across the table.

Bee shook her head. "It's not that. Aunt Marta is dead."

"I'm sorry." Hayden said in a sudden wave of sympathy.

"Mother was very close to Aunt Marta. They already had the funeral, two weeks Sunday."

"Well —"

"I know," Bee said, "but to be missing at a funeral like that is almost worse than death itself. Remember, you once said that funerals were perfect for family reunions?"

"I was just talking."

"Hundreds of people were at the cemetery, but they weren't family and it was the wrong cemetery. They couldn't get permission to bury her in grandfather's lot and now she's all alone in a strange place across the river. The last four nephews were there to carry the casket, and they all had room to gather in Aunt Anna's tiny place afterwards, and *we* weren't there."

Bee covered her face with both hands and did not speak for a long time. Hayden felt that he could not share in this sorrow, but remained quiet in its presence.

Late that night the telephone rang with the insistence of a

long distance call and Bee had a drawn-out, excited discussion with her father in New York, interrupting it to consult with her mother, until Hayden grew restless, not understanding what they were talking about. Finally, he got up and found Bee and Mrs. Saule at the dining room table composing the death announcement for the Latvian paper. Bee had printed it on a sheet of blank paper with black ink and was nervously drawing a heavy black border around it. In the quiet of the room, Hayden could hear the sharp scraping of the pen.

Mrs. Saule sighed deeply, leaving the room when she saw Hayden, who suddenly felt like an intruder. He stood there, looking over Bee's shoulder, unsure whether to ask what was the matter.

"It's almost midnight," he finally said. "Can't it wait till morning?"

"Father wants it printed right away. He's going to clip and send it to Aunt Anna and the others." Bee did not look up as she spoke. The black border was getting wider and heavier under her hand and gradually the announcement itself began to look odd to Hayden. In the right-hand corner where the names of the survivors usually appeared, Bee had printed a single word.

"What does that mean?" Hayden asked.

"Family."

"Why so?"

"Well, she said," refusing to face him, "it's because of the name. No one ever told them that I had married a foreigner."

Hayden closed his eyes and shut out thought in an attempt to escape, but changed his mind and took Bee's warm face in both his hands and turned it toward himself. All he could see in her eyes were tears. He let go, and leaving the room, walked through the house, opening windows and doors to let in the stark December air and all of Texas.

The Hoopoes' Dance (1977)
Regīna Ezera (1930-2002)
Translated by Žanete Vēvere Pasqualini

"Look, what's going on there?" one of them suddenly exclaimed. The others looked and saw them too. Out in the garden were some hoopoes, about six of them; an older pair with their four chicks from that summer. There was nothing extraordinary about seeing hoopoes in the garden — the birds often nested close to people's homes, sometimes actually in the rafters themselves. No, it was the birds' behaviour that was so odd! If only you could believe what you saw, they were … well, one pair of eyes may easily make a mistake. But six, surely not! To their disbelief, and contrary to what they thought possible, the hoopoes appeared to be dancing!

In the flaming rays of the setting sun, their wings spread wide and their spotted fan of head feathers raised into a crest, the birds were engaged in a sombre dance. With the heavy grace of elderly courtiers moving in time to an old-fashioned minuet or gavotte, the birds bowed solemnly to each other before moving apart then back together again. At times they bent so low that their wings, held out stiffly from their bodies, gently touched the ground like the starched hem of a ball gown. At other times, they leapt gracefully into the air as if throwing and then catching something; this was all done in a most unhurried fashion and with the ceremonial mannerisms of the long-past time of Ludwig.

From inside the verandah, the group of onlookers stayed glued to the window pane, watching spellbound as the dance unfolded, uncertain if they could believe their eyes, unsure quite what to think...

When the Grobiņš family had bought the Silāji house the previous year, the hoopoes were already in residence. They had no idea if the birds had been nesting there when the previous occupants lived in the house since it had stood empty for a year. The most likely thing was that these timid birds had chosen the Silāji house as a safe and comfortable place to nest and later, when the Grobiņš family moved in, didn't want to move elsewhere. Of course, they could equally well have been nesting there for years, hatching out new generations of hoopoes every summer alongside the lonely, silver-haired old lady who no doubt never went out onto the verandah with its window panes broken during the war, and its rotting, squeaking floorboards. But no matter, there was no point trying to track down the former owner of the Silāji at this point to find out. When the Grobiņš family had purchased the house the previous year, they had been far more interested in whether the Silāji had lice. But there weren't any. Only the hoopoes, and they didn't show themselves until later.

When the deeds of sale were drawn up in a notary's office in April, Edmund and Ilizāna were immediately seized with an impatient desire to walk through the Silāji as its rightful owners. It was precisely for this reason that they drove there from Riga that first Sunday. However, they didn't make it as far as the Silāji since there had been a heavy snowfall the night before and the Grobiņš were frightened that, if they tried and turned the car round at the end of the road, their Lada might well have got stuck in the snow. Their secluded new house stood almost a kilometre back from the main road, meaning it was lovely in the summer but had severely limited access throughout the rest of the year, despite Edmund already having ordered several truckloads of gravel for the driveway. Yes, a heavy truck could generally get there in all weathers, provided there wasn't a particularly heavy snowfall or thunderous downpour of rain. Indeed, after one failed attempt, Edmund and his wife had had no difficulty dropping off some new furniture using the delivery truck from work. Back then, their choice of furniture had seemed more than adequate for their modest summer house.

That had been the first time that Edmund had met the hoopoes. Or more precisely, the first time he met one of them; it must have been the cock hoopoe as later, while unloading and carrying the new furniture into the house, Edmund and the delivery truck driver heard the bird's abrupt yet gentle call, "Poo-poo-poo-poo-poo!" But maybe not, this encounter may have taken place a little earlier, as the truck turned into the Silāji courtyard.

"Oh listen to that, someone is here to welcome you!" the driver had called out, laughing, to Edmund.

Edmund looked over to where the driver was pointing but the bird had already spread his wings and was flying away from his perch on the fence in front of the verandah. With his feathered crest resembling an Indian chieftain in ceremonial dress, his spotted chest and uneven flight, Edmund recognised it as a hoopoe. The sight of the bird stirred old memories and Edmund was suddenly overwhelmed with conflicting feelings.

Back then, he had had no idea that the bird would have hatchlings right there in the Grobiņš summer house. The delapidated verandah, which had never been renovated, was not very inviting and no one spent more time there than was strictly necessary. As a result, no one spotted the hoopoe cock bringing food to his mate there, sitting on her eggs in the nest.

Of course, when the family moved in to the Silāji, it was impossible for the hoopoes to remain incognito. On several occasions, one or other member of the family noticed the hoopoe sitting on the fence by the verandah but thought nothing of it — there were hundreds of different winged creatures flying around the Silāji, just like any other country home.

And if it hadn't been for something that happened that summer, those cautious, timid birds might very well have sought another home in which to raise the next generation of hoopoes without the Grobiņš family ever knowing that the Silāji was also home to other, illicit tenants.

This is what happened. Bustling about in the garden one day, Ilizāna heard a rattling, whirring sound coming from the verandah. A speckled bird with a little tuft of feathers on its head was tottering about on the floor, wobbling this way and that. Seeing Ilizāna, it did its best to fly out through the broken window but failed, falling pitifully back onto the floor. As Ilizāna later told her family, the bird then did the most curious thing; all scrunched up on the floor, it tossed back its head and held its long beak high in the air, looking for all the world as if it were about to attack her. It did not, however — it just squinted up at her, dazed.

She didn't dare touch it all the same, preferring to leave it be, and instead went off to call Līga. Edmund was at work. When Ilizāna got back to the verandah with Līga, the bird had not flown off but was hopping round again, its claws scratching the floor as it went. This made them think it was probably a hatchling that had wandered too far from the nest and was still unable to fly. On the whole, they were right. They also concluded, quite rightly, that it should be taken back to the nest and kind-heartedly set about carrying out their mercy mission.

It was at that point that everything went sadly awry.

They were both clever enough — one a university lecturer of English, the other a student of English philology — so highly educated in terms of contemporary life and with a vast knowledge in a wide range of fields yet, as city-dwellers, they had a limited knowledge of birds. This lack of knowledge became evident when Ilizāna and Līga started searching in the rafters of the verandah, convinced that the nest must be up there somewhere. If only they had taken a good look at the floor of the verandah, they would have noticed a rather large dent in one corner. But instead, they only looked upwards and so spotted something else. There was a crack between the gable and verandah roof, about a palm's width, which happened to be right over the spot where Ilizāna had first seen the hoopoe. This led them to conclude, incorrectly, that they should look for the nest above the verandah; between the ceiling and the crack. Ilizāna fetched a short ladder and propped it up against the wall beneath the crack while Līga chased the hoopoe until she finally captured it, and shrieking that it stank to high heaven and wriggled horribly, managed to keep hold of it, too. Bravely clutching the bird in her hands, she gingerly climbed the ladder and deposited it in the gap between the wall and the ceiling. From there, they heard it hopping jauntily away over the boards; back to its nest, they happily concluded.

But that same evening, Edmund discovered where the hoopoes really had their nest. He had spotted the hole in the floorboard and lifted it up — it was rotten and loose. He was immediately assailed by the smell of mould, rot and birds' droppings along with a cacophony of warning hisses. Shining his pocket torch into the hole, Edmund peered at what lay beneath the floorboards. He saw bottles of all shapes and sizes, thick with years' old dust, some fetid-looking clothes and something alive, moving about. There were four chicks with the easily recognisable feathering of the hoopoe, with head tufts which opened and closed at will, all too small to fly. As he peered down at the nest containing four chicks, the fifth one, which had been so eager to break out of this stinking hole in broad daylight before he was ready to do so, was still pattering about above his head.

His wife and daughter were distraught at the dramatic outcome of their charitable act. There was no way of getting the chick back down; the only access to the space above the verandah was that small crack through which the chick had been poked — there was no other hatch or small window. The ladder was fetched again and Līga climbed back up, but she could do no more than push her arm through the crack up to her shoulder, grabbing blindly with her hand in case the chick happened to come within reach and she was able to grab it. All she got her hands on were some old *Atpūta* — *"Leisure"* magazines, dating back to the Ulmanis years; ancient things, still in the old style orthography. Of course, if skinny little Līga couldn't get through the gap, there was no hope of Ilizāna doing so, even less a man of Edmund's size.

But what could they possibly do? Demolish the ceiling of the verandah? They told themselves that the chick's parents, hearing its cries, would find it up there and continue feeding it. Consoling themselves with this thought, the family went indoors for dinner and later, bed. Ilizāna fell asleep as soon as her head touched the pillow. Līga started flicking through the old *Atpūta* magazines. But Edmund lay in the darkness, his eyes open, thinking about the hand they had been served by fate; namely that they should live beneath the same roof as a family of hoopoes which he found disgusting yet pitied in equal measure due to a lingering memory he had involving them. He couldn't work out which of the two feelings prevailed.

When Edmund arrived home the following day, after driving back from Riga, the two women joyfully informed him that luckily the hoopoe chick had come down on its own and was now safely back in its nest. Selflessly, Līga had lain in the garden for more than three hours, watching the verandah, and had finally witnessed a little something fluttering down. It could only have been the little hoopoe. On the floor beneath the crack, they had also found a slip of paper which must have fallen out along with the bird. The paper couldn't have fallen on its own, out of thin air, could it? There were no more pattering sounds coming from up there, either. It all sounded quite convincing. Even so, to Edmund's logical, male mind

191

there was something that didn't quite add up in this version of events. Had Ilizāna or Līga actually checked how many chicks were now in the nest — were there four or five? In truth, neither of them had; they were both great aesthetes and neither fancied poking their nose under the floorboards to be greeted by a smell as bad as a just-opened burial chamber.

This was why, in an attempt to spare their feminine sensibilities, Edmund went to the verandah alone later that evening where he did indeed find a crumpled piece of paper, yellowed with age, on the floor beneath the crack. He cocked his head: no, he could no longer hear any pattering feet overhead. As he had done the previous evening, Edmund prised up the loose floorboard, and just as before, warning hisses were heard from within. In the beam of his pocket torch, he counted just four hoopoe chicks in the nest before letting the board slide back into place. The hissing stopped instantly. A total hush fell over the verandah. Edmund looked up at the ceiling. He stayed like that, head back, looking up, for several minutes, straining to see or hear something. There was not a sound.

The *Atpūta* magazines that Līga had found in the space above the verandah led Edmund to hope there may be some other old editions up there, maybe even some books. Edmund had a great passion for reading despite reading books and the arts not being part of his education, the position he held as head accountant for a retail state enterprise didn't require knowledge of the arts. Anxious not to miss the discovery of some rare volumes, he arranged things so he would be at home to supervise the workmen on the day they were due to demolish the verandah, eaten away by years of dry rot. Disappointingly however, the space above the verandah was not hiding any valuables of ethnographic or antique interest. As the workmen pulled down the first couple of ceiling panels, two heaps of *Atpūta* magazines fell to the floor below, disintegrating as they went. The workman called down to him that there was nothing else up there, phew! just loads of dust. All the same, Edmund stayed where he was until the whole ceiling had been brought down, despite it being rather unpleasant standing so close by. The swirling dust, streaming in the autumn sun, left him feeling quite breathless.

As it turned out, his waiting was finally rewarded. Along with the rotten ends of floorboards, a strange, furry ball fell to the ground. At first, he thought it was a ball of mottled cloth. But it wasn't fur and it certainly wasn't cloth — what it was, instead, was the mummified corpse of a hoopoe, dried out in the space above the verandah in the summer wind until it was so light as to be almost weightless, virtually having lost any connection with the material world at all. He took the hoopoe away and buried it in the garden. He probably had no real need to perform this final service for the hoopoe, as is usually the case with a dead creature, as the mummified body no longer seemed in any way related to the organic side of nature.

That autumn, another verandah was constructed at the Silāji, boasting not only new walls and roof but larger foundations were dug and the new verandah, much bigger than the previous one, was fitted with wide, modern, single-paned windows. The following spring, Ilizāna planted Virginia creepers next to it so that the glazed gallery wouldn't look too much like a state-run greenhouse enterprise, as the Grobiņš laughingly said. As yet, the plants hadn't grown even as far as the window sill. And so it was from here, through the smooth glass like an enormous television set, that the family and their guests watched in amused bewilderment as six hoopoes danced in the garden; the older pair and their four offspring, all hatched at the Silāji but no longer resident beneath the floor of the verandah.

Over several minutes, the mood of the dance gradually changed and the birds' moves no longer resembled that stiff, aristocratic style where every step, turn and bow of the head is dictated by some well-established, unalterable etiquette. Their moves were becoming more boisterous and freer, their feet stomping faster and their leaps coming one after another in no particular pattern. The hoopoes appeared to be on the point of replacing their gavotte with a gallop, their minuet with the cancan, unable in the interim to keep time with the new rhythm. In the meantime, they were simply jumping about in a rather ungainly fashion, wriggling their bottoms like geriatric flirts who sadly were no longer able to get anyone's pulse racing or turn anyone's head, and whose pitiful efforts garnered nothing but Homeric laughter.

"This must be in your honour, mate!" Jorens called out to the master of the house. It was July 29th, Edmund's name day! The uninvited trio of guests had shown up on the doorstep of the Silāji, claiming that in the absence of an invitation to celebrate a friend's name day, it was quite acceptable to arrive unannounced.

"Unfortunately," Edmund replied, to himself of course.

Edmund was not the sort of man that anyone would define as either a saint or a recluse. Quite the opposite in fact. True, Ilizāna was his first and only wife. But if one were to tot up, in litres and hours, the amount of strong liquor and time in convivial company he had consumed and spent, he would score more than most other men of fifty-two. Over the last decade, since holding his present job, he had done a bit more of both than even he himself may have wanted. "It's all part of the job," he would say to Ilizāna, smiling ruefully, if she ever reproached him about it. In turn, Ilizāna had enough common sense not to nag incessantly, even if there were things about his behaviour she didn't like. Grumbling and grouching does nothing to aid mutual understanding between a married couple and can undermine a whole family. No one would go so far as to call Edmund Grobiņš a drunk or a philanderer. Chess, hockey, fishing, restaurants; he enjoyed them all as the situation dictated and never to excess. A clever woman reconciles herself with such weaknesses in the stronger sex. And maybe Ilizāna was shrewder than Edmund had ever imagined? Perhaps she was aware that many a problem loses its sharp edge when seated at the tasteful, linen-topped table of an expensive restaurant and that a glass of champagne or cognac oiled many a wheel far more effectively than anything else produced specifically for that purpose. Either way, Edmund had no wish to become better acquainted with just how far Ilizāna's understanding extended in these matters. She was a great admirer of all things beautiful and the very personification of beauty herself, from head to toe — beautiful, well-groomed, with a poetic outlook on the world and a sensitive soul. Like a real man, Edmund took care not to sully that with his own more commonplace concerns and dilemmas.

Accordingly, there was no denying that had it not been for the specific dietary requirements suddenly imposed on him that spring following the diagnosis of his liver disease, he would never have revealed his health issues to his wife. But the whole thing was in Ilizāna's hands now. No salt, no fat, nothing fried, nothing smoked, nothing spicy, not even a cup of coffee, a spot of mustard or a drop of alcohol. There was clearly no way of hiding that sort of thing from your own wife, however much he may have wanted to. Edmund didn't keep it a secret as such, he just tried to soften the blow a little. When asked what they had found, he told Ilizāna that he had hepatitis. In typical Ilizāna style, within a week she knew as much as anyone who wasn't actually a trained doctor could possibly know about hepatitis and other liver conditions. What she learned concerned her greatly. All her cooking was on the basis of specific recipes which she ate too, subjecting herself to all manner of gruels and mashes.

One evening over dinner, when Līga was out, Ilizāna expressed her concerns to Edmund. She had read somewhere that in certain cases, hepatitis could even lead to cirrhosis of the liver. As she said this, she stared him straight in the eye across the table, over their bowls of semolina. It took all his strength not to look away or appear abashed. With shocked awe, he acknowledged that Ilizāna's suspicion was spot-on. He also reflected, in horror, how very little he knew of his wife after almost twenty-five years of marriage.

That evening, they went on to discuss how it might be an idea for Edmund to go for treatment in a good sanatorium over the summer holidays. But Edmund felt tired of people. The prospect of exchanging the silence of the Silāji for the comforts of a sanatorium held no attraction for him, especially this year with his annual leave falling between late July and early August. No, the only place Edmund wanted to be was the Silāji. And judging from the ease with which Ilizāna gave in to his wishes, he deduced that she was not keen on the idea of pushing him away from their summer home, either. This pleased him, and somewhat surprisingly, touched him too. The couple then went on to discuss the dietary regime that Edmund was to follow from then on.

Throughout the entire first week of his summer holiday, he didn't touch a drop of alcohol or smoke any cigarettes. He discovered that abstaining from the former didn't cause him any great discomfort, but not smoking was a far greater challenge. Withdrawal from his habitual smoking of aromatic tobacco caused him to suffer with excruciating side effects. He was unable to find peace anywhere. His hand kept creeping to his pocket, feeling for his cigarettes. Even the rattle of the matchbox got him going, made him agitated. In the end, Ilizāna drove the *Lada* to the local store and bought him some sweets, so he could suck on them when the desire for a cigarette became too overpowering. It may have been thanks to the sweets, or maybe not, but either way, within a week his aching desire for a cigarette was abating.

And then this damned name day had to happen.

"Good god, I'm absolutely exhausted!" Edmund thought to himself, reflecting that what he wished for at that point was something totally unattainable — a bit of peace. With a mind to his poorly liver, he had given up his invigorating but rather too potent Armenian cognac, opting for a light wine instead. But the wine relaxed him too much, making him drowsy and dull-witted. "I'm not up to anything nowadays, damn it! And if that's the case, my health must be really messed up," he continued, pondering on his physical condition with a certain detachment, as if feeling sorry for someone else.

"Oh look, seems as if they're getting a bit tired!" Jorens said cheerfully from behind the verandah window, referring to the hoopoes' antics in the garden.

By this point, the birds' movements out in the garden could only euphemistically be called dancing; their mindless moves looking rather more like the capers of drunk prostitutes down at the docks or the religious ecstasy of fifty-somethings on the verge of insanity. Plucking something from the ground and tossing it up into the air, the hoopoes appeared to be performing some sort of ritual, although they rarely managed to catch whatever they had thrown into the air in their long, pointy beaks, swaying noticeably after each attempt as if struggling to remain standing. Whilst the birds' earlier moves had seemed part of a rigidly structured group performance, now they appeared to be acting independently; paying no attention whatsoever to the others, and quite possibly, not even seeing them at all. Each one was totally absorbed in its own world; leaping high as if catching something, swirling and swaying, dragging their wings on the ground and bowing their heads. They appeared to be propelled by some hazy pulsation originating deep within their own nervous system; impulses impossible to comprehend from the outside but which seemed to pull their bodies about like a puppet master manipulating the strings of a marionette. It all looked rather amusing , as viewed from the verandah window. It wasn't just funny any more. With every passing minute, the birds' peculiar behaviour became increasingly humiliating and pitiful, provoking conflicting feelings in the onlookers; feelings almost akin to quiet horror. Why horror? And what about? Or perhaps only Edmund was the only one to think this. Maybe. The others still had smiles on their faces.

"If only it would come to an end soon!" he thought, although he wasn't really thinking either of the hoopoes or the way his name day was playing out. As if the performance outside and the one in here were actually in his honour, to honour him, feeling as he did so sick and exhausted and desiring nothing but sleep.

But perhaps in thinking that, he was being unfair to Jorens? And yet he couldn't discount the idea entirely. Something told him, his sixth sense maybe, that Jorens hadn't come without reason, just for old times' sake, although that evening their long friendship had been mentioned and toasted, recalled to mind and remembered innumerable times. But was it true — had they ever really been friends? Of course, aeons ago — about forty years — they had lived close to one another and been classmates. It could mean a lot or nothing at all. To Edmund, it meant nothing at all. But to Jorens? Maybe Edmund had recently become more distrustful? Or had it been the case rather too often that he had only been looked up because he was needed for something? To authorise something... to scribble his signature on something... and wasn't it always true that their old friendship was mentioned each time, repeated over and over again, each time dealings of any sort took place, serving as some sort of miraculous oil in the machinery of interpersonal relations?

Only this year, back in the spring, Jorens Ozoliņš had been made chief of the department store. Up until then, as Jorens himself liked to say he had, "worked himself silly in the consumer associations system across various regions and in various positions". And, upon hearing that Edmund was working there, he had descended on the retail enterprise straightaway, smiling and cheerful, eager to express his delight that they would both be working in the same system whilst reminding him of a whole host of happy memories from their shared childhood. Unfortunately, the shared memories came to a halt at a later stage. Jorens' beaming delight at meeting Edmund again was so direct that it was quite disarming; he had plainly stored away so many pleasant, touching details from their boyhood in his impeccable memory. Deep down, Edmund felt a little awkward that getting back in touch with his former pal hadn't produced in him a similar whirlwind of positive emotions and he had taken to pretending a little, for the sake of politeness. All the same, Edmund later sought to maintain a certain distance between them and avoided meeting up with the whole family; something which Jorens playfully reproached him for, accusing him of becoming "proud, a bit high and mighty". Feeling slightly abashed at this, Edmund had tried to call Jorens at home, only to discover he no longer had his number. He went through the telephone directory only to find a bewildering number of J. Ozoliņš, and with a sense of relief, had given up. He seemed to recall resolving to sacrifice the rather faded and hazy memories of their childhood on the altar of looking to the future instead.

But now, Jorens had come to call on Edmund. Not only had he come out to the Silāji but he even had two complete strangers in tow, too.

Name day once a year.

Make sure your friends are fed!

The Grobiņš had issued no invitations and weren't

expecting anyone. That said, even without taking the old rhyme literally, no one had ever been allowed to go hungry in the Silāji. But from the look of things, there was no need to take it literally. Their visitors descended on them armed with all manner of food and drink — most of which, if truth be told, the party boy himself couldn't touch.

The guests introduced themselves. Jorens Ozoliņš himself. Biruta Zalktiņa, senior sales assistant at the department store, a position she looked far too young to occupy. On top of which, she was a gorgeous blonde.

"Where's his wife?" Edmund wondered initially, although realising that he actually knew very little about Jorens' personal life.

Edmund was even more puzzled by the third guest; a tall, elegant, middle-aged man with a goatee, the goods manager of the same department store with the uncommon name of Ritvars and a surname that was impossible to recall. Consequently, Edmund was also unable to recall it, so Ritvars was simply Ritvars.

"He drove us here," Jorens explained, as if detecting some kind of doubt in Edmund.

Edmund's liver may have been in poor shape but his mind was pretty sharp; he possessed excellent analytical skills, and like most accountants, was known for attention to detail and an inclination to be suspicious rather than gullible. In positions such as his, naivety paved the way in no time to being welcomed into certain well-known institutions with their nicely barred windows. It didn't take much time or effort to assess the circumstances, weigh up the various theories and come to a swift conclusion regarding the most plausible explanation as to the purpose and nature of their visit.

Essentially, there were two possible explanations.

On the one hand, this trip to see him may just have been a bit of fun with the seductive Biruta. A brief, risqué escapade; a little timeout from the home and family in wholesome, rural surroundings as a sort of stress reliever. In addition to acting as driver, the role of the third guest — the confidante, Ritvars — may well have been as cover for this romantic interlude.

Or could the handsome Ritvars possibly have been invited along for the benefit of Līga?

On the other hand, it may very well be nothing more than a bona fide business trip, which Jorens had invited his two underlings to attend quite legitimately. If so, the exact purpose of the trip would be revealed in a couple of hours when they were sufficiently tipsy but not yet drunk.

Of course, a combination of the two possible reasons could not be excluded. In any event, his name day was no more than a subterfuge behind which lurked something to do with the shop or a romantic assignation or both; yet presented in the soft and tender light of the two men's memories of a shared, oh-so-distant yet idyllic childhood.

Edmund grimaced. In his own home at least he would hope to be appreciated as a *person* whose value was determined by his traits as a *human being* rather than as a measurement of his usefulness, as if he were a car or a tool.

"I'm not going to drink a drop!" he resolved.

But later, when his head was already cotton-woolly and his muscles loose from wine, and he felt a dull ache on his right side, beneath his ribcage where his sick liver was, the six hoopoes started their dance on the other side of the verandah window, a dance that gradually became increasingly peculiar. All Edmund could think about was how tired he was and how he desired nothing but peace, peace alone, peace and nothing more.

"I'm going out to see what they are up to," he said of the birds, going into the garden. The hoopoes were bustling round the apple tree, the surrounding earth freshly turned. Although Edmund drew closer, the usually timorous and easily frightened birds made no move to fly away. Seemingly having lost all instinct for self-preservation, their behaviour was not exactly an act of courage, either. No, it appeared more as some form of obsession. Edmund couldn't shake off the feeling that the birds couldn't actually see him; it was as if they had been blinded. Their complete attention was focused on a blurred, brown smudge glittering in the rays of the setting sun. Edmund couldn't begin to guess what it was. He went closer.

He was now so close that he could clearly discern each individual feather in the birds' plumage and yet still the hoopoes made no attempt to flee. Deaf and blind to the outside world, they remained engrossed in their revelry with an eerie obsession; leaping mindlessly, circling and staggering round the chestnut-coloured smudge, pecking at unidentifiable balls on the ground and tossing them into the air. Their movements were now even clumsier and unrefined, only occasionally managing to catch whatever it was they were throwing into the air but frequently losing their balance in their desperate attempts and tumbling over on one side or backwards onto their plump rears.

At long last, they noticed Edmund and a hysterical croak

of warning sounded. Five of the birds then flapped clumsily into the air, without gaining much height. The sixth hoopoe tried to rise but failed; its flight feathers unable to lift its weak, heavy body. Unable to overcome the forces of gravity, the hoopoe could do no more than drag its wings across the ground, staggering like a man bound and beaten.

Edmund was over to the bird in a couple of steps. He reached out. As his hand alighted on the silky smoothness of the hoopoe's feathers, the bird suddenly spread its tail and wing feathers and threw back its head, pointing its long, sharp beak into the air. It froze in this position. It was an impressive show but, as Edmund knew, the bird posed no danger. All the same, he slowly withdrew his hand, feeling abashed. 'Did I really need to do that?' he asked himself.

The hoopoe didn't move from its pose of mute threat, staring at Edmund with its small but lively brown eyes, as glazed as a junkie's. Edmund stood looking down at it; the same chaotic, contradictory feelings of sympathy and revulsion churning within him as they had thirty years ago.

But it had been different then. Why try to draw comparisons? Times had changed since then; the circumstances were different. And what about him? Was he a different person, too? Maybe only his emotions…? But couldn't similar emotions be deceiving?

It had been the first time that Edmund had ever seen a hoopoe and he had been more than twenty at the time. That particular species hadn't nested in the area where he had been raised.

Along with the other sappers, he had been proceeding towards the forest, mine detector in hand. It was a sunny day in May. The air was full of twittering and chirruping, tooting and trilling. Suddenly, he was aware of light ahead of him — probably a glade or clearing. When a barren field come into sight between the trees, Edmund's mine detector started registering the proximity of metal. As he came to the edge of the forest, he came across large bundles of barbed wire. Further on, he came to a sunlit triangle with a blackish heap of stones in the middle. Edmund was about to proceed, when on the other side of the barbed wire, he noticed a human skeleton. Amongst the bright green of the lush May grass shone white ribs, faded by the sun and time, scrubbed clean by forest foragers — insects and worms. Strangest of all however, was how another form of life suddenly moved within the chest cavity of the skeleton. Taken aback, he nevertheless drew closer. It was an unusual-looking, spotted bird; larger than a pigeon but smaller than a crow, with clay-coloured body plumage and black and yellowy-white stripes across its back and wings, a long, sharp beak and a little tuft on top of its head.

He bent over the skeleton. The bird didn't bolt. Inserting his hand between the ribs, Edmund touched the bird, feeling the warm, silky smoothness of its feathers. On that occasion too, the bird didn't rise in flight, but with one brusque movement, spread its wings and opened its tail feathers. Edmund's vision blurred while the bird held its stance of silent threat.

In response to his call, a fellow mine-detector approached him.

"Is it a mine, Eddy?" he asked, in Russian.

"Look, Vanya!"

"Ah, it's a hoopoe!"

The men's voices were too much for the bird to endure and

it darted from the valve-like ribs as if escaping from a cage, flying away in uneven, thrusting flight, its wings fluttering now faster, now slower. Looking into the chest of the skeleton, the men saw a nest — carefully constructed from soft grasses, tender roots and stinking droppings of some sort — holding six elongated eggs, each one speckled with tiny white spots.

"Can you hear that?"

"What exactly?"

"The male."

Through the crisp air of the spring day, they heard soft, melodious cries, rather like a bell: "Poo-poo-poo-poo-poo."

At a later point, Edmund looked up *'hoopoe'* in a book on bird spotting; its Latin name was *Upupa epops L.* although it was also commonly known as the hungry cuckoo on account of it being so greedy.

Edmund took a step back from the apple tree, watching to see if the hoopoe, at present lying flat against the turned earth, would fly away or not. As he did so, the hoopoe lowered its beak and shook out its feathers, as though ascertaining that all was well, opened and closed the crest on top of its head and peered at Edmund with his beady eye as though seeing him for the first time. Suddenly realising it was in danger, it gave a hoarse cry and ran panicking across the brown smear on the ground, its feet sticking at times.

It suddenly struck Edmund that the smear on the ground was last year's rowanberry jam. When the weather had turned very warm, the jam had started fermenting — giving off a strong, boozy smell. Ilizāna had wanted to get rid of it but hadn't been sure how to — in the end, she must have poured it on the ground right there, under the apple tree.

The hoopoes were drunk!

He waited to see whether the birds would come back or not. And they did. It clearly took them some effort, but they did return. Just like you or I, they couldn't give up on a place where they had found something so agreeable and came back to begin their revelries all over again. Luckily, there were no cats in the Silāji! Even so, Edmund started to worry what would happen to these hapless birds if a fox or racoon happened to pass by that half-moon clearing in the forest later that night.

"Well, where did you disappear to, name-day boy?" Jorens called out. "Won't you leave these silly birds alone?"

"Ah, he's about to tell me why he's come here," Edmund thought. "My name day is clearly just a cover; I wasn't born yesterday. He's just using it as an excuse!"

And he was right in part, as Jorens Ozoliņš indeed started talking about why he had come but he didn't say it straightaway. But before one childhood friend revealed exactly what he was after to the other, and before Edmund nodded his head (maybe in agreement, maybe trying not to fall asleep), before Līga and Ritvars clinked their glasses together in the name of everlasting friendship, they all ate and drank and spoke of their friendship, both past and future and... Oh yes, when Biruta Zalktiņa pressed play on the tape recorder, they all had a bit of a dance, too.

ČIKS AND MAIJA (1987)
GUNDEGA REPŠE (BORN 1960)
TRANSLATED BY ŽANETE VĒVERE PASQUALINI

Summer was gently turning its head towards autumn. The
green trees, inebriated after lengthy spells of rain, were drying
their foliage in the deceptive September sun; emitting fragrant
fumes, damp with moisture, into the air. Scattered, sharply-
contoured clouds arranged themselves into thick, hillocky
layers, and with every passing day, the sky grew bluer and
colder. In the Katlakalns district, smoke started curling from
the chimneys and the first apples started thudding down into
families' gardens. Čiks and Maija first met each other the day
the girl and her mother came to live with Nauris. Čiks lived in
a grey, two-room house next to Nauris. Hidden away behind a
thicket of lilac bushes, the little house, with its sticky-out roof
patched all over with scraps of tar paper, tin and plywood in a
multitude of shades, resembled the sad face of an old woman
with five headscarves wrapped around her head. Čiks' mother
was rather ashamed of their humble home, which was no
doubt why they never had guests to visit any more. In fact, it
sometimes seemed that his mother truly hated their little shack

with its three box-like add-ons; one housing the toilet, another the kitchen and the third, where the wind whistled constantly, which was home to a home-made tub and piles of smaller tin tubs in the corners. Although he was such a loser, which was so unfashionable, Čiks' father did know how to mend electric cabling, clocks, transistor radios and even how to cut men's trousers. He changed jobs every six months so Čiks never knew what to say when anyone asked what his father did. His mother sent him to school in the city centre, reasoning that by doing so, he wouldn't end up hanging out with the rough local lads as far nicer people would surely be found in the centre; the families in their neighbourhood were of the most questionable sort — no nice family would choose to live in a shack like theirs. Čiks' mother even went so far as to describe his own father as a questionable sort and would always frown crossly when he started telling them, with childlike enthusiasm, about the great prospects awaiting him at his latest workplace. These were generally the only times when his father would become talkative and animated — most of the time he could be found stretched out on the striped sofa, daydreaming with a newspaper over his face.

His mother worked in a kindergarten, and over the last three years, had started going to the theatre more and more often. His father never went with her. He would wander round the garden or smoke for hours on end, sitting on a bench. No matter how hard Čiks tried to get his attention, galloping round him in circles like a month-old puppy, his father rarely emerged from deep within his own thoughts and when he did, it was only to pat Čiks on the bottom with false cheerfulness. When he did this, he seemed so pitiable, so helpless in his falseness that Čiks wanted to cry out in shame. That was why he didn't bother his father any more. But even on those evenings when his mother didn't go to the theatre, their home was as silent and miserable as a plundered church. The only sounds ever to be heard were the sizzling of supper in a pan, the rustling of newspaper or book pages being turned or the metallic clink of knitting needles. The mornings were quite different, though. Then mother would race from room to room, getting dressed and making tea at the same time, flicking through Čiks' homework book and giving his father a "to do" list for the day. His father, too, often seemed livelier in the mornings, as if he had resolved to do something of importance. But by the afternoon, as Čiks' mother stood in front of the mirror putting metal curlers in her hair, everything changed. Looking out of the window, Čiks saw Maija creeping round long beds of dahlias in Nauris' garden; her dark head flashing now between the yellow blooms, now by the bright purple ones. He went quietly out into the garden, and hidden from view behind the lilac bush that separated their plot of land from Nauris', started making growling noises. Unperturbed, the girl continued to pick up dahlias. She was wearing amazing trousers of the sort Čiks had never seen before — covered in colourful patches, so rather like the roof of Čiks' house, only each patch had a gold button sewn on top. Čiks' growling grew louder, then switched to a wheezing sound. In the end, he put two fingers in his mouth and whistled. The girl looked around, as if about to run away but by then Čiks was standing in front of her so he gave a deep, theatrical bow and said, "Hello!"

Maija saw a boy with white-blond curls, an adult-looking chin and a mischievous look in his kind eyes standing in front of her.

"You look like a fox terrier," she said.

The girl slowly took in Čiks' face, his worn, bobbly sweater and his legs, squeezed into thin sports trousers.

"Have you moved in here?" Čiks asked.

His back was dripping in nervous sweat. He had no friends. There weren't many questionable sorts in that neighbourhood and if the ones that did live there popped up from time to time, they just passed Čiks over as if he were of less interest than a blowfly. At the city-centre school, on the other hand, everyone seemed to think he was some sort of half-wit who was given good grades for that same reason. A while back, he had had a friend, Nikolay, who lived nearby but then the boy's family had moved to Moscow. Nikolay had promised to write but a year had gone by and he still hadn't heard from him.

"So that was you wheezing like that just now," the girl went on, still looking him up and down.

"Don't hold it against me. It was just a silly prank. My name is Čiks."

"Maija."

Čiks' mother was also called Maija. But this was quite a different Maija. She had a way of looking at you that was calm and collected, indifferent almost, but she seemed to be quite keyed-up on the inside, too. Skinny, with absolutely no womanly curves to speak of. A teenager, but of an undefinable age with a smooth, pale face. Čiks liked her. He wasn't sure why, but he felt sorry for her, too, which made him suddenly feel angry, making him shout with more than a hint of bravado, "Let's go!"

"Where to?" Maija asked in surprise, unable to take her

211

eyes off the boy.

"You'll see. Or do you have to report back to Nauris?"

Čiks hated his neighbour. While his mother was at the theatre, it was Nauris who filled his father's head with nonsense which would later send him to the tavern where he would get drunk. Of course, Nauris always went with him, and when they came back, Nauris would be holding his father up under the armpits like a good boy, roaring with laughter and flashing wide-spaced, yellow teeth from his wide, gleaming mouth. He hated his neighbour, despite the fact that every so often he would slip a bar of chocolate or biscuit into his pocket. Čiks was quite convinced it was all Nauris' fault that his mother disappeared off to the theatre while his father dozed and their home always felt deserted.

"They won't notice I'm gone," Maija answered, ready to go.

After circling the streets for a while, the pair reached an overgrown apple orchard. They were assailed by the sweetly oppressive smell of apples rotting in the grass. The hut itself was hidden amongst the trees.

"I spend some time here," Čiks announced with pride, hurrying to open the door. "It used to be a woodshed. The house itself burnt down but the shed survived. I don't have anywhere to go and think in my house," Čiks finished, gesturing to the girl to go inside. Glancing sideways at Čiks, Maija stepped over the threshold. The floorboards were rotting in places but the walls were adorned with art prints cut from magazines. "This is my Purvītis," said Čiks, lighting a candle and pointing at a winter landscape. "And look here at my paintings, *Girls in national costumes,* one by Tabaka and the other by Polis.

See?" he said with pride. "Of course, they are not originals but one day, when I earn lots of money, I'll buy the real paintings."

Maija said nothing. What a know-it-all! So she didn't know who these reproductions were by, but so what? It had been bad enough when they had gone to the museum on a school trip and the teacher had made them look at black and white chalk drawings of men and women for a whole hour. Oh, how the girls had blushed and the boys had sniggered! Maija's life revolved around moving from place to place, the ever-present smell of nail polish remover (her mother was a manicurist, and as she said, offered her services from home) and a stream of faces that before you had a chance to memorise them were already out the door, waving their red, violet and orange nails as they went. That's how they moved around, going from place to place. In fact, Maija didn't really know where their real home was. Maybe it was that narrow room, smelling of mothballs and strawberry soap, which Aunt Cilda had had put down as mother's place of residence when she had first moved from the countryside to the city to train at the beauty school? In addition to Aunt Cilda, who was widow-like and rather frightening in her chaste sterility, the apartment was also occupied by a very noisy family with two children and at least another two planned. When Maija's father came on the scene, Aunt Cilda feared being poisoned and her room was given to the newlyweds. Indeed, she conjured up such refined, psychological scandals and intrigues, while the neighbours in turn seemed keen to smoke out both arguing parties, that Maija's mother eventually decamped to her fiancé's lodgings in the workers' dorms. And there they stayed under tough conditions but in a state of romantic elation until Maija was born. This, however, was followed by her mother's return, head hung low in shame, to the aunt's apartment as Maija's father went to Magadan to make his fortune, from where he failed to come back at all, either with bearskins and bags of money or poor as a church mouse. Until the age of seven, Maija lived with her mother in the tiny room in Aunt Cilda's apartment where she would not permit her mother to have ladies for manicures for fear of them all ending up in jail. As a result, Maija's mother spent her life dashing from one well-to-do apartment to another, trying to make up for the lost riches which had never arrived from Magadan.

Then Roberts came along — a gentle giant. Night after night he would come and sit in their tiny room, bearing gifts of apples and fiddling sadly with his wedding ring on his big, white finger. Aunt Cilda interfered again, threatening to sue them for amoral living. Big Roberts took Maija and her mother to his attic lodgings, saying it was where he did his writing; he lived elsewhere. Her mother was unable to host paying clients up there in the attic so she sold her parents' modest country house which had become redundant since their death, and the pair spent a pleasant year with no financial worries at all. They bought furniture, dresses, went to puppet shows and the ballet. That year, Maija's mother smiled from noon to night. Roberts was happy, too, spending the weekends with them in the attic. Maija's mother never pretended or asked anything of Roberts, as if she knew that they weren't going to be together forever. With a shudder, Maija recalled her mother's tearless moaning (that grated in her ears like the scratchy head of a bottle brush) when Roberts was killed in a car accident. His wife and two daughters then showed up, telling them to vacate the flat which belonged to them. They stayed a little while longer as her mother was reluctant to beg her aunt to have them back. She would sooner have gone to Magadan herself than go back there. At that time, her mother had been twenty-seven years old, Maija eight. And then, to Maija's surprise, her mother underwent a complete change. Her voice became sharper and harsher, her gait more militant and her chin more pointed. Her friends kept giving her comprehensive advice on her rights and on housing councils, courts and executive committees. On one occasion, Maija's mother tried to persuade her daughter to go and live on her own with Aunt Cilda. Maija would rather have died than do such a thing — how could she live with that sanctimonious sneak who poked her nose into every jar of jam and every drawer, muttering prayers for days on end, being a nuisance to both her and her mother whom she would have reduced to a nervous wreck had it not been for Roberts appearing when he had. What happened next came about in a very fast, business-like manner. Valdis and now Nauris. Mother hugged her daughter more often and told her, as if in consolation, that there were so many kind people in the world. All the same, she now realised that never before, not even in the presence of the kindest person in the world, had she felt the surge of exciting cosiness, quiet cheerfulness and inexplicable magic that suddenly emanated from this hut and this boy. She didn't feel guilty or in the way as she had often felt since Roberts' death. Here she was free. Free from it all. Čiks had put on an old, brown velvet jacket, embroidered here and there in silver thread.

"My dear lady, would you like to take a seat? Would you care for a little afternoon tea?"

He put one hand behind his back and, from behind his chair, pulled out a packet of rusks and a pot of jam.

"You are amazing!" Maija gasped with joy. "Where on earth did you get that? And the jacket!?"

"My father used to work with the seamstresses at the opera house. When he left, he asked for it as a gift. Tuck in!'

"Mother always tells me to beware of boys I don't know," Maija suddenly said in a teasing voice.

Čiks looked away in displeasure. "Now you are acting like the girls in my class. They smudge block mascara on their eyelashes and speak about men as if they knew all about them. It drives me mad,' Čiks muttered indignantly, clearly disappointed in the girl. Oh, how he hated the way girls chattered on! He had heard something similar from Nauris, who had shared his knowledge of women with his father. At school, too, he heard boys and girls competing in the exchange of witticisms along the same lines, sharing rude anecdotes and infantile imaginings, both parties blushing whilst enjoying the whole thing enormously. Čiks never joined in and so was considered wet behind the ears.

"Don't be cross! It's lovely here. Things are just moving a bit quickly. We haven't settled in yet and we're already on the move. I want to go a bit slower," Maija told him, her head bent. Her thin, white fingers were chapped across the knuckles. Her nose was straight except at the tip, as if it had decided at the last minute to shoot upwards. In the candlelight, the gold buttons gleamed on her patchwork trousers.

"Is your mother a goodtime girl?" Čiks was unsure how to ask in a more polite way.

"Don't you dare say things like that, you little fox terrier.

I'll go away if you do," Maija said with slow menace. In the twilight, she didn't even look very childish any more.

Čiks was embarrassed. "I'm not as clever as you are, I don't know as much about such things. But don't be angry with me, will you? We are friends, now, aren't we?" Čiks said, feeling his voice becoming gruff. He had never spoken like that before. Generally, the only time he opened his mouth to speak was when he was being given an oral test at school. Never at home. Maybe just a few words about school, washing, eating. Things hadn't always been that way. Two or three years ago they had all gone mushroom picking together and when father played his harmonica at Christmas, mother shoved her nose into father's ear and everyone laughed. Back then, his father had a job mending clocks and had given his mother one for New Year — a chiming clock with a glass front which came packed in a huge box. But those times were over and it seemed now as if they had never even existed. To Čiks' mind, everything had happened at the same time — his mother had thrown the little hammer at the clock, started putting curlers in her straight, shiny hair and developed a love of the theatre at about the same time that his father had started dozing on the sofa and chinwagging with Nauris. In the past, they used to have friends round and mother never used to say that she felt ashamed of their home, that it wasn't halfway decent. That said, Čiks had started to receive excessively cordial, suspiciously warm greeting cards on his birthday. On these occasions, the silence was even more tormented than usual as they all sat round a freshly baked birthday cake that Čiks ate as if it were horsemeat balls that had gone off. He did his utmost not to let this show; his mother's eyes so moist they looked fit to overflow and his father so impotent, his sorrow so hopeless, that it all seemed on the verge of collapse after which nothing would remain. This was precisely why he kept quiet now as Maija, still talking, seemed to see him for what he was.

"You're really cool, you know. Don't snigger and call me names, pretending to be so grown up. You can't talk to them normally; they are so self-important. But with you it's different — I feel I could tell you anything," Maija went on seriously.

"Go ahead! I've got nothing in particular to share about myself. I might have done, when I was little, but I haven't any more. My father keeps himself to himself, never says a word, and all my mother does is go to the theatre or quiz me over my maths homework. We don't have a home in the country or summer holidays. Father never gets any holidays nowadays as he changes jobs all the time. He lives in hope of us being assigned an apartment somewhere. Mother works right through the summer as we need the money. Quite a sorry situation, all in all," Čiks finished with a half-smile, biting off a bit of rusk. Sitting there with Maija, he had the same sort of feeling he had only ever witnessed before in paintings — the glow of candles without any candles actually being there, warm faces and dark figures seemingly emanating a sort of inner smile; a reflection of their souls. Only thing was, he couldn't remember who had painted what. There had been hundreds of books on paintings in Nikolay's home, belonging to his parents. Sometimes, he used to call on his friend when he knew his parents were out and leaf through the expensive, illustrated volumes while Nikolay bit his fingernails in boredom, waiting for Čiks to stop wasting time and go down to the basement with him to play charades. Nikolay was a tsar, or at least that was what his parents called him — the tsar of the family. But that was a long time ago. A year had passed since Nikolay had moved away.

"I don't have much that is cheerful to share, either," said Maija. "But something is always happening. I keep getting a new father, or going to a new school. In some ways it's quite fun, but it's very hard on my mother and she cries a lot," the girl said.

Čiks realised that it wasn't easy for Maija to talk about these things — she was ashamed. "How many fathers have you had so far?" Čiks inquired carefully, rather taken aback.

"Well, proper ones — I'd say three. I don't remember the first one. Mother said that I never actually met him. The second was a writer. He was such a big, kind man."

"What was his name?"

"Roberts."

"Don't you know any other writers?" Čiks pressed her.

"What?"

"Well. The ones we study at school. He wasn't one of them."

"Then you'll still have a lot to read," said Čiks, in a fatherly tone.

"Don't be such a know-it-all. You sound like a twenty-year-old ninny. Roberts was killed. It was terrible, mother wouldn't stop wailing. Then this woman came along and chucked us out of our home. After that came Valdis, the guy from the TV shop. He never stopped talking but he never had anything of the slightest interest to say."

At this, Maija gave a laugh as if remembering something amusing. Čiks didn't take his eyes of the girl for a second. She looked like someone who might have been cruel to cats when she was little but no, that was hardly likely! She had such a kind smile. All the same, little silver daggers darted from her eyes.

"And what about that drunkard, Nauris…? Does he count as a new father now?" Čiks was finding it all a bit difficult to get his head round.

"What? Of course, he does! Although I don't actually call him father, I didn't call Valdis father, either, come to that. But I guess he counts as a father, seeing as we live with him. I can't make any demands or ask for anything seeing as I'm still a minor. And the fact my mother is so unhappy is probably all my fault. I'm to blame for the whole sorry mess." Maija spoke slowly, as if every word she uttered caused her pain and yet she needed to get them out, Čiks realised. The boy just shook his head in silence.

Maija then suddenly came around, saying, "I'd better get going."

"How about going fishing in the Daugava River tomorrow after school, it's not far. Have you already started at school?"

"No, my mother is still getting the paperwork sorted out. She's quite worried about all the formalities. She got everything she needed from my last school but hasn't had time to enrol me at this new one yet. Next week, maybe."

"So you're not actually going to school at the moment?"

"No."

"Right, I won't go either!" said Čiks, jubilantly. "It's not as if we were little kids any more."

Evening was slowly descending over the houses and gardens. Čiks sat in his family's tiny kitchen, weaving something out of strands. His parents were not speaking.

Mother's curlers clanked on her head; she was getting ready for the theatre. His father was lying on the striped sofa, a pillow over his face. There was something rather menacing about the glint in his mother's eye and the way she was moving about, so Čiks took himself off to the kitchen. Shortly afterwards, his mother called out, "Bye!" her lips smothered in bright red lipstick, before prancing off down the road in that joyful, dancing way so characteristic of her. Her spotted silk scarf fluttered in the evening wind. Čiks was suddenly assailed by an unfathomable pain, burning in his heart, but he didn't go after her. Maybe people stopped talking to each other when they hit thirty, or a little more, Čiks thought. And what do they do then? Scrub each other's backs, cook, light the log burner, work out their expenses so they would stretch to the end of the month... perhaps thirty-year-olds only talked at night when their children were asleep? Čiks was no child, he would have heard that.

Maija lay in her bed and heard laughter coming from the next room. A crumbled wafer had been put on her bedside table. Čiks handed things to her, whereas Nauris left them in a bowl for her as if she were a dog — never actually giving anything to her himself. There were no books. At least in Roberts' attic there had been novels that her mother didn't let her read. Valdis had owned collections of the current affairs magazines *Dadzis* and *The Thistle*; Nauris had nothing. She wondered what he had done with himself when he lived on his own. Did he use to grow flowers? At the moment, he had her mother to talk to, but could two people keep talking indefinitely? In addition to which, most people slept in their beds but she noticed that they were very restless at night. She was woken by Nauris' laughter, coming from the kitchen. Her mother stuck her head round the door and told her, rather sourly, to come and have breakfast. She saw that she had grey circles round her eyes, as if traced by a compass. The kitchen table was covered with a green, checked wax cloth. Nauris smoked, smirking oddly every so often into his wiry, red moustache. Her mother fluttered between the kitchen sink and the gas stove and back. Maija was struck by the thought that she was behaving rather like a hen when, really, she should be seated on a white chair, like a princess, while Nauris served her a cup of coffee. Čiks would definitely do that. And he would place his hand behind his back before bowing as well. Nauris attacked his bowl of salad like a pig. Maija felt like kicking the greedy hog — for the circles round her mother's eyes, for her sharp voice, for everything, for the whole lot of it.

"Thank you!"

The girl got up. Someone was growling by the front door, then a blond-white, curly-haired head appeared wearing a broad yet secretive smile.

"Let's go!" Čiks exclaimed.

Maijas temples throbbed in pain. She felt filled to the very brim with fresh, joyful air so eager to escape it could blow her apart. Who was this Čiks?

"Didn't your parents notice that you didn't go to school?" Maija asked.

"No, it would never cross their minds to check up on me. After all, I always get top marks."

"Oh, I hate swots!"

"I'm not a swot," Čiks said, his pride hurt. 'But I'm not an idiot, either."

When school was over, they spent entire afternoons sitting on the rocks by the river, dangling their feet in the water for hours. Čiks made boats out of colourful scraps of paper and floated them on the Daugava.

"Let's go to Italy in this one. There are museums there," Čiks said dreamily, gently lowering a boat made from the purple cover of an exercise book into the water. "And this one will take us to see the animals in Africa," he said, sliding into the water a boat made from green desk paper. "Where would you like to go, Maija?"

"Heaven, maybe? I hear there is all you could wish for there; no need for a father or a mother."

"What rubbish is that?!" Čiks shook his head in disapproval. "Listen, Maija, I've been thinking. Why don't we dig a hole under the woodshed and make another room."

"What for?"

"So we would have a small shelter of our own. What if something happens in the world? We could pinch some hay from a garden somewhere, get hold of some plywood, maybe find some glass we could use for a window…"

"But why? Would it save us, somehow?"

"It would just be the two of us. We would definitely survive! We could have a family of our own. How many children would you like?" Čiks asked.

"Three, perhaps." Maija said, thoughtfully.

"We could get married. What do you think?"

"They wouldn't let us." Maija shook her head. But what a life it would be! They would walk hand in hand for miles. They would go to school together and shop for milk and sweets. Maija could go fishing and fry her catch for dinner. No, she would read books and find out who Purvītis was so Čiks wouldn't think he was the only clever one. In the evenings, Čiks would put on his velvet jacket, she — her pink blouse, and they would go out dancing somewhere. And they would sleep quietly, ever so quietly, at night. So quietly that you could hear a pin drop. Not like Nauris and her mother.

"Well, will you give me your hand — I'm asking you for it," Čiks said, getting to his feet, and after rummaging in his pocket for a moment, pulled out a ring woven from strands of plastic. He threw it up into the air then put it onto Maija's finger. "Let's wait a couple of hours before we get married, shall we? We don't need more time than that, do we?"

It was hard to tell if he was being serious or not. His straight shoulders were quite at odds with his rounded mop of curly hair. Everything about Čiks seemed as though it ought to be rounded, complete. He knew so much and always came across as being so sure of himself. The boys at school talked differently, they even walked differently — strutting about and showing off. A green plastic ring. Wasn't that simply amazing? And he had woven it himself. Maija had never owned any jewellery, not even a badge; unless you counted the one for October Children or Pioneers. Envious and miserable, she would stare at the beringed hands of the ladies whose nails her mother filed. But she had never seen anything like that. What a boy!

"You can take more time if you need to; I believe it's a bit different for women," Čiks suddenly said. They roamed the streets; passing through gateways, walking through the parks, scaring pigeons and eating the bread they had brought for fishing. And so it went on, seemingly for eternity. Maija and Čiks, side by side. Then, Čiks started going faster; as if forgetting he was holding hands with Maija. "Slow down, Čiks, or it will all be over too soon."

"No it won't, not at all! Don't judge us by the standards of adults. They can't see what lies at the heart of things. Like, for example, how my mother didn't come back from the theatre. I didn't want to tell anyone about it, actually. My father got very drunk — he's probably still sleeping it off. That means he'll have to look for another job. Where's the sense in any of it? Just because they are adults. They can't afford anything any more," Čiks had grown increasingly angry as he spoke.

"Do you know what I think? Adults do what they want. My mother is a manicurist but once, after work, she cut Nauris' toe nails. And, sweetly smiling, told him that she didn't want him to scratch her. Well? What do you have to say about that?"

"Let's go to our den." The woodshed was invisible in the overgrown garden. The nose of a crane was moving menacingly up and down quite close by, a digger was tossing up the earth.

"Is this area going to be built on?" Maija asked him.

"Probably. My friend Nikolay used to live there."

"Where does he live now?"

"In Moscow. He doesn't write to me. He didn't leave his address, either."

"Don't worry, I won't leave you," Maija said, her eyes cast down to the ground. The sweet smell of apples blended with hay hung in the air.

"Yesterday night I made you a veil," Čiks said, smiling shyly, and pulled a strip of polythene, tied in a rose-shaped bow at one end, from behind the wardrobe. "So, untie those silly pigtails. Let me comb your hair for you."

"There you go! And the veil. Oh no, the bouquet! Silly me! Never mind, we can make one from a handful of hay. Your trousers are just perfect! I don't like long dresses on girls."

Maija stood there, confused, staring at Čiks in silence. And that was exactly how they did it! Clear as day. There was nothing funny about it whatsoever. Only the two women in national costume looked at them askance, their wreaths on their heads slightly crooked. Čiks put his velvet jacket on. On a chair, he had placed his pocket knife and an apple.

"There should always be an apple. It has something to do with weddings and so on, I've seen it in paintings." Then, he took a deep breath and said, in quite a loud, booming voice, "Maija, do you take Čiks to be your husband?"

"I do," the girl exclaimed, before asking him, rather hoarsely, "Čiks, do you take Maija to be your wife?"

"I do," said Čiks before looking away. "And now, my children, you must prove that you will be faithful with the exchange of blood and the eating of the apple," Čiks intoned in a low voice. It started drizzling outside; leaves rustled and windfalls fell from the apple trees. Maija and Čiks made small incisions on their fingers. With steady expressions, standing before the plywood wall, they pressed their fingers against the dark area between the cut-out art prints.

"A lot of blood isn't called for, even if we are getting married," Čiks said, sucking his finger. Then they shared the apple, which they ate with great solemnity. "And now, to bed," Čiks said, a slight question in his voice. Maija looked at him with frightened eyes from beneath her polythene veil. "You do want three children, don't you?" Čiks asked.

"Well, not immediately. First you have to kiss me."

Obediently, Čiks went over to her, and lifting her veil, placed a dry-lipped kiss on her forehead. "We'll make our bed in the hay," the boy decreed. Čiks appeared to be growing in confidence as he bustled about. In the candlelight, the threadbare blanket looked like a small, leaded verandah window.

"Listen Čiks, thirteen-year-old girls don't have babies, you know."

"That's only because no one loves them enough," Čiks explained with conviction. Sitting on the loose heap of hay, Čiks put his arm round Maija's shoulders. The look she gave the boy was full of trust and assurance. She nuzzled her head into his neck.

"So, do you feel something big now?" Maija asked.

"Yes," he replied quietly, quite choked with happiness. It felt as if a great, warm knot was rolling across his chest. "I'm scared I will grow up myself. I'm scared because I feel something big," he said forcefully.

"I think that, instead of sitting, we should lay down," said Maija, pulling Čiks down into the hay.

"Now we will definitely have three children," Čiks said.

"Definitely, with all this excitement!" The polythene had steamed up in the warmth. "Shouldn't I take my veil off? I'm not a bride any longer, am I?" Maija said pensively.

"You know, we'll let our own children get married when they are thirteen, whenever they are ready, if we ever get too much for them. No doubt we won't have any understanding of such things ourselves by then."

"No, you know there is a way that we could make sure we

don't get too much for them. You could read to them lots and I'd make scrambled eggs."

"No, Maija, it's not just that. There has to be something else. Like in that painting with the warm light. I just don't remember who painted it. No, no scrambled eggs. Or else what would happen is that, over time, we would only ever speak of eggs. Now, listen carefully to everything I tell you and I will remember everything you say. I don't trust adults. I won't trust you or even myself when we grow up. The most important thing is that we remember everything. You are my wife. Do you hear me?"

"You're speaking so strangely. It's all so complicated," Maija replied quietly.

Čiks hugged her to him; their entire life experience seemed to flood into that embrace as though they were saving themselves from a fate worse than death, from something never ending yet simultaneously vanishing. The next morning, no one came growling outside Maija's door. The night had passed amidst nightmarish dreams that mingled with the joy of wakefulness. In the next room, mother babbled falsely, Nauris laughed every so often. On her bedside table sat a plastic duck that he had given her, along with some sweets. Čiks didn't come. The girl recalled how her mother used to peep into Aunt Cilda's mailbox in the apartment block, hoping to find a letter from her father. It had been miserable, awful. Later that evening, that terrible sense of not knowing combined with fear reduced the girl to tears and sent her creeping out into the neighbours' garden. She crept up to the window and tapped at it, but no one answered. Nauris had gone somewhere with a bottle of wine. Her mother came into Maija's room; tired and without her façade of happiness, she looked old and pitiful.

"Life is dreadful. I'm so sorry, darling!" mother cried. It happened all the time when they were left alone at home.

"Don't cry, mother," Maija said automatically, more than once, distractedly patting her mother's shoulder.

"Such a dreadful life could be the end of you, too," her mother whimpered. "No doubt it's the fault of this miserable life that our neighbours' boy has fallen ill. It surely can't be pneumonia; they must be lying about it. They took him away yesterday. Oh Maija, if anything similar were to happen to you…" at this, her mother lost all self-control. Maija pulled away from her and dashed outside. Čiks! We promised each other that we would never be parted, do you hear me? Remember everything I'm telling you now and I will remember everything you say. I do remember, Čiks! Don't be afraid! She raced to the apple orchard. Three weeks later, a pale Čiks, still with dark circles beneath his eyes, knocked on Nauris' door.

"Where's Maija?" Čiks asked, breathlessly.

"Maija who?" Nauris asked, stroking his wiry, red moustache.

"Your daughter," Čiks replied, falteringly.

"Oh, that Maija! They both left." Nauris sighed, looking into the distance over the boy's head.

"Where did they go?" Čiks shouted, his lips trembling, his chin jutting into the air.

"I don't know, they didn't say. They won't be coming back."

He waved the boy away with a heavy, weary hand. Čiks fled. The cranes were already busy in the orchard. The apples trees had all been sawn down. The air in the hut was cold and stale; hay and apples rotted in the damp. The match refused to be lit. Taking a long stare at the print of the snowy winter landscape and the one of women in national dress, Čiks began rolling them up after taking them carefully off the wall.

"Čiks!" He heard a shout from outside and Maija launched herself into the hut. "Čiks, you must believe me, I came here every day! They're going to demolish our hut. I prayed every day that they would hold off until you came. Aunt Cilda died. I won't have any new fathers from now on. Čiks, dear Čiks, do you remember what you have to remember? Do you?"

The girl shook him before Čiks in turn clasped her tightly to himself, both pairs of eyes fixed, unmoving, on the spot on the slatted wall, penetrated forever by two drops of blood…

A DAY IN HER LIFE (1996)
NORA IKSTENA (BORN 1969)
TRANSLATED BY MĀRA ROZĪTIS

She still doesn't understand what actually happened that day.
She remembers sitting in a train, opposite an affectionate
family — husband and wife taking the seeds out of rosehips
and feeding the rosehips to their young daughter. Make sure
there's not a seed left, the seeds have tiny claws — the wife
kept on reminding her husband. Gods of the train trudge up
and down the carriage, some timid, others brash, with offerings
of the day's yellow, pink or red press, songbooks, cheap beer,
bitter mineral water, bibles in two languages, slowly melting
ice cream, handbooks on love and faith, ugly plastic dolls,
the purchase of which would support orphans... a deranged
woman sits down next to her, and embarks on an endless
monologue. "I had a son, it was bad, I have no son now, it's
still bad, it won't get better, I'll starve to death, I'll freeze to
death, I'll be unburied, who'll bury me with my son gone, he's
dead and buried, I scattered black earth on the sand, I collected
mosses and lichen, all kinds of flowers, pebbles, I put them
around his grave in rows and circles, circles and rows, planted

four lilacs, when they come into flower, I look for lucky five leaf flowers, they're my son's luck, I loved my son, but he was unlucky, didn't love me, until he died, I had a son…"

The affectionate family was quick to escape to another seat. She is left alone with the old crone, who falls silent only to draw a breath, then begins once more, "I had a son…" the woman's mutterings slowly blend into the monotonous clatter of the train. An old man with a basket of frozen mushrooms gets on at a small station. In her agitation, she tries to focus on something outside, and through the window, she sees rust coloured caves of forest. It's late autumn. She presses her smarting eyelids closed and remembers a night in spring. It was raining, Kirje was barefoot and splashing in the puddles, while she, whoever would have thought, took off her jumper, and laughing, strolled half-naked through the village. It was dark then. At first, Kirje was embarrassed, but soon they were shyly kissing each other's earlobes. She can still remember the taste of rain. The train has sped up, the tireless sun flashes in the windows, blocks of cloud in the sky, bright toadstool clusters on the edges of ditches. Her eyelids are sore but she feels a sense of lightness, of happiness. She has never felt anything like it before. With no questions that she couldn't answer. They were all just one question — the question of love. Does love exist or not? It does, and she can testify to that. Fear has disappeared. The fear that had almost destroyed her, that lay in wait in her fitful sleep, that hounded her in a nightmare of days. There had been an overpowering bodily sensation of duality — though she was never sure which two parts of her were in contention, flesh and spirit, goodness and evil, deception and honesty, but she fled through the streets, with sweating palms and understood that she couldn't escape. But everything had ended just as suddenly as it had begun, although the fear that it could happen again, still haunts her. Her body remembers this fear so vividly that shivers run down her spine. In the meantime, the deranged woman has ended her monologue about the dead son and is muttering about something else.

She listens… your son is gone, reverend, let's hurry on as fast as we can, a true God and a man, a saviour of crowds, let us meet Jesus, let it be in prison, Judas, his disciple, betrayed him, a crowd of enemies took him away, but we will serve him with all the strength we can muster, my son is gone, reverend… you haven't been thinking of God — she recalls this seeming reproach, from a close friend, a theological seminary student in answer to her despairing plea, to help her cope with the fear of the frightening splitting apart. They were sitting on a bench in the seminary courtyard, it was late autumn, as it is now outside the train window. Her friend had changed markedly, and asked her to call him Timotej. He saw that she was suffering, that she was in abject fear and did not know what to do. Timotej reminded her of the parable of the forbidden fruit and whispered in her ear, in all seriousness, about how he had brought the works of his beloved Nietzsche to the seminary in his backpack. Now the books were well hidden, in a place known only to himself, but occasionally he still had to struggle with the urge to leaf through them again, but up till now, he had succeeded in suppressing these urges. Do not think about lust, begin instead to think of God, her friend had encouraged, paternally taking hold of her hands.

At first, she had wanted to answer proudly, that thinking

about Kirje was the same as thinking about God, but she was suddenly confounded and wished that she could remind Timotej that God is love until finally, her anger exploded, and words just spilled from her mouth, unrestrained and loud. As she spoke, she felt an almost evil thrill. Timotej had started to look around nervously, and pat down his blond, short-bristled hair. She still has a detailed recollection of the very words she had spoken to Timotej — what you call my lust, has actually lain in me for some time, even before I started thinking about it. It continues when I think about Kirje or when we sink into deep discussions about guilt and death, profess our love or our disbelief that we can profess it, touch each other, not knowing what awaits us, see allegories of our emotional trials in our dreams until we finally wear ourselves out with doubt, but now and then we ascend to the dizzying heights of choice, humiliate each other as much as we are able so that afterward we can relish deification... it feels like she has a sheet of paper glued in her head, on which someone was tapping with typewriter keys in the same rhythm as the rattling of the train, writing out the words that she had allowed herself to say to Timotej.

She wants to put a stop to this writing and feverishly looks at the bright sky and rust forests that flash past, the woman has fallen asleep, freed briefly from her endless monologue. Before her feeling of joy returns, she still sees Timotej's pursed lips and wringing hands and hears her last haughtily shouted question, "Do you even know what rain on an earlobe tastes like?" Timotej had turned pale, but three other seminary students that were passing nearby, turned their heads to look.

It seemed to her it was a look of pity three times over. Just one more station. The frozen mushrooms in the old man's basket were slowly turning brown and he sat looking sadly at his pathetic bounty.

She thinks about that very cold winter and the bouquet that Kirje had given to her, that she had to keep on the edge of the snow-covered balcony. While she was coming home, the flowers had frozen, that was why they couldn't be put in the warm, where the stiff petals would have thawed, drooped and quickly turned brown. She had been so happy each chilly morning, as the first thing she saw when she awoke, were the bright flowers in the snow, now it seems to her it was an allegory of the deception of joy and beauty, or maybe bitter truth and sweet lies, the love of faith or the faith of love, the short term of joy, of dreams and reality…

She imagined that the window through which she looked at the flowers each morning was a wall of glass. On the other side was the deceptive beauty of frozen petals, on this side, there'd be the veracity of the ugliness of the thawing flowers. But the truth of the flowers stayed on the glass. Now she has almost found a description of her feeling of joy — she can clearly see reflections of the glass wall and the reason for that is love. Perhaps Timotej sees them too, and the reason is God. She is ashamed again about her outburst in the seminary courtyard. She gets up to make her way to the door but the deranged woman who has woken up is shyly stretching out her hand with something hidden in her tiny fist. She puts out her palm and feels the fist open and sees a peppermint sweet. Instead of a thank you, she smiles and quickly walks to the carriage door. She waits on the platform until she is alone, then steps over the railway tracks and makes her way over the meadow. The peppermint sweet held tight in her fist. She knows the way. It will lead to the cliff from where there is a good view of the surrounding countryside.

She will certainly want to lean up against it and fly a little. But once again she will discover that it is impossible. Standing on the crag, she nevertheless flaps her arms around, birds fly overhead between the cloud banks and forest towers. Abashed, she stops flapping and sits down in the damp sand right on the edge of the cliff. Looking down her head swims. She turns towards the columns of still sky and half-naked trees, slowly sucking on the peppermint sweet. Kirje had once said, give me a shipkin, as he sat opposite her at an oval table. She didn't understand. Kirje took her hand and showed her how to give a *shipkin*, a little ship — it was exactly as the madwoman on the train had done. You hold your hand in a fist and then open it gently and secretively like children do, Kirje explained. Then they gave each other invisible *shipkins*, keeping back what they were really giving.

The barman became so engrossed as he watched this strange game, he started giving out change to his customers in *shipkins*. In her next night's dream giving shipkins grew into a whole series of events. She dreamt that she was expecting a child. The baby was born easily, in a shop filled with shoppers, but it wasn't the usual kind of delivery — someone placed the baby in her palm like a *shipkin*. She remembers how curious she had been, how slowly she had opened her hand and the enormous disappointment she had felt when she saw a small ugly plastic doll in her palm. She felt ashamed in front of the shoppers. Despondently she carried the squashed doll in her hand to show to her relatives, at the same time telling herself and fervently believing that such an ugly child could never have been born. In the doorway, she opened her hand and saw instead that she was holding an amaryllis flower, so she happily ran up the stairs. On the edge of the cliff, sucking on the peppermint sweet, she remembers the relief that had washed over her as she awoke from this dream of the baby, that was born of a *shipkin* in her palm and changed from an ugly plastic doll into an amaryllis flower. As well as the firm conviction she'd had in the dream, that the ugly plastic doll would be transformed into something radiant and delicate.

Normally she would have gone looking for Kirje, so that they could both wonder and be carried away by the parable that had grown from the innocent game of *shipkins*. But instead, she decided to go to the seminary to ask Timotej to forgive her violent outburst. Birds fly over the forest towers and she hardly knows what to do with her newly discovered emotion, no, she isn't at all afraid, just full of doubt, would life still have any meaning after such a revelation. She thinks of long-gone saints and recites their names, Gregory of Nazianzus, Teresa of Ávila, Ignatius of Loyola, Rose of Lima… Timotej knew the names of all the saints and she feels that at this moment, here, on the edge of the cliff she is one of their number. Timotej would never countenance it, he would just declare in his calm voice, that held a warning — seeing love does not mean seeing God.

She remembers the morning after the dream of giving *shipkins*. The way on foot to the seminary was long — along narrow cobbled streets, past the wooden Roma houses — a young Romani woman was breastfeeding a child, sitting in the sun on warped wooden steps, black hair with a centre parting shining in the sunshine, engorged brown breast, legs spread apart provocatively, she smiled and called out to the workmen across the way. "Come on over," she said, uncovering her other breast. "Can't the old man handle you any more?" a workman laughed. Paul Delvaux. Sleeping Venus. "Oi Yolla, I've no old man, this child is the Holy Spirit's," the Romani woman brayed back, black toothless gums in a gaping mouth. She continued walking, past derelict arbours in an overgrown park, where tea had been served in the time of the tsar, past family vaults in deserted graveyards, where the homeless and drinkers now sheltered themselves to sleep or make love, at the small orthodox church she wanted to turn back and find Kirje. She saw an old woman sitting on the low wall by the church — in her lap bunches of dark crimson amaryllis flowers, with a small spray of the tree of life carefully tied around each flower.

The woman summoned her, she remembered her dream, so for a few paltry coins she bought an amaryllis and continued on her way to Timotej. As she had to wait some time in the seminary courtyard, she sat down on the same bench where she had sat that time, the time she had screamed at Timotej, "Do you even know what rain tastes like on an earlobe?" She has a memory too, of the three seminary students and the pitying look. This time no one noticed her except a young boy running across the courtyard who grinned when he caught sight of the dark red amaryllis in her lap. Through an open window, she heard the sound of singing — *"Di-riga-tur Do-mi-ne, oratio mea Si-cut in-cen-sum in conspectu tuo..."* The sound of two boys' smoothly overlapping voices filled the seminary courtyard, the monotonous waves of sound turning into an emblem of sanctity.

She thought of Kirje. "God bless you," said Timotej instead of good day. He was polite but reserved. Without greeting him, she asked, "What are the boys singing about?" "May my prayer, O Lord, be directed as incense in Thy sight," recited Kirje and fell silent. She hastily embarked on the tale of her dream of the child put in her hand like a *shipkin*, of its miraculous transformation, of the old woman with a lapful of amaryllis, of the provocative Romani, of the flowers in the hard frost outside the window… "To see love does not mean to see God," Timotej interrupted. He avoided looking at her and gazed instead at the window through which the boys' singing was flowing. "Renunciation and humility have brought me happiness. When I was a child, I played the violin quite proficiently and my father always told me: 'If a backyard bully ever hits you, don't hit back, because you have to save your fingers for the violin, my boy.' "

She felt that she was looking at Timotej just as she had looked at Kirje's frozen flowers through window glass. Between them too was a transparent wall. "Please forgive my outburst that time," she said, "but I must tell you what it was I was weighing against God. You know that people have died together for it…" Died together? Timotej regarded her with surprise and compassion. "No one dies together with another, we each die alone. With only God present," Timotej smiled, laid his hand on her head, and walked away over the courtyard cobbles… *"Con-spec-tu tu-o."* Beyond the seminary gates she could still hear it. *"Con-spec-tu tu-o." "Con-spec-tu tu-o,"* she tries to sing on the cliff edge. Mixed with sand and pebbles the sound trickles down the cliff face. This cliff is a giant sand clock that no one is strong enough to turn over, but it isn't needed for it will never run out of sand, and time will never run out. She has a small sand timer in a sandalwood frame.

She pulls it out of her pocket and inhales its perfume — she feels Kirje. When they saw each other for the last time (She feels now, it didn't happen in her lifetime), their love trickled through this sand clock. While she slept, Kirje had sat at the round table in the feeble light of the waning moon and kept time with this sand clock in its sandalwood frame. She awoke too in the middle of the night and sat down at the table opposite Kirje. The shadow of the timer fell on the table. The sand trickled soundlessly, Kirje waited patiently and turned it over. When she laid her head on the table next to the timer she could hear the quiet and regular movement of the sand. Kirje bent over and breathed in the perfume of her hair. His face next to hers, he said, "While you slept I stood guard over time. I wanted to feel how it flowed when we are together." They spoke no more — Kirje followed the time of the sand.

She lay stretched on the table listening to the subtle sifting. It seemed that light was dawning quicker than usual. She had closed her eyes and seen a whole narrative, how together with Kirje — two blighted lovers in the Middle Ages, who had crept past midnight guards into a stone building with a tower, recklessly possessed each other and then taken turns in keeping time, until they parted in the darkness and unseen, gone in opposite directions along the cobbled streets. When she opened her eyes Kirje had gone. Kirje could vanish without a trace. Now on the edge of the cliff, it seems that darkness is falling quicker than usual. The damp of late autumn is seeping into her bones, the forest towers are blending into the sky, no birds fly. She should get up and go, but she wants to linger here because it seems she will never understand what actually happened this day. In the darkness, the sandy cliff is peacefully sifting — a giant sand clock.

NETTLES (1998)
INGA ĀBELE (BORN 1972)
TRANSLATED BY LAURA ADLERS

They set out onto the mud-soaked road — an old, plump woman carrying a milk pail and a young girl with a little stool. Everything around them stirred in the swirling wind. The sky above — abandon your illusions, girl, if you don't look up, you get the impression the sky is made of solid grey lead, in places darker, but above the hill — lighter. Look up, look up, girl, and you'll see the sky is moving too, those aren't clouds, that's a grey mist of the most translucent material, being struck and struck and struck. The leaves are whipping the branches, the treetops are bending, the cows' tails are lashing against their sides. The old woman stops looking. Look, girl, before you must also look away. And that summer is ending — that's just a delusion. The mud will still dry up, the treetops will still sparkle, perhaps we'll even have blue skies for a couple of dry months. Cows' muzzles are carved from ebony, their ears from yellow acacia. The old woman places the stool near the side of the cow and puts the milk pail between her legs. The girl is crouched on the other side watching the fat foamy streams bending in the wind before landing with a splash into the pail. A couple of drops of the white milk land on the green dandelion leaves, others are thrown onto the cow's legs. The cow chews her cud and looks away into the distance. Then she wants to leave and kicks the bucket away from between the woman's knees with her hoof. A devil amongst the cows, aren't you! Satan herself! Ha!

Grab her chain! And the girl grabs it, but the cow is stronger, the steel chain slips through her hands. She tries to restrain her by the head, but the cow turns away and hits her captor in the chest with her horn. Someone drives up and stops the car beside the pasture, right in a patch of black mud. He opens the door and quietly watches how both silhouettes on the hill are struggling with the cow. She is finally milked and the older woman stands up straight and tall, blesses the cow once more with some choice words, then takes her white kerchief and pulls it onto her forehead. The hair around her kerchief is dishevelled from the wind, silver with black curls like a witch. She heads for home with the milk pail and stool, but the younger one heads slowly towards the car. Come here, boy. A brown dog licks the girl's ear when she bends down to pick some bent grass. The wind ruffles his jacket, his trousers, blows back his hair, the dog's tongue dries in the warm breeze. Well, hello, darling! Hi, bunny. He rumpled me, he ruffled me, he held me in a warm place under his arm and stroked my hair. He asked me something and turned on the music, which the wind swiftly stole away through a crack in the door to be sown amongst the blue-black cabbages. Why are you crying, darling? Did the cow butt you? Yes, that too. Did the chain graze your hands? Yes, that too. He kissed me, trying to kiss the tears from my eyes, but I told him to leave me alone. The fog above us was thickening, the wind blew creaking into the greenhouse, the moaning yellowed wooden frame swelling like the sides of a dead animal. But I looked out at the trees far off on the horizon, where the sun was setting red and bright, while the edge of the cloud sprinkled yellow drops down on the trees. And suddenly he is speaking so close to me that I can feel his breath on my face. You were already crying at the beginning of summer. Why were you crying, darling? She's dancing with her father, crazy twists and complicated steps. It's Midsummer's Day, warm and lovely as the smell of a newborn baby. Nearby people are eating at a table, shiny cutlery clinking on the plates, the sun's sparkling forehead settled right in the middle of the table. And then her father whispers something in her ear, right at the moment when the dancing is at its highest point, like the tide. Her dishevelled hair falls back onto her shoulders, she presses the palm of her hand to her cheek and cries like an old, tired wife. A wedding followed, but she looked happy at the wedding. What were you crying about that time, bunny? What did your father say to you? He told me about the ash tree. Yes, it will always be standing here and I will always have to fear it when there is wind. Wind like today, darling. I promised to cut down the tree. That very day I promised your father I would cut down the tree. Is that something to cry about? No, of course not. Where were you today, where are you, when you are gone for so long? No matter what you're doing, it's so hard to wait for you. The young woman suddenly jumps out of the car, and that's how they return to the farm — her in front of the car, with her eyes on the trees in the distance, he behind her slowly following in the car, trying to hold his patience in each of the tightly clenched fingers on the steering wheel. Later his mother asks him to pick some nettles and pour scalding water over them in buckets to prepare an iron brew for the cows. The girl says that nettles don't sting her, and she goes to the edge of the deep green prickly forest and starts pulling up nettles with her bare hands. People at the dairy stare silently, but leave a little while later. What are you doing, my bunny? Are you lying for my sake? It really doesn't hurt, she says. It hasn't hurt for a long time, since I was a child. He walks away, embarrassed, and sits down under the huge ash tree with the hollow trunk. The wind has chased the clouds away and curled up to sleep under a bridge. The evening is gently drinking raspberry-pink light from the ponds. What did you teach your daughter, strange man? He came in late at night, lying in bed next to her, carefully on the very edge. I had put my hands back, far above my head where they burned white hot all night. In the moonlight he caressed my body with his gaze, but he had no fingers with which to touch me.

Push Push (2004)
Andra Neiburga (1957-2019)
Translated by Ieva Lešinska

As I light the stove I only think of firewood. That's all. Firewood. And not about the forest or the trees or the people who cut these trees down, big deal. I'm only interested in the firewood, in how dry it is and is this fucking stove going to light or not, will the chimney cough the smoke back like a wheezing old geezer from the poorhouse.

Meaning of life? Go fuck yourself. There is no meaning to life. None.

Okay, so the snowdrops are cool and so are all those, you know, rivulets of spring. Those streamlets. The sun. It's okay, really. And when you walk out in the morning, in your galoshes and nightgown, you're quite warm although there is a thin crust of ice on the water in the tub, warmth from the bed preserved between your flushed skin and the flannel, when you survey the yard — all pathways raked neat, everything more or less in order, sap from the birch reluctantly dripping into the vat: drip drip drip. A bird chirping to itself. You draw the crisp air as yet unspoiled by the day into your lungs — oooh — crouch behind the outhouse, watch your piss disappear shimmering into the moss — ecstasy.

That's where perhaps there is meaning. In that one instant. That single instant where there is time to look around, look at the sky, for instance. Just look at it, without any thought even. Without wondering if God is or is not, if there is a storm gathering, if the laundry should be taken down.

But see, all that already is, simply is, without you and not for you. You simply happen to be here, by sheer accident. To be happy or sad over this fact — well, that's everybody's private business.

Planets rotate? Let them.

The Universe is expanding? Say what? — it's contracting again? So let it contract, about time it did. Contract and cease. Peace and nothing.

But fuck the universe. I have no use for it. If the universe has use for me — here I am.

Just like in that dream where I was chosen to continue mankind as some sort of an ur-mother. Our civilisation was doomed, a nuclear war or something like that. The earth and the sky were red, red dust everywhere and you couldn't understand where top or bottom was. And out of that redness, there floats out something like a ship, a spaceship, you know, like a flying saucer, and a voice thunders from the sky (I am not sure if there weren't even flaming letters in the sky, but I wouldn't bet on it, it's possible I came up with that later): "Andra," it says, "get ready!" "Here," it says, "it will take billions and billions of years until life on earth starts from a molecule again, but you have a chance to start a new life over there."

Where?!

They wouldn't say. I woke up.

As they say, your own trouble makes you contract, another man's trouble makes you expand.

So I contract, I withdraw into my house in the middle of the forest, by the cemetery. The road is bad, the bus goes to the regional centre twice a week, the store-on-wheels comes around once a week. If it don't break down.

What's that, there's no such place in Latvia any more? Of course there is, you bet there is.

And I am fine here. No problem.

I think only about firewood. I think about grub. And about Gramps. In winter I also think about spring, in summer, about autumn. In autumn about winter. But not philosophically or metaphorically, no. Very simple — winter's coming, so got to get firewood. Spring: rake the old leaves, dig up the vegetable garden. Autumn: put mushrooms in brine.

Meaning of life.

He made me real mad yesterday with all that talk about the meaning of life! Really mad.

I thought we'd have a drink and such, I haven't had a man in a couple of months. But he is, like, 'I have these questions.'

So we didn't even make it to bed.

"Where," says he, "can one find the meaning of life?"

"Well, don't look for it," says I, "relax. Then you won't have to worry you can't find it."

Well, you know that old saying: seek and you shall find? A stupid saying, if you ask me. To seek is to hardly ever find anything but those who don't seek will just stumble upon something. For example — go into the forest and try to find a mushroom knife. You can walk for a week, for two weeks, and you won't find shit. Or a fiver on the street? Not a chance! Whereas all you have to do is just squat in that same forest, no reason, just answering the call of nature, or just kick an empty beer can on the street — and bingo! here's your knife, here's your fiver.

It's been a long time since I've sought anything.

You have what you have. You don't have what you don't.

My neighbour — not even really a neighbour — a whole kilometre counting from the ditch — does herself up like the Queen of Sheba every Friday night and off she goes to the regional dance. She's seeking. A guy, of course. She'd do better to hide herself, the dumbshit.

Oh, I'm just ranting.

Have to give Gramps gruel. Gruel with jam.

Milk, butter, grits.

And thanks. Not thank God, thank myself that I can still make some money. With physical labour.

Others make art, write music, play theatre, teach, but you (meaning, I) push a wheelbarrow. Go ahead, honey, push. With your higher, almafuckingmater, education.

Life straps you down. If you kick too much, the strings will simply get tighter. So you better relax.

No guy?

No.

So what?

I can manage.

My hands are all cut up — see, here with a knife, here with an axe. And this came from that fucking metal broomstick that my ex left broken and sharp as a sword, I stumbled; good thing it didn't slash my belly wide open.

I do as much as I can. What I can't do I don't. Just let it be.

See, the mutt's not vaccinated, I just didn't have the time.

See, he sits there and stares at me with those weird eyes of his. Maybe he's mad already, he runs around the marshes and the forests, who knows. And you can't cure that disease. Who cares about death, but the torture of it all. I'm really afraid of pain. And rabies, they say, is awful. Three days of agony. Why don't they simply give those who have it a shot? You know, to put them out of their misery. And they call themselves doctors.

Phew.

I don't think about the forest, don't think about the sea, don't think about the sky. I look right through you, I don't see you, get it.

I don't see!

The morning gallops along like a horse foaming at the mouth, can't manage to get anything done. Look, the fire in the fucking stove is out, but Gramps is calling from his room: he has to have his gruel and someone has turned his antenna.

I haven't touched your goddamn antenna, you old fool! Fuck. I have no time for TV anyway. I have my own reality show, my own "farm" here.

You must have turned it yourself.

He doesn't believe me.

Throws a newspaper at me; angry.

Rolls his eyes.

How far can you throw a newspaper, dumbshit?

"Sure, sure, you know best, you're the smart one."

"Of course, I am. Not you. Here's your gruel, eat, you can watch TV in the evening."

Gruel for the dog as well. A different one. Water as a base, plop in a cube of beef broth. So you don't think I feed Gramps and the dog the same gruel. There is some humanity left in me. But whether that is a good thing is subject to doubt.

"What kind of a jam is this?" Gramps yells from his room.

"Lingonberry."

"What kind of a lingonberry jam is that?! A lingonberry jam should be properly cooked, there should be no berries!"

"There are none."

"So what kind of a lingonberry jam is a jam without the lingonberries?!"

"Same one as yesterday. Eat."

" 'Twas a different one yesterday. But sure, you know best, you're the smart one." All the same, he eats.

It's over. Relax, relax.

The fire in the stove has gone out again.

And the rage.

Fierceness is a form of humanity.

You think not? Meaning, an animal is fierce too? Sure, but not as fierce as a person. Me, I'm pissed at the birch. At the rock, at the pond.

'cause I'm getting old.

What are you lookin' at, mutt? Shoo, you bastard.

The floors.

The dishes.

Take the laundry down.

Hang the laundry up.

Put what's dry into the wardrobe.

The floor again. When did that happen?

Gramps is on a roll again, has uncovered another Jewish conspiracy in the paper.

"Eat," I tell him, "stop yelling. The gruel's getting cold."

I've long since stopped discussing Jews with him.

"Peace," I tell him. "Here, in the middle of the forest, we have no Jews. We take care of our business, the Jews take care of theirs. End of story. Besides, a Jew — he's human too."

That's all he needs. Throws the paper at me again. Palestine and Israel really bother him.

"Better hold on to your paper. Next time I won't give it back."

"What?"

"Nothing. Eat your gruel before it gets cold. There won't be nothin' else until five, I'm off to the store-on-wheels."

The meaning of life. Let those who have time look for it. I don't. I'll take the wheelbarrow and roll it to the store. On the way there through the forest, back along the sea.

And my period has started. Cramps.

What do I need the goddamn period for? What the hell for?! Better if it were over and done with.

Yeah, better if it were all over. All of it.

Gramps gets up in the middle of the night, every night, and goes to Australia to see his brother. Supposedly there's a million and a girl waiting for him. Really. Almost feel like tying him to the bed. I scramble like a cockroach all day long, and then I can't even get any rest at night.

"D'you hear, Gramps?"

"What?"

"Do you want anything from the store?"

"Thugs, that's what they are!"

"You want some boiled sweets?"

"I don't have no teeth, how am I supposed to eat them," he says crossly. Impossible to please.

"That's okay, you can suck on them."

Old folks crave sweets, don't they.

Okay, that's it, just have to get the wheelbarrow and go.

"Stay, mutt, stay, guard the house! I'm going. Be good, Gramps."

"Just don't stay out too long, I get scared alone. What if the Gypsies come."

"Be back in a coupla hours. Don't be silly, we have no Gypsies around here."

"Sure, sure, you're the smart one, you know best."

He'll take a two-hour nap and won't even notice I'm gone. Lately he sleeps all day long.

Three kilometres through the forest.

Yesterday he was driving me nuts with that meaning of life stuff.

"This kind of life," says he, "it ain't for me."

"Of course, not. You're the boss."

"But the Bible says: ask and it shall be given."

"Sure, go begging by a church in Riga and you shall be given."

I put out a bottle of vodka, and got nothing. Didn't get him in bed. Am I old or somethin'? Or perhaps just don't know how. As my old and educated city friend used to say — sex takes place in your head. Or as my neighbour likes to repeat: guys need to have their brains fucked, then they will stick around. They both say the same thing, really. Just in different ways.

Actually he's always been that way, ever since we dated in school: he prefers philosophising to action. On lofty matters. Though it was I who ended up a student in Riga, not him. And studying made me give up philosophising for good. What's the point? Got my degree, but the accent remained. And I guess something different in the thinking. As that same lofty friend of mine said: no, I don't like those country girls. I seem to have even blushed — although at that time he could have hardly known. That I'm one. There must be something written all over our faces, we, the country bumpkins. Don't do what you were not made to do, right.

So that's how I've turned out — neither here, nor there, neither fish nor fowl. *Blyad'* and *fuck* in the same sentence. Country folk are too uncouth for me, I'm too uncouth for city folk. In terms of, as they say, serious relationships. But actually I don't really want a serious relationship. I have enough to push along. Don't expect that a man will make it easy for you — I've learned at least that much from life.

Rolling my wheelbarrow through the forest I do an expert evaluation of a fallen tree. True, it's on Teodors' land, but who cares. Some time, when it's dark, I'll come over with a saw and the wheelbarrow — push, honey, push. And then we'll have free firewood to last us for a while.

I couldn't really get used to the city. The city, yeah, that's the place where thoughts about the meaning of life will just bug you to death. Hot water just runs through the pipes, don't have to lift a finger — everything just happens on its own. Got a job at a school, but could barely make enough to cover the rent and the kids just drove me nuts. They are not the same as before, in my day. And not the same as in the country. Just yelling at them will not shut them up. No way.

And then those parties, those long evenings, all that blah-blah-blah.

No, thanks.

Me, I think about firewood, get it?

Not about the forest.

So I returned home from the city.

Mother, in the meantime, had taken off with some German agronomist, leaving Gramps all alone, heaven have mercy upon us sinners. So she keeps sending pictures from her German village. Doesn't look happy at all. But she now knows the meaning of life. *To live a life worthy of a human being.* Ha, that's exactly what she said in her glossy Christmas card. Decided not to even show it to Gramps. If it only had occurred to Mother to ask — years ago, when Gramps still had a grip on it, when he worked, when he made for free furniture for all our village neighbours, when he would read newspapers by the hot stove in his garden shed and dry mushrooms on the stove — that shed still smells of Gramps' mushrooms — so if she had the presence of mind to ask then, he would have been able to tell her more about life worthy of a human being than this sausage-eating Kraut. About how to avoid becoming a broken man in Siberia. How not to betray friends. How to love one woman all your life.

Though I didn't ask either. Too late.

Shame on me.

So I'll never know.

Not long ago, in the paper, somebody went on and on about consumer society etcetera. Basically put us all where we belong. All of us. Those who don't look for a meaning but simply eat and drink, if they have enough money. And work. Work, believe it or not. And listen to Raimonds Pauls. I don't, personally, but still: I demand that others have the right to be free to listen. Is that clear?

Otherwise it seems that only the five or ten or fifty smart ones up there know what the meaning is. But who, may I ask, has left the rest of us without meaning? What asshole has taken the meaning away from us? Or has forgotten to give it to us?

That hurts.

They know but they won't tell us.

'cause we supposedly won't understand.

But perhaps — to each his own. And my meaning is completely different from the one that smarty-pants has. Somewhere.

But I refuse to look for it, so leave me alone.

Look, those crazies have ploughed the Gulbīši road. Could only happen at a time like this. Difficult to get the wheelbarrow across that mess. Good thing I live by the cemetery, at least they won't build camp sites there.

But these days — who knows.

Old women gathering by the store-on-wheels. Not very many. Can't get a big crowd here in the village before the season has begun. I lean against a pile of logs, light a cigarette. Will stay here while there's a line. No wish to shoot the breeze with the crones.

The smoke tastes good. My fucking back hurts. The scent of damp wood in the air. There's still smoke by the garbage dump, yesterday there was a fire, even the fire brigade came. I didn't tell Gramps, so as not to scare him.

Actually, this is kind of a special place here by the woodpile. This is where three paths cross: to the sea, to the cemetery and to my house. Not much to see here: junipers, crooked pines in clusters, the forest on the other side of the road, the big sky, the meadow, the white-coloured cemetery gate. In the early evening there's usually fog. If you stand perfectly still, completely motionless, so that even the grass doesn't rustle underfoot, draw a deep breath and hold it so that you don't betray your existence with some hissing or wheezing, just stand there and see and nothing else, just listen and look, for three to five minutes, then you can imagine how it all will be when you are no more. And to get the feeling of how you will be without being.

Oh, hogwash.

Robis had also helped put out the fire. Maybe that's why he seemed so tired. I even sat on his lap. We even sort of kissed for a while. I even poured Gramps a glass of vodka so he'd quit coughing and sleep. But nothing came of it. He just talked about the meaning of life and hobbled home.

A warm body next to you — I haven't felt that for months. So you can just stretch out your arm and touch and feel he's there. There. Warm and breathing. Yours. Muttering something in his sleep. Feeling you are there and hugging you. Throwing a heavy arm around you. Or a leg, doesn't matter. Perhaps that's where the meaning is.

Phew, the smoke is getting in my eyes.

My fingers are frozen stiff. Standing like this in the norther, handling cigarettes with gloveless hands will do it.

The crones have dispersed, just a couple left, time to push along.

Okay, here we are. Just old Kārta remains. Her name matches her looks: tall and stiff, she walks as if she's got a broomstick up her ass, in an oblique angle to the ground, as if bent by the wind from the sea, and she looks at you obliquely too, from below and never straight in the eye.

"Robis apparently came home from your place yesterday only around midnight."

"On whose authority?"

"Authority? His wife's the authority. God only knows what he wants from you, a scrawny bitch, when at home he's got a woman who's a real looker."

What he wants... he wants to talk about the meaning of life.

"Phew."

Canned goods. Bacon. Noodles. Flour. Bread, the 'brick' — five pcs. Margarine, economy size, boiled sweets for Gramps. No, orange-flavour, he likes those the best. There. Champagne? Champagne.

I want to drink, so I drink. So what.

Push, honey, push. Nice and easy along the shore.

On the shore the wind grabs at skirts and hair, a good thing I brought Gramps' old quilted jacket.

Why not make a detour to the other end of the village, there I can get back on the road, by the church?

And let's pop open the champagne to make it more fun.

And the champagne is good, sweet, the world looks brighter with every sip. Blood starts circulating, even hands get warmer. The wheel of the wheelbarrow keeps sticking in the sand, should get closer to the water, there the beach is firm like a table.

I am thinking about the wheelbarrow. I'm thinking about the bubbly.

I push and I sip. Push and sip.

And no seagulls, you know, that bring letters like in that old song.

The wind throws tiny, icy drops of water in my face, can't tell whether it's rain or just moisture from the sea.

Where the road leads back to the dune, there's a huge wooden spool, it's been there for years. Like a bobbin enlarged thousands of times, as large as the big old oak table. When I was at university, I was fantasising about bringing my friends here. And that guy. For whom sex happens in the head. A picnic, so to speak. Like sophisticated people would have. And the spool would be used for the table. The lower part of the spool was completely covered by sand even at that time, but the top, bleached by water and the sun, was smooth and firm. It would be appropriate to have champagne and canapes with salmon, juicy red strawberries, the bluish sheen of blackberries, beautiful black-haired women in white dresses, with cherry earrings, the shrieks of white seagulls, yellow kites in the sky, the rustle of the waves.

And conversations about poetry, about literature, about… well, the same thing. About the meaning of life.

Ha, I must have watched too many films.

Decadence.

Yes, I know that word, I didn't go to university for nothing.

I can actually talk like from a book. But I don't want to. I don't pretend. I only use the words that become me.

Still, a young person sure can have their fantasies, eh?

And the champagne has made me sentimental. Should have bought wine.

Look, this year the spool has almost disintegrated, only a few boards remain from the top, everything else is buried deep in sand, only rusty cables stick out.

That's okay. Dreams should be fulfilled. Who said that? I did.

In the shelter of the spool it's quite warm and the bottle is still more than one-third full.

Gramps' jacket instead of the white dress, but who gives a shit.

Style is not important, it's thirst that matters.

Let me close my eyes for a minute and just listen.

Not think anything.

Although I didn't think anything before either.

Despite the rain and the damp cold, the monotonous lullaby of the wind and the sea make me sleepy, my eyes won't stay open.

There is something like voices talking. Some like Kārta's voice, then kind of like Gramps'.

Big drops of rain wake me up, the air has got darker and denser, the wind has died down — for a minute.

The bottle's been empty for a while, a disgusting taste in my mouth, and my head feels deadened.

And the meaning of life is just as remote as before.

Hard to get up, back hurts, legs have gone to sleep.

Push, honey, push.

The rain gets fucking stronger, the wind returns even more fierce, right in the face. Cold.

That's how it is with dreams.

I guess I'll pull instead of push.

It's easier to pull, at least for a while.

The light house, painted white, thrusts into the dark sky.

Poor Gramps must be worrying all this time.

The roof of the church, covered with tin and painted white, stands out sharply against the sky. Looks like it's covered with snow. A crowd of jackdaws is whirling around the spire. As if they were drunk. The church has its lights on, inviting warmth emanates from the windows. Like goddamn Christmas.

Shall I go in?

Nah, nobody wants me there.

God lives elsewhere.

And don't say I'm drunk.

And meaning… perhaps it's in the voices of jackdaws and in my ability to hear them and in the silhouette of the cross against the sky and in my ability to see it.

And to hear music in the sea.

My legs are teeter-tottering a bit, but so what. There's no one to see.

And I must hurry, Gramps is waiting.

Why not trek through the forest.

The path starts out wide and firm but then all but disappears in a muddy mess, the forests are boggy around here. Where it's most sloppy, somebody — bless their heart — has thrown down some boards, I just have to steer the wheelbarrow so the wheel hits the boards. Not an easy task. The bog to the left looks like it's from a black-and-white Russian fairy-tale film from my childhood. Witches lived in such places — places where the dry lower branches of big firs are reflected in the still, unmoving marsh water. At any moment could appear such a witch, smacking her evil lips, sniffing through her long nose, and with her feet clad in bast shoes not so much as crinkling the surface of the puddles, wobble off to some witches' business.

You're that witch yourself now. I'm that witch myself now.

I fear nothing any more. Neither the living, nor the dead. So strange to think that I was so afraid as a child. Of bad, recurring dreams. Of ghosts. Of pieces of furniture that moved in the dark and seemed to have a life of their own. Of door handles that used to turn in the twilight and doors that used to start opening silently without ever fully opening.

And of death, of not being, of eternity.

"Gramps, would you sit with me, I have those bad thoughts again."

And Gramps, exhausted after work and second jobs, smelling of fresh sawdust, sat with me, holding my tiny hand in his own large, dry hand crisscrossed with veins, until I fell asleep. The little bedside lamp was always burning.

Good thing there comes a time when it's over.

It's all over. And nothing can be held back.

Nose leaking, I must be getting old.

Gramps also tends to have a drop hanging from his nose.

Wonder how he is.

The house is dark — of course, forgot to turn on the light when I was leaving.

"Brought you some boiled sweets, Gramps!"

I turn on the light.

Gramps lies motionless in his bed. His head at a funny angle. Facing the wall.

Dead??

"Gramps!"

Whew, alive.

He turns his head.

"Where the hell have you been all day?"

"There was a big line by the store. And it was hard to push. Those crazies have ploughed the road."

"What for? Are they gonna plant potatoes or what?"

"It's for tourists."

"Bull."

"Camp sites. Ecologically sound recreation."

"Bull. Sure, sure. You're the smart one."

"Here, Gramps. Boiled sweets," — I stretch out my hand, and I touch his hair.

"Leave my hair alone. Go pet a dog, don't pet me."

"Who's petting." Your hair's dirty, I have to wash it. Have to light the stove, heat some water. I am thinking about firewood.

Lichens (2015)
Inga Žolude (born 1984)
Translated by Zan McQuade

"What are you trying to do there?" Reval laughed as Brita shoved her rubber boots aside in the trunk of the car to make room for the case. "You're not going to work on holiday, are you?"

"There'll be samples to collect," Brita said, her head still in the trunk.

"Do what you want, but leave me some room for the beers!"

"We'll buy groceries on the way." Brita closed the trunk. "Switch off the sprinklers." She pointed to the left side of the lawn. "And anyway, no one waters their lawn in the middle of the day." She headed for the open door of the house.

"Look around! Everyone is watering their lawns!" Reval called after her. "You want to come back to dried-out grass?"

Walking into the house from the bright light of day, Brita couldn't make out anything until her eyes adjusted to the light in the room. It was cool in the house. After a moment, when the dizziness from the heat had passed, Brita went to the kitchen and inspected the contents of the refrigerator. She pulled out a crumpled aluminum foil parcel, unwrapped it, and with a knife cut a slice of spinach pie. Reval's voice approached, cursing. He stood at the threshold of the kitchen, and Brita, leaning over the frying pan, heard Reval breathe explosively in anger.

"I turned off the sprinklers, but look at me now!" he sighed.

Brita turned, swallowing the pie. Reval stood there, arms held out from his body like penguin flippers, wet shorts clinging to his thighs, his heavy dark plumage visible through the wet fabric. He sucked his stomach in so that the front of his wet shirt dangled, not touching his body. Water dripped onto the floor. Not saying a word, Brita leaned under the counter, pulled out an old grey t-shirt that they used to wash the floors, walked up to Reval and dropped the cloth at his feet. She laughed ever so slightly.

"Poor thing!" She went back to her food.

"Brita!" Reval shouted, but Brita fished out a piece of pie from the aluminum packet and put it in her mouth. "Aren't you going to help me? This is your fault!" Reval erupted.

Brita leaned against the edge of the counter and looked at the pitiful Reval. "Darling," Brita said soothingly to the enraged man, searching for the words... "you must get undressed, you are completely wet, I'm sorry." She picked a crumb from the pan with her fingers and put it in her mouth.

"Goddammit, then help me..." he pleaded, angrily heading to Brita with splattering steps, "...undress!" And he fell painfully to the ground, his wet slippers slipping on the kitchen tiles. He didn't move.

Brita exhaled and went to him. "We're never going to

leave like this," Brita said, reaching a hand out to him. Reval sat silently on his bottom, hurling one slipper into the room, and smacking the other one against the wall next to him, leaving a wet streak. As she got him to his feet, Brita pulled his shorts down to his ankles.

"Do you even love me?" Reval asked, seeking approval.

"Love, love…" Brita muttered in a vague tone — either reiterating the essence of the question, or perhaps confirming its answer.

Reval grabbed Brita's hands as she caught hold of the edge of his polo shirt to pull it over his head. "Come here." Reval pulled her closer to him. He tried to kiss Brita, but she turned her head, dissuading him, saying they had to leave. He let go of Brita's hands, and she helped pull off her husband's shirt, he noticed how ruthlessly she did it. He was naked. "Come here…" he stumbled, catching Brita again by the forearm, she twisted it, but realised that it was stuck in Reval's grip.

"Well?" Brita looked into Reval's face, eyebrows raised, not knowing what would happen next. He sucked at her lips, blowing air through his nose in short intervals, but Brita just stood there, ambivalent. Reval placed Brita's slender hand on his balls, he grew harder, hotter, but he noticed that Brita wasn't overcome with passion. "What is up with you?" Reval whispered, half leniently, half in reproach.

"I don't want to," Brita answered and attempted to step back.

Reval didn't let her go, he was looking into Brita's eyes now, pupils darting right to left, right to left… and he leaned in again for a kiss… "No, Reval!" Brita dodged him more vigorously, and he let her go.

266

"Your breath stinks," he stung furiously, "from that compost you're always eating!"

Brita swallowed silently, folded the almost empty foil packet and shoved it back in the refrigerator. Stepping back, she felt Reval standing there, and she tried to pass by him without touching him. But he deliberately pushed himself against her. Pushed her against the counter. She said nothing, just stood there calmly, feeling how the edge of the counter pressed against her stomach and hip bones with more and more force. "You didn't answer me," Reval said quietly, "but you're right, words mean nothing." And he shoved his hand into Brita's underwear. Brita closed her eyes as Reval started to fuck her, she grabbed onto the edge of the counter and thought of moss saturated with moisture, becoming fleshy and almost transparent.

When he finished, he let his head fall for a moment on Brita's back. Catching his breath, he kissed Brita on the cheek, holding her by the chin and turning her face closer to him. "You know that I love you…" he said.

"Are we going now?" Brita asked, and out of the corner of her eyes saw the round muscles of Reval's bottom headed upstairs. Brita picked Reval's shirt up off the floor, squeezed it, it was wet and heavy, she could no longer squeeze another drop from it, and so she used it to wipe her crotch.

When Reval came back downstairs, he was dressed, he'd put on a watch and sunglasses, and was ready to go. Brita was nowhere to be seen, he went round all the rooms and noticed that she had placed his wet clothes and slippers out on the terrace to dry. Closing the windows, he picked up a few more things along the way and went out to the front of the house.

Brita sat in the car next to the driver's seat, the door was open, and her knees were covered by a map on which she was making a few marks.

"There you are!" Reval said. "Are you going inside again?"

Brita shook her head, not looking up from the map. Reval went to the car and closed the door on Brita's side. The car rocked as Reval settled into his seat. He started the motor, and Brita put on her seatbelt, watching the closed door of the house receding as they backed out of the courtyard. Reval turned on the radio.

"You're not buckling up?"

"What are you, the cops?" He laughed.

"No, it's just…" Brita was rattled. "It's safer."

"Well, if we crash, at least you'll survive," Reval teased, pulling Brita's seatbelt and touching her breasts. As Reval removed his fingers, the strap tightened against Brita's body, and he asked: "What time will they be there?"

Brita looked at her wristwatch. "They're never on time. No need to hurry. We still have to go to the shop."

Reval turned up the music. After a moment, Brita turned it back down to be almost inaudible. "Do you mind? That 'music' is horribly aggressive."

"It's made for driving! For overtaking all these shitheads who pull in front of you, this one, for example! Look at what that idiot is doing! He doesn't even realise he's on the road yet, instead of shuffling slow-motion around the room in his felted slippers! How did they let him have a licence?!" Reval performed an overtaking manoeuvre. Brita glanced back at the car behind them with a sympathetic gaze, sending apologetic thoughts to its driver. It was a grey-haired gentleman, next to him sat a white husky, its muzzle shoved out of the open window, catching the passing breeze and the scenery along the road.

Brita picked up her phone.

"Ask them how much booze they bought? Maybe we need more!"

"I'm not calling them."

"Who then?"

"I have to call Dahl. About the forest."

"What… about the forest?"

"I told you there will be samples." Brita had already lifted the phone to her ear.

"You're really going to the forest? But it's our holiday! I don't like that Dahl…" Reval shut up, as Brita had already started to talk. Reval pulled into the shop's car park, and Brita, still speaking, pointed to a parking spot. As soon as the car had stopped, she finished confirming her plans with Dahl for their hike and hung up the phone.

"He's a faggot, right?!" Reval looked at Brita.

"What's got into you?" Brita grabbed the door handle. "Sometimes I think you're a different person."

"Well if he isn't a faggot, then should I start worrying, or what?!" Reval shouted over the roof of the car after they had both got out.

"Since when did you decide that you should be bothered with other people's sex lives? Doesn't that seem a bit mean to you?" Brita scowled.

"Since you two started calling each other and… surely my wife's sex life still has something to do with me?!"

Brita shook her head as if dizzy and glided through the shop's doors. When she had retrieved a shopping trolley, Reval joined her.

"Do you want anything in particular?" Brita asked like it was nothing.

"Yes, I do want something in particular," Reval spat out, looking intently at Brita.

"I meant from the shop. What should we buy?" Brita put her hand on his shoulder and pulled it diagonally across his chest. "Stop…" she whispered and smiled.

Reval was restrained.

"I'll call Pietro about the alcohol, it'll be stupid if we have to sit there sober. You want some wine?"

Brita shrugged ambivalently. She headed to the leisure department, where Reval's voice could still be heard, laughing into his phone.

Reval looked over the items gathered in Brita's trolley and added a thing or two that he fancied. At the checkout, Reval stood in line with his wallet in his hand while Brita placed her purchases on the conveyor belt.

"Do you really need new wellies?" Reval stared in disbelief at the boots standing at the very end of her purchases. Brita stared blankly at her husband.

"These aren't even professional, they're some kind of supermarket brand!"

"Well then they'll be suitable for gardening…"

"With flowers on them!"

"It's a rare species. *Swertia perennis*. I really like them." She smiled.

"You don't say! Then your forest brother will appreciate them too!"

Brita shook her head, unable to believe that Reval had said something like that, and took the boots down off the conveyor belt.

"No, no!" Reval cried. "I'm sorry. If you like them... then okay, put them back."

Reval looked at Brita as she quietly sorted and packed the shopping in cardboard boxes. Brita walked slightly ahead across the car park, Reval pushed the shopping trolley a few steps behind, watching Brita all the while. "Are you wearing those diamond earrings I gave you?" he asked suddenly.

Brita turned in shock, eyes wide. "To the woods?!"

"You see! See how you answer me! Can you not simply answer me when I ask you something. You always talk back to me or dodge the question... I don't know how I'm supposed to talk to you!!!"

Brita laughed. "Then don't talk to me."

"You want me to not talk to you?!" Reval tried to look Brita in the face, but she turned away. "I can *not* talk to you if that's what you want," Reval said.

"Stop..." Brita forced a smile. Recently she smiled a lot.

As they drove Reval concentrated on the road, and Brita looked out of the window on her side until she suddenly spoke. "It's just..."

Reval turned the music down. — Say it. Say it, sweetheart.

"No, nothing... it's just... you know, we're different. You've changed..."

"I haven't changed!"

"...and I've changed. Not really changed, but... I notice

271

those things… for example, when I'm in the woods…"

"In the woods like at work? What do you mean, in the woods?"

"That's just it! You can't understand it, but I don't blame you."

"I can't understand again? It seems like all I've done my whole life is try to understand." Reval had started to drive more slowly, more closely concentrating on the conversation.

"But maybe you don't have to try. I believe that there are people who understand you without trying. They just get it, because they're on the same wavelength."

"And I'm not on the same wavelength as you, is that what you're saying?" Reval smacked the steering wheel. "Goddammit, for once just say what you want to say — do you want a divorce?"

"Do *you* want a divorce?" Brita looked at Reval, her husband. Reval was silent, his gaze on the road unbroken, he began to slow his speed. There was nothing ahead of them, and Brita squirmed uncomfortably in her seat. Reval pulled to the side of the road, not saying anything, and got out of the car. Brita pulled up her knees and pressed them to her forehead. Reval opened Brita's door. He could have hit her. Brita had always retained a tiny morsel of fear of Reval, it seemed to her that Reval was the type who could hit a woman given the right situation. Reval pressed his hands on the roof of the car and stared at Brita.

"Brita," he said, afraid, "are we having a crisis?"

"A crisis?" Brita forced out. "Are you fine with how things are?"

"But what do you want? What do you want from a person?

From people? We've been together a long time, and it feels like… you want romance? Then say it!"

Brita let out a bittersweet laugh. "Romance… you know, the point is that I don't even want that. There's nothing I want. To want is an extravagant thing."

"So what do you want?!"

"See, again! Are you even listening to me??"

They were quiet for a moment, the space was filled with the horn of a passing car. Reval craned his neck. "I think that's Pietro's car." He followed the SUV with his glance for a few metres until it stopped. "We'll finish this later." Reval said, and stroked Brita's upper arm.

The car in front of them approached in reverse, its door already open, from which emerged Anika's voice. Then her leg appeared, and a figure in a long, orange dress jumped out onto the side of the road. She leapt like a gazelle up to Reval, and embracing him, kissed him on both cheeks. Pietro, in a striped shirt and dusty shorts, shook hands with Reval and the three of them looked at Brita, still sitting in the car. She reached her hand out of the open door and shook it, trying to thaw out the stiffness that had come over her after their conversation, and the path their day had taken. She got out of the car and joined the trio as if nothing had happened. There were about fifty kilometres left to go.

Reval and Pietro parked the cars as close as possible to the cabin, and before they started to bring the things inside, uncapped some beers and greedily finished them off in a few swigs. Brita, meanwhile, got her belongings out of the boot and carried them into one of the rooms. So, this will be their bedroom. There were two beds in the room, spaced apart, that could also be pushed together. Brita hadn't looked into the other bedroom and didn't even want to know about the arrangement of its beds. In the aisle between the two beds, she placed her equipment box and her new boots. She looked them over and tore off the price tag, then set them next to each other and looked with pleasure upon this still life.

There was activity downstairs, fortunately they didn't come upstairs, and Brita leisurely indulged in her solitude, arranging her clothes in the dresser drawer, leaving a few items on the bed. She and Dahl exchanged a few texts, and then she turned on the shower. Even though she had washed before the drive, she thoroughly scrubbed her crotch and inner thighs. Washed clean, fearfully listening for sounds, she emerged from the bathroom into the bedroom, now even emptier. She took a deep breath, it had been hot in the shower, Brita looked out of the window, the woods were within a hair's breadth. Brita picked up the black seamless underwear, waterproof pants and jacket she'd left on the bed and got dressed, fastened her rucksack across her chest and, smoothing her hair at the top of the stairs, gathered herself, then went downstairs. The trio's voices were in the yard, and she went up to Reval to kiss his forehead and muss up his hair, and announced she was off for a short evening jog.

Pietro and Anika's presence and the beer had released the tension, and Reval smacked Brita on the arse and said that he'd be waiting impatiently for her to get back. Brita shifted on her toes, stretched for a few lunges, and started to run, hair swinging, leaving the seedy laughter behind her.

At first, Brita ran easily and quickly, not thinking about roads, a map, Reval, or meeting Dahl. In this moment she was the only person running along this satisfying terrain, Brita quickened her steps to melt her rage, she looked only at the monotonous rocky path of earth, then around her the silence became deep and satisfying, and the birds sang, sounds from the tops of the trees echoing over the lowest part of the forest floor. Brita stopped, left the path and stepped onto the earth of the forest. She tilted her head up to the crowns of trees that joined and melted into the clouds, then peered back at the ground and saw the reason she had come here — low and soft moss and lichens. She smiled, gasping. Something was recovered in that moment. Brita glanced over at the road, the stands of trees and cliff ridges in the distance. Everything was blanketed in the quiet of the early evening, there was no one around. Brita took a map from her rucksack. On the map she'd marked the rental cabin and the place where she was meeting Dahl. She drew her finger along the cartographic lines, every once in a while, looking up to see if the surroundings were right. She resumed her way out along the road, she wasn't late yet. Brita spotted the traveller's hut from a distance; it must be the right one. Arriving at the tiny hut, she opened the door. Inside was some firewood and a bucket. She set her rucksack down against the side of the hut and took out some accessories. The forest resembled the sound of a seashell. It was a big seashell too — twisted from serpentine hills, on the other side of which you might emerge into a valley.

Dahl wasn't there yet, so Brita decided to climb the steep slope. Under the moss, dormant bits of rock crumbled under her steps and slipped downward. Brita grabbed at the new shoots and thicker roots of bushes. From the bottom, the highest point had looked attainable, but now Brita felt the effort of that short climb. As she climbed the green, moisture-soaked wall, she noticed she hadn't even reached the very top, the wall continued higher in increasing steps. She decided to sit down on the flat rock terrace. Brita looked back; the thicket had drawn in impenetrably behind her. The slope opposite was overgrown with giant spruce trees, their tops heavy with cones. Brita walked to the edge. At the bottom flowed a river, which hadn't been visible from the way Brita had come. The water was brown, here and there larger peaks of rock rose up from it. Brita walked around the viewing area, watching the path of the river's flow until it turned in a bend. She went back to the other side and listened intently, hearing a rustling gathering strength. She headed in its direction, until she caught sight of a waterfall. It fell between black cliffs, where it collected into a small, peaceful pool of water that had been carved out of the dark stone walls. Brita stretched out onto an axillary of twisted larch trees growing out of the slope, leaning forward towards the ravine, and for a moment, letting her body relax, she imagined herself to be like a blanket draped over a horse's back. On the opposite wall streamed a tiny jet of water that poured from the rocky protrusions downward in a rapid stream, and the drops were white. There was something soothing in this cascading water and with a hypnotic force it extinguished the embers of unrest inside Brita, although they returned in a different form as soon as Brita heard someone calling. She looked at her watch, leaning against the tree trunk. It had to be Dahl, and she got up and walked back, calling his name. She saw Dahl standing at the bottom, they waved at each other.

"I'm coming down now! Move to the side, in case I

dislodge any stones!" Brita cried from above.

Dahl nodded and stepped back.

"I knew you by your equipment!" Dahl said when Brita came down. She remembered her discarded open bag with some of its contents removed. "You didn't come here to work, did you?!" He laughed.

Brita tipped her head to the side and grinned good-naturedly. "What else am I supposed to do, if my... if they're all staying in!"

"Well, I didn't bring anything with me... I'd intended to take you to see the waterfall."

"Yes! I saw it from above!" Brita said delightedly.

"You already saw it? Well, what am I going to do with you? A real scientist!" Dahl remarked playfully. "Then we won't go to the waterfall? I had thought perhaps from the bottom..."

"Of course, we'll go!"

Brita packed her bag, and they slowly headed in the direction set by Dahl.

"I should have told you not to bring the whole lab with you — you won't find anything in this flora that you haven't already seen. The common *aspicilia cinerea*, although rather uncharacteristic for them to still be here, given the development of infrastructure and the influence of urbanisation, however they won't likely let go of their long-time place so quickly. Up there, though, there might be some of the more interesting *rhizocarpon geographicum* species..." Dahl glanced at Brita, "well, we already have them in our catalogue, but they look impressive in nature in such numbers."

"Yes, definitely, let's look at them!" Brita lit up.

"But not today. Today — the waterfall. I hope we don't get our feet wet. There's not really a path there, but I think we're used to wading off-road!"

Brita smiled and nodded.

The path wasn't easy. It had rained during the day, and the moss was soaked, and the stones were slippery. In places, the stone-wall bank along which they hiked jutted out convexly. Dahl went first and tested each leap from rock to rock. He appeared sure of himself, he wasn't daring, but stable. Dahl waited for Brita at the most dangerous places and helped her if necessary. He extended his hand and held hers firmly and for a long time as Brita made her way across.

"Let's rest," Dahl said, pressing his back against the wall of the cliff. Brita agreed. She was a bit winded; she smoothed the strands of her hair, that caught in branches along the way, had come undone across her forehead. Brita glanced at Dahl and pressed with her rucksack too against the wall behind her. It was the same place where she had stood up at the top, opposite the drops of water that fell downward over the blackened stones.

"I like waterfalls, don't get me wrong," Dahl turned his head to Brita and waved with his right hand, "but water dripping from the rocks... there's something special about it."

This had been Brita's thought, and it seemed silly to her to agree. If she did, it would be as if she agreed with someone else's thoughts, but she'd come up with this thought herself. But she didn't want to deny it either, so she said: "That's exactly what I thought, up there. I don't know what's so special about it... maybe the rhythm... it's soothing." Brita closed her eyes. Now the murmur of the water surrounded her as completely as if she were in the middle of the waterfall and there was nothing else, not even a road back. For a split second, Reval's face flashed into Brita's thoughts — as if she were walking down a street filled with people and glanced at him like a stranger, continuing onward. Brita listened to her body, and it felt like it burned in the very place Reval had pleasured himself. Suddenly she opened her eyes, and for a moment the landscape was blurred, until she looked at Dahl, immersed in calm right there with her, the water tumbling down on the opposite stone embankment.

"Shall we go?" Dahl asked, and Brita nodded. There was detritus stuck to her palms and she rubbed them against each other. Dahl resumed walking along the edge. In places he lingered longer, assessing the opportunity to move from stone to stone, stones that looked too far apart from each other, but he always managed to get across and bring Brita over with him.

"Are you afraid of getting your feet wet?" Dahl asked.

Brita opened her eyes wide. "Why do you ask?"

"It looks like we can't get any farther."

"No? I wanted to see the waterfall from the bottom…"

"That's why I asked. It can be reached by water. It's just there."

To Brita, turning back and not reaching the waterfall would be devastating — they would demur silently without any satisfaction, say their goodbyes, and Brita would have to head back to the house and Reval, Anika, and Pietro. And so completely casually Brita tossed out: "Then let's go in the water!" and sat down to untie her boots. Feet bare, they tied their shoes to their rucksacks, rolled up their trousers, and Dahl stepped into the water. He looked back at Brita and offered her a hand.

"Is it cold?" Brita asked.

Dahl smiled. "You'll get used to it. Just like people get used to every…" But Brita wasn't listening any more, she held her breath and briskly stepped into the icy water. She saw that Dahl was expecting her cry of shock, but her mouth stayed mutely closed. She raised her arm and placed her hand into Dahl's waiting outstretched hand. Slowly their feet made their way upstream, and Dahl led them away from the shore. The river was up to their knees in some places, in others shallower or deeper, the rocky river bed made the water appear brown, its flow wasn't strong and yet occasionally Brita imagined her body being tugged by the stream's current and carried downstream, the thin, submissive and empty frame of a human body. She tightened her grip on Dahl's hand. Dahl climbed out of the water onto a flat outcrop of rock in the middle of the river. Brita felt his strength lift her, and they squeezed together on the small surface that rose above the water. The stones parted the ribbons of water into undulating tatters that were reunited again farther along only again to be separated in an endless delta. Dahl stared at the waterfall right there in front of them. They shouted to each other through the deep and continuous rumble.

Brita's eyes twinkled with delight. "Thank you…" she gasped, but Dahl brought his ear closer to Brita's face — he hadn't heard.

"Thank you!" Brita shouted into Dahl's ear.

Dahl smiled and hugged Brita. Brita was confused, but Dahl's embrace was unbroken, and Brita clung to him. Over

Dahl's shoulder she stared at how the blade of water crashed from above into a serene pool at the foot of the cliff. Its flow dispersed into an uninterrupted avalanche of droplets that raced to reunite with the river, and then Brita comprehended the warmth that flowed between her and Dahl's still unparted bodies, and she glanced at Dahl's face, the skin of his cheek so close, as if seen through a microscope. Brita had put her fingertip under a microscope several times. There turned out to be much, much, much more there than what we can see. What we can see is nothing more than a distant and blurred view, a tiny part of reality that, since this revelation, Brita felt she could no longer rely on. Dahl's skin covered something much greater and deeper, and she let her hands go, moving her body away from his, which seemed to have begun to grow, clinging to the roots of the shoots that were looking for somewhere to latch onto.

They watched the falling river for a while. Brita would have liked to walk through the waterfall. Dahl said it wasn't possible here, he'd already tried. Brita believed him.

They had to go back.

After their embrace, neither of them knew how to behave. Did it mean something more… for one moment they had been so close. Dahl's hand was like a lifebuoy to Brita, surrounding her in a protective, closed circle and holding her up over the depths, into which she might have allow herself to be devoured if she were alone on the river. Her life had been changed.

It seemed to Brita that Dahl was helping her more than he had on the way there, his hand gripped Brita even more firmly, meaningless touches became more frequent and more meaningful. Brita felt like an insect stuck to a sundew, unable to escape or to understand what's happening to it. Their palms slid against each other, and this imperceptible friction warmed Brita's chest. She felt like it was getting harder to breathe, and several times she slipped on the rocks. Her clothes were soaked, Dahl lifted her up, she couldn't speak, the stately fir trees were flowing from tips to roots with the darkening dusk, mossy layers shimmered before them — *sphagnum, pleurosium schreberi, hylocomium splendens...* suddenly everything seemed so tiny — what kind of job was that — to study lichens? Who did it serve? Brita had shrivelled like a falling drop on the stem of a haircap spore and was threatening to dry up and disappear.

Brita hadn't noticed how they were walking, her legs carried themselves to the point where everything began, this excursion. The excursion with Dahl to the waterfall. It had grown dark. Brita avoided Dahl.

"Your cottage is that way?" Dahl waved his hand down the road.

Brita nodded her head.

"I'll walk you there."

If Brita were to say something she would refuse, but she couldn't even say 'no' to Dahl. As if the icy water had paralysed her tongue and voice, but she still kept herself above the water that carried her like an empty boat where it pleased. Brita couldn't resist. Anyone. As if she had no will — Reval used her like a holidaymaker at a resort, riding a dinghy across the lagoon, while Dahl steered her like a pilot through a harbour canal.

Lights flashed. They got closer to voices and the bark of a dog from some distant cottage. Dahl slowed his pace. Brita had begun to think feverishly about this evening. "Maybe you want to come in?" she asked shyly, not understanding what her offer and his possible consent meant.

"Me?" Dahl was confused. "I don't know…"

"Of course, come!"

"But your husband?'

"Come anyway, he's nice!"

Brita didn't know why she'd said something like that. First — is he nice? Second — that meant that she loved her husband and had suddenly set up a border for Dahl. Of course, she hadn't been planning on any kind of breach, but…

They had continued to walk as they spoke, approaching the house. Neither Brita nor Dahl stopped, as if it were already too late. They entered the yard, Brita heard Reval's drunken voice. Entering the house through the door that stood open, Brita heard Anika's laughter and Pietro's babbling, too. Brita took off her shoes, and Dahl did the same. They set their rucksacks on the floor. Unpacked belongings stood gathered all around them. All the lights were on, even though the trio sat in one room, where Dahl was headed, following Brita.

"Everyone! Meet Dahl!" Brita said loudly.

The trio turned and fell silent.

"My colleague from work," Brita threw out. "He has a house nearby."

— So, THIS is Dahl? — An intoxicated Reval stood up, obscuring the fire in the fireplace that had overheated the room. Brita walked up to her husband and placed her hands formally on him.

"And these are our friends — Anika and Pietro."

Dahl nodded.

"Finally, I get to lay eyes on him!" Reval set his drink on the table, attempting to take a step. Brita pulled him back from behind the chair. Reval shook off Brita's hand. "Surely, I have the right to shake the hand of my wife's colleague!" He laughed loudly.

Dahl also attempted to step towards Reval and stuck out his hand. "What a great holiday cottage! Mine's not so lovely. You'll have to come over one evening if you aren't too busy. Do you fish? I have a few extra fishing rods."

That cheered Pietro up, he liked to fish. He and Reval used to go to the Faroe Islands. They never managed to bring home anything they may have caught after a week of fishing, but they were worn out. Most of the time they spent drinking, some ten men squeezed into one room, their local guide right there with them, who they paid in bottles of alcohol. They went into the sauna and walked around half naked, wrapped in dirty towels that came undone to reveal their manhood, which they weighed against each other enviously with thieving glances.

Pietro offered Dahl a drink, Dahl didn't refuse. Reval hadn't yet released Dahl's hand from his stiff grasp, looking him in the eye.

"Oh, let him go now!" Anika cried compassionately; she had mascara smeared under her eyes. Dahl turned toward her. Brita laughed. Brita, Reval, and Dahl stood standing until Pietro finally suggested everyone sit down. Reval fell into a club chair warmed by the fire, his cheeks were red and hot, moisture protruding from his forehead.

"It's hot in here," Brita said and turned away from the fireplace, fanning herself with her hand. "How can you stand it?"

She pulled off her jacket and set herself down on a chair near the wall, away from the fireplace. Reval looked at her with a burning glance that Brita found incomprehensible. Meanwhile Pietro was talking with Dahl, Anika was drunk and giggled non-stop. Her long orange dress had ridden up and revealed tanned legs with thin ankles in strappy sandals. Reval turned away from Brita and observed Anika's legs.

Brita watched the fire. It changed, though it wasn't as interesting as the falling drops of water projecting from the surface of the rock as if from its depths. The water could extinguish whatever had burned in Brita, in spite of the fact that she had still loved Reval and swore not to let anything come between them — a gap grown over with the smothering vines of a jungle could no longer be restrained or traversed.

When Brita glanced, unnoticeable and fear-filled, over to him, her body relaxed in a liberating breath — Reval had fallen asleep. Brita stood and went to her husband to take the crystal glass from his limp hand, the contents of which had dripped onto his lap. He didn't move. The other three noticed Brita's presence. She put a finger to her lips and they lowered their voices.

"Time for me to go," Dahl said and stood, and for a moment he and Brita looked at one another. "Can I help you?" Dahl asked Brita, gesturing to Reval. Brita shook her head and after a moment answered: "Let him stay there."

"Yes, let him sleep it off!" Pietro laughed and put his hand on Anika's waist. They both said goodbye to Dahl, and heading upstairs, turned off the light in the stairwell.

"I'll walk you out," Brita said to Dahl. He moved closer, Brita stepped back ever so slightly, but Dahl only bent down to the fireplace to douse the red coals. Setting down the poker, he looked at his palm, it was black. He stood, rubbing at the coal mark, and Brita grabbed his hand, casting a shadow over Reval's sleeping body. "Was it hot?" she asked.

Dahl shook his head. "Just black."

Brita placed her hand on his dirty palm and allowed her tired eyelids to close. Brita thought that she could feel the radiating energy of the black cliffs through this black hand. Suddenly she heard Anika's voice instructing Pietro to go downstairs and pick up their things, and Brita pulled her hand back from Dahl's hand. She headed to the entrance. Dahl followed her. He put his hands on Brita's shoulders, but she shook them off. She put on her shoes and managed to close the door behind them before Pietro had noticed them. They both stood outside silent, dark as ink, Brita opened her mouth slightly, and it was filled with a stupefied, swelling blackness. Brita didn't know what Dahl intended to do. Dahl didn't know what to do. But they both knew what thoughts coursed through the both of them. Brita shifted: "How are you going to get back? It's dark."

"I'll get back," Dahl whispered, touching Brita's hand that calmly hung at her side. Her fingers answered, gently sliding into the skin of the recess of his palm. Brita took a step, and Dahl followed her, not letting go of her hand. They went to the road. In one of the distant cottages a dog barked several times then grew silent.

"Brita…"

"Thank you for the waterfall," she said in a casual voice, pressing his palm more firmly and then letting it go completely.

"Please…"

"Good night." Brita stepped backwards, small pebbles grinding treacherously under her soles.

"How long will you all be here? Maybe…"

"Yes, let's meet up again for sure!"

"Yes?"

"How are you going to walk home now?! I didn't think about you!" There was guilt in Brita's voice, she could have offered Dahl the couch… but she shouldn't let him stay the night.

"I have a flashlight." He rifled around in his bag for a moment, and a halogen beam pierced the darkness.

"Good night, Dahl, and thanks."

Dahl shone the beam up to the door of the house, and Brita headed along the light's path back inside. The door closed, and Dahl cast the beam ahead of him, to head homeward along his light's path.

Brita locked the door. From the entrance, she could hear Reval's snoring. Pietro and Anika were quiet upstairs. Brita glanced over the bundles of things and set her shoes next to them. She went into the room, where her husband slept with a wet lap and a pink, calm face, and turned off the light. Brita tiptoed, turning out the lights elsewhere and headed upstairs. She closed the bedroom door, pulled her pyjamas from the dresser drawer, changed into them and slid into the bed farthest from the door. The sheets were matt-white and pilled, like hotel sheets used to be, the synthetic pillow was like a sponge, and Brita tossed the decorative sand-coloured cover to the ground and wrapped herself in a blanket, letting herself be encompassed by it as if it were a warm white stream of milk, perhaps. Closing her eyes, Brita saw alternating scenes of the day, figures and words like a thicket which she imagined Dahl wading through. Brita saw the flickering beam of the pocket flashlight ahead of him, which grew more and more faded and became shorter and shorter. Brita had known him for several years now, they worked in the same department. They had formed a good bond, and possibly not just because of a mutual affinity but because of their circumstances — they came to work together every day, they were both interested specifically in lichens, and their other colleagues were either much older or much younger — for them, life meant worrying about the things that suited them. And he knew that Brita has a husband, that she's happily married. So then why did she run away from her holiday to the waterfall with Dahl? And let him embrace her? And play with her fingers against his palm only a few short moments ago? And invite him inside? Brita waved it all off, but it came back and back again, and she concentrated on all the species of *peltigera* she could think of, forcing them to surround, to overwhelm what she saw, until she fell asleep.

Brita was woken by Reval's moaning. He had dragged himself into the room, rubbed his face and squeezed his neck and shoulders, which were sore from sleeping in the chair. Reval noticed Brita's eyes, open and staring at him.

"I walked in on them!" Reval threw his hand at the next room.

Brita heard Anika and Pietro's grunting and fidgeting.

"What time is it?" Brita asked.

Reval collapsed seating himself at the foot of Brita's bed. "It's morning," he forced out.

Brita stretched her arms and closed her eyes for a moment.

"You could get up," Reval hinted, "and make me some

coffee. Or juice. I'm thirsty."

"You were all drinking last night."

"Oh really, were we! We're on holiday! Just massage me."

Brita looked at Reval's fat, red fingers, squeezing his shoulder, waiting for her fingers to take over. The back of Reval's neck was wrinkled and greasy looking. Brita furiously got out of bed, and entering the bathroom, locked the door. She went up to the tap, and leaning against the sink, looked into the mirror. She saw her face, eyes wide open in desperate inquisition. What happened? What am I doing here? She shoved her fingers under the stream of water and splashed them around so that Reval would hear that she really was washing herself. And after a while Brita did wash her face. Several times. Submerging it in handfuls of cold water, waiting in hope for the passage of time when something might happen, when something might work out, when some kind of *deus ex machina* might descend and lay out everything right there on the shelves of the medicine cabinet hanging on the wall, holding tinctures of calendula and valerian. Allowing the water to dry from her face, she went to the tiny bathroom window and pulled aside the curtain. The sun was shining, Brita sensed that it was hot outside. The road was light grey and pastel brown, the lawn, faded by the sun, seemed to be light blue in places, but elsewhere golden, the meadow in the distance — the colour of dried firewood with pink droplets, surely some kind of flower, maybe there were thistles or poppies here. Brita opened the window, letting in a burst of fresh air. So, then it wasn't hot. At least not as hot as Brita had imagined. Brita leaned out of the window until she was overcome by the chill air, and she caught sight of someone sitting there, sheltering in the shade... Reval was in the room, or at least he just was, and it wasn't Pietro either. Brita leaned out farther, clinging to the floor with the tips of her toes. There, leaning against the wall, eyes closed, sat Dahl.

Brita ducked back into the bathroom. She wanted to close the window quietly, but she leaned over again, his eyes were still closed, and she cleared her throat. She cleared it again more loudly, until he opened his eyes.

"What are you doing here?!" Brita asked quietly, realising that the shirt of her pyjamas flapped freely in the breeze, possibly exposing her breast to Dahl's gaze, and with one hand she pressed it against her body.

Dahl jumped to his feet. "Brita! Wonderful!"

"I'll be right down!"

Brita unlocked the door and went into the room. Reval had taken off his shirt and was lying on his stomach, and was poking at his back to show Brita where she should press.

"I can't! I'm going downstairs! We have a guest!"

"A guest..." Reval dragged out, "what guest?"

"Dahl is downstairs, he's sitting by the door, and I'm going to let him in!" Brita dressed quickly, hurrying, casting off her pyjamas in a hurry.

As she reached the staircase, Anika, wrapped in a towel, was pushing shut the door to the next room. Brita knocked and let them know that Dahl was downstairs and they should get dressed.

Brita ran down the stairs and ran through the dawn-filled ground floor, where last night's beer-sticky glasses and the lingering smell of a hangover still remained.

"Come in!" Brita chirped across the threshold, leaning

out with the door handle in her right hand, not wanting to go outside in bare feet.

Dahl lifted the handle of a fishing rod in greeting and smiled widely, starting to say he thought this might be an excellent day for fishing, but Brita had already gone back into the house and started to busy herself opening curtains and windows, collecting glasses from the table and putting them in the dishwasher.

"We haven't eaten breakfast yet," Brita said, when Dahl came inside.

"Really?"

"Yes. Did you sleep well? Your house must not be that far."

Dahl laughed. "It was just a short walk away."

The voices of Pietro and Anika grew louder as they continued their conversation heading down the stairs.

"Good morning!" they said.

"Coffee, everyone?" Brita asked with the kettle in her hand over the sink, not looking at them.

They cheered yes, and Brita asked Anika to help her with the breakfast. Dahl nervously began talking to Pietro about fishing, and they went out through the open door, to where Dahl had left the fishing rods in the yard.

Brita pretended as if nothing had happened. She made sure that her behaviour gave no rise to suspicion. And nothing had happened anyway… when Brita, asking how strong to make the coffee, turned back to Anika after her answer, she saw that Anika had already managed to apply make-up and looked gorgeous. Brita looked at her own hastily pulled on clothes. She suddenly felt that she didn't look beautiful, she needed to try harder. And she remembered her new wellies with their *swertia perennis*.

Reval only managed to stomp his way downstairs once everyone was already seated waiting patiently at the table and Anika had called him repeatedly. There were four identical plates on the table and one smaller, which Brita claimed. But Reval declared that she deserved one of the four normal plates, since she was the one staying in this house and he was the one paying for it, and so the fifth plate belonged to the fifth person — Dahl. Dahl stood up to trade plates, but Brita didn't want to agree to that, and they stood firm, until Dahl calmed Brita down, saying it was only a plate.

Reval mopped his plate with bread, and shoved it into his mouth after licking the sauce from its surface. His teeth ground the food to a pulp. Suddenly Brita pictured herself at work in thin gloves, plucking fragile specimens from herbariums and filing cabinets with tweezers, easily transferring green moss with a trowel to the examination table and to the microscope, where they lay patiently and calmly. Pietro was talking about going fishing, and Dahl immediately concurred. Dahl seemed to think fishing was the best possible thing you could do in a day, even though Brita knew that the fishing rods were just an excuse. Pietro wanted to fish, and Anika wanted to go with them to tan and swim, but Reval said no and dissuaded Pietro as well. It was supposed to be the first day of their holiday, and doing nothing was the best form of relaxation.

"Fine," Brita didn't object. "Then I'll use your relaxation to do a bit of work. The department gave us an assignment to collect some new lichens, and this is the best time for collection, right, Dahl?"

Brita could see Dahl trying to remember if there really was an assignment and precisely which lichens Brita was talking about.

"Right, Dahl?" Brita asked a second time more insistently. And Dahl nodded his head. "Yes, yes. The lichens!"

Reval let out a burp and struggled up from the table. He shuffled into the living room, slumped onto the couch and turned on the television. After a moment he called Pietro to show him some match on the sports channel. Pietro headed from the table to the room like a dog after a sausage. Brita began to collect the dirty dishes, and Dahl helped her. Anika lifted her legs onto Pietro's empty chair and placed her coffee mug on her chest, drawling: "Then I'll probably finally get to sleep in the sun. I feel so good afterwards. *Joie de vivre* literally radiating right into me!"

Brita nodded and carried the stack of dishes to the kitchen sink. Dahl talked distractedly with Anika while simultaneously watching Brita scrape the remnants of food from the dishes into the bin, rinse them and put them in the dishwasher, open and close the refrigerator to put away the food remaining from breakfast, carefully wipe the kitchen surfaces and the edge of the sink with a sponge, shake from her hands droplets of water that flew off out of sight beyond the sink, then hesitate in the middle of the kitchen looking for a towel.

Then Brita said she was going upstairs to change her clothes.

The outline of Reval's body was pressed into Brita's unmade bed. She lifted the blanket by its corners and spread it evenly over the bed. Opening the dresser drawer, she realised that she hadn't brought any nice clothes with her, only comfortable ones. She put on the rubber boots she'd bought at the shop and walked them around the soft flooring of the bedroom. Pulling on tiny shorts and a tight-fitting t-shirt over a worn-out seamless bra, she went to the bathroom mirror. A greyish yellow face, expressionless. She pressed her hands on her cheeks and tugged at her skin. Ten years younger. She sprayed nettle extract on her face and tapped the sides of her face and under her chin. Brita pulled the rubber band from her hair. She looked strange. Unlike herself. Typically, she wore her hair tied in a knot or clipped in a bun.

Heading downstairs, Brita went to Reval. "So, we're going. See you later!"

"Yeah." Reval thoughtlessly brushed her off, moving to one side to see the screen.

"Let's go then," Brita said to Dahl, entering the kitchen.

Dahl said goodbye to Anika, who lazily stood and said she was going to get her swimsuit. Her lipstick-marked mug still remained on the empty, crumb-filled breakfast table.

Brita asked if it was worth bringing her instruments with them. Dahl cocked his head and shrugged. Brita stared into his eyes. "I'll bring them in any case," she said. Dahl stood to put on his shoes, and noticed Brita's rubber boots — *swertia perennis!*

Suddenly Reval hurried out from the room. "Hang on, hang on, where are you going?" he asked, disturbed.

"What?" Brita tilted her head in amazement and frowned in confusion. "I told you… you even said!"

"And?"

"I just went in there, and you said — okay!"

"Really?!"

"Yes, really!" Brita snapped. Dahl waved at Reval, went to the door, and went to the fishing rods, they toppled as Dahl attempted to gather them.

"You really meant to go fishing, huh?" Reval called out to Dahl from behind Brita.

Dahl nodded, unwinding the tangled fishing lines.

"Are you two going to fish?" Reval asked Brita, stunned.

"No, not that. Dahl wanted to go fishing with the rest of you, but since you aren't going, we're going to look for lichens. For work."

"What do you mean 'since we aren't going'? It's our ho-li-day! I want to relax!"

"Fine, darling," Brita smiled, "I won't say anything. Relax! You've earned it."

Reval shook his head. "Okay, okay, okay."

"Okay," Brita confirmed.

"Well, you could stay here too…"

Brita placed a conciliatory hand on Reval's shoulder. "I'm on holiday, too."

Reval interrupted her: "Exactly! Then come and relax!" He pulled Brita by the shoulders.

"I relax best in the forest." Brita looked Reval right in the eyes and didn't see her husband. "Do you remember what we talked about on our way here?!"

"I remember! Do you remember?!" Reval fumed. "And I remember that we didn't finish our conversation. Do you remember that???"

Pietro's shouts of celebration rang out from the room, something had happened on the television. "We're ahead!" he shouted. Reval looked back towards the room, Brita looked at the door, where Dahl stood with the fishing rods in his hand.

"See you later," Brita said quietly, and stroking Reval's upper arm, departed. Reval went back into the room and sunk into the couch next to Pietro.

Brita and Dahl walked silently along the road. Brita looked at the powdery dirt of the road inlaid with tyre tracks and footprints. She glanced at her own pale thighs overgrown with small, fine colourless hairs like the spore stems of a *polytrichum splendens*. Dahl yawned.

"You look tired," Brita said.

Dahl looked at Brita, not turning away. They stopped. "Brita…" Dahl said. "Let's walk further," Brita interrupted him. Dahl nodded. They walked along further and came to the place where they had met the day before, and walked down to the river along which they had walked to the waterfall. They stood for a moment by the water, until Dahl climbed higher, set the fishing rods down, leaning them against a pine tree, and sat down right at the foot of the tree. In the twilight of the forest, goosebumps appeared on Brita's skin and several mosquitoes landed there. Brita stood next to Dahl, brushing off the insects, Dahl looked up at Brita and grabbed her ankle with his hand, sliding it upward. Brita's leg began to tremble. "You're shaking," Dahl said. Brita pressed her lips together and felt Dahl pulling her downwards to him. Brita sat on the wet bog-moss and felt the moisture soaking her skin through her shorts. She stared at the river — how the stream leapt over the rocks.

"Brita," Dahl said to her again.

Brita hadn't noticed it approaching, but now she felt a strange eddy of force swell in her, pulling her into her own whirlpool. And she chose to avoid it. "Everything okay, Dahl?" she asked innocently.

Dahl put his arm around her shoulder. To Brita it felt as if she was carrying a piece of dried out rotten wood on her shoulder that she knew was fragile, only held together on the outside. And her stiff, resistant shoulders were squeezed by this wooden arm. "I think about you all the time," Dahl said, looking at Brita, she felt Dahl's breath against her cheek, gently fluttering her hair. Brita bowed her head so that her hair covered her face. "Ever since we parted last night, all I've been able to think about is coming back to you." Brita covered her eyes with her hand. Dahl stroked her back and the nape of her neck, but Brita sat firm, not letting her body be swayed, to swing into his touch. Dahl placed his other hand on her lower leg and moved it caressingly higher and higher. Brita stiffened. Dahl's hand had slid up the inside of her thigh and sneaked under the edge of her shorts. "Brita, I've been watching you for so long, we're so alike…"

Brita interrupted him, shrank away, broke off. "Dahl! I can't."

"You can't… what?"

"I can't. I just can't." Brita lifted Dahl's heavy arm from her leg and let it drop on the moss between them. "Maybe I gave you the wrong impression… if so, I'm sorry, but… I have a husband, you saw him."

"I saw that the two of you are as far apart from each other as… as…" Dahl searched for the right words. "As the two banks of this river."

Brita blew air through her nostrils, laughing bittersweetly. "What do you know… you think that you know something!

297

But you know nothing... NO-THING! You see how people celebrate the first day of their holiday for one night, and you think we're each on our own planet?! Well, that's how it usually is, only we're all on our own planets! You, too." Brita turned to Dahl and scrunched the soaked moss in her hand, tearing it with her fingertips and rolling it in her palm. "And what does 'far' mean anyway?!" She threw the ball of moss towards the river, but it didn't make it to the river. "Is that far?!" Brita exclaimed defiantly and leapt to her feet, her rubber boots sinking and slipping, she pointed her legs towards the water, and arriving there, stopped still as if rooted. The cool stream flowed past her, white on the surface, russet brown underneath. She pulled off her boot which had been stuck to her foot and wouldn't give. Wobbling, Brita took off both boots and turned to steady herself for the fight facing her, suddenly these rubber forms decorated with *swertia perennis* seemed so pointless. Brita spread her arms to balance herself and fumbled her way closer to the water.

"What are you doing?" Dahl called.

Brita shook her head, pausing for a moment, then dipped her foot in the water and clenched her jaw. She waded in deeper. Dahl pressed his palm deep into the bog-moss with force, as if trying to squeeze out its last remaining moisture. He pushed his palm deeper and deeper into the earth, until he released his hand, leaving his imprint in the moss. He lifted his glance, but he didn't see Brita in the river. He froze and held his breath, but the gurgling of the river filled everything all around him, preventing him from being able to make out Brita. Dahl scrambled to his feet and rushed down to the bank, tripping over Brita's boots. Brita lay in the water, caught by her arms in the long strands of *chlorophyta*. There was no risk of her drowning, the river was shallow here. Brita jerked in the air compulsively, as if gasping for breath or crying.

"I'll help you," Dahl said, suddenly filled with guilt, realising that he was the one who drove her here, into this icy despair. Without removing his shoes, he entered the water in big steps and his hands took the heavy weight of Brita's body under her armpits. She didn't help, she could almost slip from his grip, but Dahl managed to carry Brita to the bank. He laid her on the carpet of green. She lay there calmly, occasionally shaking from the cold. Now, Brita thought, now you can embrace me, lie next to me and warm me, now.

"You're completely wet," Dahl said. "Are you cold?"

Brita nodded, opening her trembling lips. Dahl hopped over to his bag and brought back a jacket. He quietly handed it to Brita and she quietly took it. She sat up and grabbed the bottom of her shirt. Dahl turned and stepped away, then saw the discarded rubber boots and headed to get them. Taking the boots, he stood for a moment, not turning back, almost as if he were lingering to give Brita time to change her clothes. Then he noticed a particularly long *bryoria* and went to look at it.

Coming back to Brita, who had wrapped herself in his jacket, he handed her the twig with long grey-haired threadlike lichens.

"Thanks," Brita laughed, "I can never tell the difference right away between *bryoria* and creeping thistle." She turned to Dahl. "And this is…" she guessed uncertainly, *"…usnea filipendula?"*

Dahl cocked his head, took the lichen twig from her and held it up to his face. "It's *bryoria*," he declared.

"See!" Brita exclaimed, clapping her hands. "I never know which is which!" She reached out her hand for Dahl to help her get up. "Which is right, which…"

Dahl pulled her up, and Brita almost bumped into his chest, but he set her body straight and sighed. "Look at us."

"Yes?"

"Look at yourself."

Brita examined herself, her feet were still bare, and she slipped them into the boots Dahl had retrieved.

"You probably can't go back like that."

"What are you proposing?" Brita replied defiantly.

Dahl looked her in the eyes. "I'm sorry."

Brita's head sank.

"I'm sorry that I tried to propose anything to you, I was… I don't know…"

Brita bowed her head.

"I can't go back like this," she sighed after a moment.

"What are you proposing?"

"I don't know," Brita grinned and looked up, and their glances met. "You don't live far, and you must have dry clothes…"

Dahl knitted his brow. He rubbed his face with both hands a couple of times, then said: "Come on. Let's go then."

And they started to go, not taking any bags, or fishing rods, or Brita's wet clothes that she had thrown over a branch to dry.

Dahl walked along the carpet of green, and Brita followed in his footsteps, they went silently, carefully, as if there were a boundary they might cross and fall into the abyss. As they left the forest, Dahl's gait became smoother, still they didn't talk, and Brita continued to walk slightly behind, and it was as if Dahl was leading her and she was following, not letting her deviate from this trajectory.

And suddenly she returned to her conversation with Reval. No, before their conversation. There, in the kitchen, before the drive. She is bent over the table and he is pressed on top of her. And then that conversation on the way. Were they having some kind of crisis? Of course, we're having a crisis, darling. Does she want a divorce?! Hard to say. Hard to say to yourself.

"My house!" Dahl gestured towards the house. Brita nodded. With each step she was getting more and more aroused, and all of these realisations and declarations echoed like gong strikes pulling her into a strange trance.

Dahl unlocked the door. Brita stood at the bottom of the stairs and looked around at the house and its surroundings, she noticed that her shorts were almost dry. She sat down on the step.

"There!" Dahl exhaled, reappearing in the doorway. "I tidied as much as I could. You can come in to my…"

Brita looked at Dahl, eyes blinking from the sun, and suddenly said: "We left everything in the woods! Everything."

"Do we need it?" Dahl shook his head. "Do you need those fishing poles?! That wet shirt? I'll buy you another one! Just come in!" And he took Brita by the hand and pulled her up to her feet and she stumbled to the threshold, and Dahl drew her into the sandy-lit wood decorated rooms, filled with the scent of dried grass. Brita's glance fell here and there, to the plants that lay drying out on paper on the ground, to a book on dendrology left open, but Dahl led her downstairs into the furthest room of the house and opened the closet. "So then, what do we have here?!" Dahl laughed, and pulling some crumpled clothes from the depths of the closet, pressed them into Brita's hands. "Dry shirts! As many as you want!"

Brita stared at the pile of clothes, then carefully placed it on the ground at their feet. She pulled down the zipper of Dahl's jacket. She had nothing on under the jacket, and Dahl moved away. Brita managed to catch him by the hand. Dahl stood there, not turning away. Brita pulled him closer and stroked his palm with her finger.

"I'll never forgive myself for starting this," Dahl said firmly, forcefully removing his hand from Brita's. "I shouldn't have done it." Dahl went outside, intentionally kicking the dried plants on the floor, stirring up a cloud of dust that shone in a beam of light sliding in through the door.

Brita turned her back. She sunk to her knees on the layer of clothes on the ground. Lifting her head, she saw the open closet with its emptied shelf and she stood up, picked up the clothes, folded them neatly and placed them back in the closet, then closed the door, but when she let go, the door creaked open again until Brita locked it shut, leaving the key dangling from the lock. She tiptoed to the window in the hallway. Dahl was sitting on the steps and staring off towards the woods, in the direction from which they had come.

Brita didn't want to talk to Dahl. Not now, not ever. She went back to the room with the closet, quietly opened the window, and dangling her legs over the edge, jumped out onto the grass. She went around the corner of the house and began to run across the meadow. As fast as she could. In the complete opposite direction. Whatever, make it to the forest, then make your way around that. Get your shirt, your bag, though what difference would it make if you left them behind. Now she saw in the meadow that those weren't poppies, but thistles, the needles of which she was now running over, let them scratch her, let them sting, let it bring her back to her senses, homeward. Brita heard Dahl calling her in the distance, but didn't see him standing there, and so that he wouldn't catch sight of her either, she threw herself to the ground and crawled to the edge of the forest.

She found the place by the river; their things were still there. She pulled her damp clothes back on, folded Dahl's jacket and placed it in his bag, wildly grabbing any moss and lichens she could find along the way and stuffing them into her bag.

Taking a deep breath, Brita went inside the house and rushed straight up to her room, calling out along the way. "Hi! I'm back! Gonna take a shower!" The house seemed quiet to her. She dropped her bag in the bedroom and ran into the bathroom, locked the door, turned on the water, hot. Her pink, mosquito-bitten cheeks, hair mussed and strewn with the bark of trees and bits of flowers, needles criss-crossing her forearms and thighs, Brita pulled out a few of the tiny needles, bits of soil stuck to her knees. She peeled off her clothes, threw them into the laundry basket, stepped into the bath, and closed the shower curtain.

She emerged from the bathroom wrapped in a towel and was startled. Reval stood in front of her with a bunch of *cladina mittis* in his hands next to Brita's open bag. "You really were gathering moss?"

"Husband, that's lichen…" Brita said calmly, taking a step towards him.

"I don't know which is which!" Reval laughed and put the sandy cap of lichen back in Brita's bag. "And what's the difference between them anyway, I don't know!"

"There's something else you should know..." Brita opened the chest of drawers and pulled out a grey cotton bathrobe, which she pulled on, letting the large bath towel slip from her body to the ground. "We need to talk," she turned to her husband.

Reval exhaled. "Just don't say that..."

Brita interrupted him: "But first help me push these beds together." They moved the things that had stood between the two beds to a corner of the room. And they pushed the two single beds, once spaced apart, into one large double bed. "Thanks," Brita whispered and lay down on one side of the bed, gesturing for Reval to join her. For a moment they lay there calmly, Reval looked at the ceiling, Brita looked at Reval. Reval turned to Brita and on her hip, he placed his large hairy paw, which had so often created a sense of security in her, now it lay there, heavy and lazy on her as if on a bounty he wanted to make sure wouldn't run away, and Reval said: "You know that I love you." Brita blinked, placed her hand across Reval's on his hip and said: "I still love you, too."

"Still?"

"Still."

They reached out to each other, and ever so slightly and gently, kissed.